Make It Sweet

Make it Sweet

Hearts Are Wild
Book Two

MARISA SCOLAMIERO

Make It Sweet

by

Marisa Scolamiero

Cover Art by Dane Low
Editing by Kelsy Thompson
Formatting by Erik Gevers

For my grandma
Thank you for my name

Songs to listen to while reading...

Make It Sweet - Old Dominion
5-1-5-0 - Dierks Bentley
Craving You - Thomas Rhett ft. Maren Morris
Miss Me More - Kelsea Ballerini
Before He Cheats - Carrie Underwood
Fix - Chris Lane
Forever's Gotta Start Somewhere - Chad Brownlee
Have Yourself a Merry Little Christmas - Michael Bublé
What Ifs - Kane Brown ft. Lauren Alaina
Simple - Florida Georgia Line
Love Your Love the Most - Eric Church
Love Ain't - Eli Young Band
Love Someone - Brett Eldredge
Anywhere With You - Jake Owen
Die a Happy Man - Thomas Rhett
Diamonds or Twine - Ryan Hurd

One

Danny Moreau stood up from the conference room table and shook hands with the two men sitting across from him. He'd been selected as the architect for a building of luxury condos by a well-known developer. When the project first came about, Danny had never thought that his name would make it onto the list, but apparently his designs were what the developer was looking for. He exited the conference room and headed for the elevator. He felt a surge of pride as he got into the elevator and leaned against the back wall, but at the same time he was also filled with a sense of, well, he wasn't quite sure. Being selected for a job like this meant that he had established himself, and while that was a big accomplishment, Danny felt like all of his jobs were starting to blur together.

He stepped onto the elevator and let out a deep breath. When the project first came up for formal presentations months earlier, he thought it was a good opportunity, but that was just him being practical. Danny liked knowing there was a steady payday coming in so that he didn't have to stress about bills or his staff getting paid, but designing luxury condos seemed to be a trend, one he couldn't seem to break away from.

For as long as he could remember, Danny had always loved building things, and then as he got older, he grew to love designing things. He could see the way a room should look or how an older house could be redesigned to look brand new. In his mind, being an architect was the only career for him.

Of course owning his own company hadn't happened right away. After college, Danny took a job at an architectural firm and spent the next three years working and learning. Right before he turned twenty-five, he decided it was time to set out on his own. It had been a risky move, but in the end it had been well worth it.

He pulled his phone out of his pocket and saw he had a message from Zack, the architect who worked for him, wanting to know how the meeting went. Danny sent him a text letting him know everything was settled. He exited the elevator and the building and made his way to the parking lot. As he climbed into his truck, he dialed his assistant to check in.

"Moreau Architectural Designs."

"Hey, Nat, it's me." He closed the door to his truck as he held the phone to his ear.

"Hi, is the meeting over?"

"Yeah, the contracts are all signed. They're going to send a copy of the jobsite details over—probably sometime next week."

"That's great! Did they say when they want to get started?"

"They have a civil engineer taking a look at the plans. If there aren't any issues, I'm sure things will get moving within the next couple of weeks. I think they have a contractor lined up too."

"Things are moving along nicely. Why don't you sound excited about it?"

Danny let out a sigh. "I wish I knew. This is a great project—it's the biggest thing we've ever done—but it feels, I don't know, like something is missing. I know people need a place to live and creating a great space in a great location is ideal, but I thought I'd be doing something more meaningful."

"I understand. Sometimes we envision ourselves doing one thing, and we end up doing something in a completely different direction. It doesn't mean that you're stuck; it's *your* company. You can take it any direction you want it to go."

"It would be great if I actually knew which direction I wanted to go." Danny shook his head and let out a sigh.

"You'll figure it out. You have the rest of the week and the weekend out of the office. Take the time to clear your head," Natalie replied, trying to bolster his spirits.

"Yeah, maybe." He ran a hand over his face.

"Are you on your way to the airport?"

"Yeah, I'm leaving now. Is my sister's flight still on time?"

"It is."

"If nothing else is going on, close up shop."

"Okay, sounds good."

"Have a happy Thanksgiving, Nat."

"You too, Boss. I'll see you next week."

He ended the call and started up his truck before he pulled out of the parking lot. One thing he was very grateful for was his good fortune in finding Natalie and hiring her as his assistant. In his first year of business, he'd managed to land lots of new clients but it all became too much for him to handle on his own. When Danny interviewed Natalie, all he saw initially was the lack of office experience on her résumé. He knew he needed someone who knew what they were doing. Just as he was about to thank her for coming in, she started asking *him* questions about how he kept his schedule on his computer. Before he knew it, she was behind his computer, showing him how to better organize his calendar.

"How do you know how to do all of this?" he'd asked her.

"My mom owns a hair salon. She had no idea how to get her schedules on a computer, and I just had a knack for it." She shrugged.

Danny had leaned back, trying not to look as stunned as he felt.

"I know I have no office experience, but I'm a quick learner and a hard worker. I promise if you take a chance on me, you won't be sorry," she'd told him. Danny couldn't say no to that kind of enthusiasm.

Four years later, she had more than made good on her promises. Natalie made everything run smoothly in the office. She kept him and Zack from missing appointments, built the company's social media presence, and even did the bookkeeping for the company. It made Danny's job a lot easier knowing that he had someone he could trust to watch his back.

He pulled into the Charlotte airport; it was almost five. His sister's flight was supposed to land at quarter to five so he was right on time. Charlie and her boyfriend, Nick, who was also Danny's best friend, were coming in from New York for Thanksgiving weekend. Charlie had moved to New York after college to pursue a career in magazine publishing and to get out of their small town of Belmont. Danny had fully supported her move. He had honestly believed that there was nothing that could ever make Charlie consider moving back home, but once she and Nick got together everything changed.

Nick was an orthopedic surgeon and he was currently in a yearlong fellowship program in New York, which he'd chosen so he could be closer to Charlie. Once the year was finished, he had a job lined up as one of the orthopedic specialists for the Carolina Panthers, the NFL team Danny's older brother Jason played for. While Danny was excited his sister and his best friend would be home for good, at the same time it reminded him of what was missing from his own life—someone to share it with.

It was the first time he felt like the odd man out when it came to his siblings. Charlie had Nick, and Jason had married his girlfriend Kate six months earlier—while Danny was still going home to an empty apartment every night. He'd spent several years focusing on establishing his business but had always had his eye on Tess, Charlie's best friend. The girls had been practically inseparable since kindergarten, which meant over the years his feelings for Tess had grown, and he'd become an expert at keeping them to himself. He was convinced that Tess only saw him as a friend, so he saw no reason to complicate things.

His thoughts were interrupted by the sound of his passenger door opening.

"Hi, Danno!"

Danny smiled at the sight of his little sister. Her long dark hair fell in loose waves around her shoulders and she held her coat in her arms. A large bag was slung over her shoulder.

"Hi, Ace. Where's Nick?"

"He's getting the bags with Will."

"Will?"

"Yeah. Will ended up on our flight, so I told him we'd give him a ride back to Belmont and invited him over for dinner."

The sound of bags hitting the bed of Danny's truck jolted him. The tailgate closed and then Danny saw Nick and Will come around to Charlie's side of the truck.

"All set. Hey, Danny," Will said, climbing in the back of the truck.

"Hi, Will." Danny couldn't help but grin. As much as he never thought he'd see Charlie and Nick dating, he absolutely never thought he'd see Will, Nick's younger brother, in a car with all of them.

Will and Charlie were the same age, but they didn't exactly run in the same circles in school. Will was the king of the popular kids while Charlie was the nerdy bookworm, a fact Will and his friends liked to remind her of as often as possible.

As fate would have it, Will and Charlie had both ended up in New York City and after almost ten years, they ran into each other. Charlie had transformed from the nerdy bookworm into a head turner, and Will didn't know who she was the first time he saw her. She thought she could get away with giving him a blunt reminder of who she was and then never have to see him again, but the next day Will showed up at her office as her company's new legal counsel.

Will was determined to prove to her that he'd changed and that he was worthy of a second chance. After a lot of doubt, she decided to give him a chance. At the same time that Will and Charlie decided to give dating a shot, Nick told Charlie he had feelings for her, creating an emotionally charged triangle. Charlie ended up spending extended time at home when their mother had heart surgery, which meant that she spent more time with Nick. The more time they spent together, the more obvious it became where her feelings truly lay. Unfortunately, before Charlie had the chance to come clean with Will about her feelings for Nick, he had showed up in North Carolina and caught her at Nick's apartment wearing nothing but one of his brother's T-shirts. Needless to say, that sparked an explosion that left everyone hurt and not speaking. It took Charlie almost dying in a car accident for everyone to realize what really mattered.

"Hey, man, thanks for the ride!" Nick said, getting into the back of the truck.

"Good to see you, Doc."

Charlie sat in the front seat once the guys settled in the backseat and then they were off. "It's so nice here!" she exclaimed.

Danny chuckled. "It's cold in New York, huh?"

"It snowed last night," Charlie told him, rolling her eyes.

"It was only flurries, it didn't stick." Nick laughed.

"Whatever, snow is snow. It's sixty-three degrees here and it's almost five o'clock. It's glorious." Charlie smiled as she sat back in her seat.

Danny grinned at his sister's comments and asked, "How is New York besides the weather?"

"Good," they all replied.

"The way they get New York ready for the holidays is something else. I thought these two were exaggerating," Nick said, gesturing to Will and Charlie.

"Nah, no one does the holidays like New York. There's no

exaggerating that." Will laughed.

"Who's coming tonight for pre-Thanksgiving dinner?"

"Jason and Kate, I think aunt Mary and uncle Julian. JJ said he'll probably come by after his shift," Danny told his sister. JJ was Mary and Julian's youngest child; they had a daughter, Casey, who was Jason's age. JJ was a year younger than Charlie.

"I texted Tess earlier about coming over. The bakery was busy but she said she'd try to come by after she closed up," Charlie added.

Danny nodded and avoided his sister's glare.

"Have you spoken to Tess lately?" she asked.

"Can't say that I have," he told Charlie.

"Why? Ever since Jason and Kate's wedding you two have been weird." Charlie studied her brother, waiting for a reaction.

He shifted uncomfortably in his seat. "We haven't been weird. She has been avoiding me. I've tried to talk to her a bunch of times, but she always finds a reason to cut me short or ignore me completely."

"Something had to have happened at the wedding. You guys had that dance together and then you disappeared."

Sometimes he really hated how observant his sister was. "She knows how I feel, but she thinks we're better off as friends. What am I supposed to do?"

"You don't give up. You two would be perfect together," Charlie told him.

"No argument here. You're going to have to try telling your friend that because she won't listen to me."

"Tess is my best friend and I love her to pieces but she doesn't exactly have the best track record when it comes to men. She's used to assholes. There is nothing I'd like more than for her to be with someone who knows how to treat a woman right, and I certainly hope that you would. She just needs a little sense knocked into her."

Danny let out a sigh. He knew how guarded Tess was and he had no problem being patient, but he wasn't sure that she was going to give him a chance no matter how long he waited.

Nick laughed from the back seat, which made Danny laugh too. Charlie turned to look at her boyfriend and then her brother. "What are you two cackling at?"

"Nothing. I just think it's funny, you saying that Tess needs some sense knocked into her. You didn't exactly come around quickly when I made my intentions known, Moreau."

"That was different. You spent years annoying me! All we did was fight. Danny and Tess aren't like that. They make googely eyes at each other and think no one else notices."

"Now that's true," Nick said.

Danny rolled his eyes. "We do not make googely eyes at each other. Will, I'm sorry you got stuck riding with these two nuts."

Will chuckled. "It's all good man, I'm enjoying the entertainment."

Charlie turned to her brother. "You deserve to be happy, Danno, and so does Tess. She just needs to remember that." She smiled at him and then sat back in her seat.

Danny felt comforted by Charlie's pep talk. Maybe he'd been going about it the wrong way. Maybe he needed to be very clear about what his intentions were toward Tess so she knew he wasn't going anywhere and that he was nothing like those assholes that she'd dated in the past. He pulled up to their parents' house, feeling better about the situation than he had in a long time.

"Okay, are ya'll ready for pre-Thanksgiving dinner?" Charlie asked as she unbuckled her seatbelt.

"Let's do this thing," Danny replied. They got out of the truck and headed inside for what was sure to be a good night.

Not far from the Moreau house, in the center of town, Tess Carmichael stood behind the counter of her bakery holding a fresh tray of lemon cookies. She slid it into the case and took a look around. The bakery was filled with people wanting dessert for Thanksgiving. They'd had tons of orders the whole week, which was great, but now Tess was starting to feel the strain of all those long hours.

In the five years that Sweet Southern Treats had been opened, Tess had made its success her sole focus. When she'd started out, she primarily sold cupcakes and cookies but then slowly expanded to other desserts and even breakfast treats. They had orders for parties, events, and even weddings on a pretty steady basis, which made Tess feel confident her baking.

The sight of all the people in her shop made her so happy. As she moved some of the empty trays out of the way, she started softly singing along to the music playing in the bakery. It only took a few seconds before she realized what she was doing and abruptly stopped. That voice telling her that her singing was annoying and nothing but a distraction echoed in her ears. She cleared her throat and went back to what she was doing.

"Hey, Boss, do you know if Betty has Mrs. Perry's order ready?" Leanne, her manager asked.

Tess checked her watch. "Uh, she's supposed to pick it up at six and it's only five."

"Well, she's here now," Leanne said with a forced smile.

Tess looked to the end of the counter and saw Anita Perry in all her southern glory, probably trying not to look impatient while she waited. She didn't quite pull it off.

Mrs. Perry was a good customer, but a demanding one. The woman didn't understand the word "no"; she was notorious for getting her way and doing it with a smile. She was your typical old school southern woman: she was always dressed as if she were going to meet someone important, her hair and makeup were flawless, and she had no problem speaking her mind while sounding sweet as pie. Tess had no doubt Mrs. Perry was the last person anyone would ever want to cross.

"I'll just run in the back and check," Leanne said.

She nodded as Leanne disappeared into the kitchen and approached their customer... "Good evening, Mrs. Perry. Leanne just went to check on your order."

"Thank you, dear. I know we said six, but I was out so I thought I'd pop in."

"Not a problem." Tess smiled as she leaned against the counter.

"Where are you spending the holiday?"

"At my parents' house. My gram will be over and so will my sister. Leanne and Penny will be there too."

"Oh, that's nice. Still no man in your life then?" Anita asked, pursing her lips.

Tess cleared her throat. "No, ma'am, there isn't."

"Honey, you aren't getting any younger, and you really are very pretty. It seems like a shame to waste those good childbearing years."

Tess felt her cheeks get hot. "Well, thank you. I'll, uh, keep that in mind."

Just then, Leanne came out of the kitchen holding a large box.

"Okay, here we are. Two dozen red velvet cupcakes, Mrs. Perry."

"Thank you, girls. The rotary club will be thrilled." She handed Leanne her money and gave a wave.

"Happy Thanksgiving!" they yelled as she walked out of the bakery.

"Ugh! She makes me want to drink five cocktails all at once." Leanne grimaced as she watched Mrs. Perry walk back out onto the street.

Tess laughed. "She's not that bad."

"You're too nice," Leanne said as she rang up the sale and put the cash in the register.

"She's a good customer."

"That may be true, but that doesn't mean we can't say she's a pain in the behind once she leaves."

Tess shook her head and laughed. One of the many things she loved about Leanne was her brutal honesty. Four years earlier when the bakery was just getting off the ground, Leanne had walked in and spent several minutes just looking around. When she finally stepped up to the counter, she said, "You have a wonderful place here, but it sure looks like you could use some help back there."

She wasn't wrong; back then the only employees had been Tess and Betty, an older woman who had been basically running the kitchen so Tess could be out on the floor. While Tess enjoyed being out front and interacting with her customers, her heart was always in the kitchen, baking.

Leanne explained that while she couldn't bake a thing, she was excellent at managing after spending years waiting tables and managing a bar back in Texas. Tess knew she could use someone whose main focus would be making sure things ran smoothly, so she was happy to offer Leanne the job.

In a short time, Leanne had proven why she was the right person for the job. She took charge with things like taking inventory, she developed a more efficient way to take and record orders, and she redesigned their website and set up profiles for the bakery on Facebook and Instagram. Tess knew that she would be lost without Leanne and not just in the bakery. Over the past several years, they had also become friends

"Hey, Tess, Betty wanted to know if the pumpkin cookies for Mrs. Finley were ready to get boxed up?" Penny, her assistant, asked as she pushed her glasses up her nose. Penny was twenty-three and one of the happiest, sweetest people Tess had ever met. Penny, like Leanne had wandered into the bakery one day, checking out the display cases. She ended up ordering two lemon cookies and then asked Leanne if they were hiring. She explained that she was in need of a job while she figured out what she wanted to do about school. There was something about Penny that made both Tess and Leanne want to hire her.

It wasn't long before they realized that Penny had a knack for baking and a great eye for decorating. They encouraged her talent, and soon Penny was taking baking classes to improve on her skills. Tess felt lucky to have her and her talent.

Tess nodded. "Yes, they're all ready to be boxed up."

"Okay, I'll let her know."

"Don't you have somewhere to be tonight?" Leanne asked, placing a hand on her hip.

"Do you know something I don't?"

"I thought I heard you mention earlier you were texting Charlie about dinner."

Tess waved Leanne off. "Oh… that. It's just pre-Thanksgiving dinner at her parents' house. It's been a tradition since before we were teenagers, but it's not a big deal. I told her I'd try to stop by if I didn't get out of here too late. She landed a little while ago so I'm sure they're starting soon."

"Well, why are you still here then?"

Tess glared at her. "Last time I checked, this was my place of business."

"We're almost done here. Besides, your best friend just flew into town and you should go see her. I'm willing to bet that gorgeous brother of hers who just so happens to have the hots for you will be there too, so even more of a reason to get a move on!" Leanne waggled her eyebrows.

"Oh good lord! Danny does not have the hots for me!" She rolled her eyes and groaned.

A smile flirted across Leanne's lips. "He sure does, and you're being dumb if you think otherwise."

"Who has the hots for Tess?" Penny asked, coming over to ring up a sale.

"Danny Moreau, Charlie's brother."

"Oh yeah, he totally has the hots for Tess," Penny agreed with a big grin.

Tess covered her face with her hand, trying to hide her embarrassment. "We're working here and it's not like that between me and Danny," she whispered.

"That's only because you won't let it be like that."

"Lee, we're just friends. We've known each other forever, and it's just better to keep things simple."

"Simple is overrated. He's hot, you're hot, and he's into you. You work all the time and never do anything for yourself. Would it kill you to have a little fun?"

Tess felt her palms start to sweat. The last time she told herself to have some fun, to not think for once, was at Jason and Kate's wedding. That had turned out more complicated than she had anticipated.

"I do have fun. I don't need a man for that."

"Baking doesn't count." Penny giggled.

"Tess, as someone older and wiser, believe me when I tell you when you have a good man in front of you that looks the way Danny Moreau does, you need to quit coming up with excuses about why it can't work and just give it a chance. You owe it to yourself to have fun out of the confines of this building or a kitchen. Just go home, take a shower, get out of your flour-crusted clothes and get your butt over there. We'll close up."

Tess looked from Leanne to Penny. They both gave her encouraging smiles. "Okay, I'm gonna go but it's only to see Charlie."

"Sure thing. Have fun!" Leanne said.

"I'll see you both tomorrow for Thanksgiving dinner."

They nodded and then she disappeared into the kitchen. As she walked toward her office, Tess tried to push thoughts of Danny out of her head. She'd always had a crush on him, but since Charlie was her best friend, Tess had put him in the "can't have" category long ago. When she pulled her phone out of her pocket, there was a text from him reminding her about pre-Thanksgiving dinner. Tess did what she did with all of his other texts: she deleted them and pretended that they'd never existed. She knew how much focus was required to run her bakery and if she let herself get wrapped up in Danny, she would lose her focus and that was something she wasn't willing to do.

No one understood her need to keep her focus on work and to steer clear of love. Tess had a history of liking guys who were selfish assholes, for lack of a better term. They had all seemed nice and sweet at the start but then everything became about them and she'd ended up tossing aside what she wanted in order to please them. She had learned the hard way not to forget that her dreams were important, and she was willing to sacrifice having a relationship for the sake of her bakery.

She reached for her keys to unlock her Jeep and was so distracted by her thoughts that she didn't hear someone approach her. "Hey, Tess."

She jumped and clutched her chest as she turned around. She was relieved when she saw a familiar face. "Oh, Cooper, hey."

"Sorry, I didn't mean to startle you. I was walking by and saw you coming out so I wanted to say hi."

Cooper Witter owned a sandwich shop a few doors over from Tess's bakery. He'd been open for less than six months and was doing well from what she could see. His shop was always busy and the word around town was that everyone liked his food. Cooper had made his way to Belmont from somewhere near New Orleans. His previous business hadn't worked out so he'd come to Belmont looking for a fresh start. They'd become friends over the past few months and she enjoyed his company. Cooper understood what it took to run a successful business and it was nice having someone to talk to who understood the sacrifices and hard work involved. He was close to six feet tall with dirty blond hair and hazel eyes. He had a good build, so he definitely stayed in shape. Though Tess couldn't imagine when he found time for that since he always seemed like he was at work.

"It's okay. I don't usually scare so easily but I was lost in thought, I guess."

"You're leaving early tonight. You're usually the last one out."

"Yeah, well, Charlie is home for Thanksgiving so I'm going to see her. Things finally slowed down, and Leanne and Penny said they could handle closing up. I'm sure you were busy today too."

"We had a bunch of catering orders and then the shop was full until about four. I can't complain, you know how it is, busy is always good even if your feet are killing you." He chuckled.

She nodded in understanding. "Well, I should get going."

"Okay, yeah, don't let me hold you up. I meant to ask you the other night when we grabbed a drink after work if you were planning on going to the Pulled Pork and Whiskey Festival?" He gave her a small smile and never took his eyes off of her.

"Oh yeah, I'll be there. Charlie's mom entered and she asked me to bake cupcakes to compliment her table. You should come by. There will be a big group of us there. It'll be fun."

"That sounds great. I guess I'll see you there."

Tess nodded and gave him a smile. "I'll look for you."

"Have a happy Thanksgiving, Tess."

"You too, Cooper." She opened her door and climbed in. She gave him a wave as she drove out of the parking lot.

Two

Pre-Thanksgiving dinner was in full swing. Danny, Charlie, Nick, and Will were greeted by Danny and Charlie's mom, Alice Moreau, who was beaming at the sight of having all of her children in one place. Chief Moreau walked in a few minutes later, still wearing his police uniform and carrying enough Chinese food to feed the entire neighborhood. Jason, the oldest of Alice's children, and his wife, Kate, came in right after him along with Danny's uncle Julian, his father's older brother, and his aunt Mary. Everyone headed for the kitchen to help unpack their food and then went right to filling their plates before settling between the kitchen and family room.

Jason had a home game on Sunday so the conversation was about the game up until Mary wanted to know when Charlie and Nick were moving back to North Carolina and settling down for real.

"Nick finishes his fellowship in June, and we'd like to live either in Belmont or Charlotte since he's got that job at the hospital and with the Panthers. We need to start looking at places soon."

"It's been a long time since all of us Moreaus have made North Carolina our permanent residence. Batten down the hatches." Jason chuckled.

"Danny, did you get the condo project you were telling me about?" his uncle asked.

"I did. Over a three hundred luxury condos in downtown Charlotte."

"Why don't you look that excited about it?" Charlie asked.

"I am. It's a great project... I don't know... I guess I'm just looking to do something more than condos."

"There's nothing wrong with expanding your horizons, Danno."

Danny appreciated that his sister always seemed to be attuned to how he was feeling. He took a bite of an eggroll and smiled.

"I'm here!" They all looked up to see JJ walking in. "Oh, that food smells delicious! I'm starving!" He greeted everyone and then went to fill up his plate. Danny got up and grabbed him a beer. "Thanks man. I definitely need this today," he said taking a sip.

"Long day?"

"I worked a double so I could be off tomorrow but I may work seven to seven tomorrow night to help out one of the guys with two kids." He shrugged.

"Sounds like a lot of hours," Danny replied.

"Yeah, but the overtime is good. Besides, the chief likes to keep me on my toes." JJ smiled looking over at his uncle.

"Damn right, and if you're lucky you'll make detective by the time you're thirty," the chief retorted.

"Oh good. Only another four years until I get promoted."

"Sounds about right to me."

They all laughed, but Danny knew his father thought JJ was a good cop. He'd always had good gut instincts and he liked helping people.

"Charlie, when does your next blog post come out?" Kate asked.

"After this weekend. I'm going to feature Momma's pulled pork for the blog and use pictures from the festival."

Saturday was the annual Pulled Pork and Whiskey Festival in town. Their mother had entered for the first time last year and won third place. Now she determined to win first place.

"I'm glad to see the blog is doing so well. It certainly was a good investment, Ace."

"Thanks, Jay. I'm still amazed at how many people who just started up businesses want me to write about them and feature their products or their clothes on my blog. It's still kind of crazy to me," she said with a laugh.

"If you can show people things that they wouldn't see otherwise that sounds pretty awesome to me," Danny said.

"Hello!"

He heard the familiar voice and tried not to show his excitement. Charlie dropped her plate on the coffee table and jumped out of her spot on the couch and quickly made her way into the kitchen. "Yay! You're here!" she said wrapping Tess in a big hug.

"Yes, and I brought dessert."

"You didn't have to do that!"

"Although no one is complaining that you did!" Jason called from his spot on the couch.

Tess dropped the box on the counter and made her way into the family room to say hello. Danny knew he was staring, but he couldn't help it. He thought she looked good no matter what she wore, but he was used to seeing her in her bakery clothes. She looked really good in a pair of dark jeans with a few rips at the knees, an off the shoulder black sweater, and short black boots.

He stood up from his spot on the couch and waited for her to turn toward him. "Hey."

"Hi, Danny." She tried to avoid eye contact with him, but he took three steps closer to her.

"Glad you could make it."

"Yeah, me too," Tess replied still avoiding his gaze.

"You must be starving. Let me grab you a plate," Charlie said, leading her into the kitchen.

Danny returned to the couch and took a long pull from his beer. When he looked over at his brother and his cousin, they were both grinning at him. "What?"

"You've got it so bad man." JJ chuckled.

He shook his head and tried to ignore them. Charlie and Tess returned and flopped down on the opposite couch. They chatted about Tess's bakery and how busy she'd been with the holiday.

"You're not open tomorrow are you?" Alice asked.

Tess shook her head. "No, I like to give my employees off for the holiday. Leanne and Penny will actually be at my parents' house for dinner tomorrow."

"What are you baking for tomorrow? I know you're not gonna let someone else bake," Charlie said with a smirk.

"I think just three pies." Tess laughed as she shoved some lo mein in her mouth.

"Are you coming to the festival on Saturday?" Danny asked her.

"Oh yeah, I'll be there. Your mom asked me if I'd bake cupcakes to go along with her pulled pork, kind of like a double whammy of savory and sweet."

"That's perfect! I'm doing my next blog on the festival, and I'd love to feature you too."

Tess's face lit up. "That would be great. Anything to bring good press to the bakery."

17

Danny knew how hard she worked to build her brand, and she was definitely successful for it. Her work ethic and her dedication to her business was one of the things that attracted him to Tess, but he'd been attracted to her long before she started her business. There was so much more to her than just baking, but he felt like work was the only thing she truly focused on and as a business owner he knew how the grind could wear you down.

JJ stood up and looked at the group. "Are we gonna sit around all night, or are we going to get this party started?"

"What did you have in mind?" Jason asked.

"I'm pretty sure there's a beer pong table downstairs just waiting for us to use it."

"Oh, are ya'll looking to lose?" Charlie asked with a laugh.

"Whatever! Let's go!"

They grabbed their plates and headed into the kitchen to drop them in the garbage before making a beeline for the basement. Danny hung back, waiting to get Tess alone.

"Don't get too crazy down there. Ya'll are adults!" Alice said.

"Bring the cupcakes!" Jason called out.

"Don't take all the cupcakes!" the chief said.

"Don't worry, chief, I'm leaving some up here for ya'll."

Tess turned around and placed a few cupcakes on a plate on the counter before grabbing the box and a butter knife to bring downstairs. As she made her way toward the basement, Danny was waiting by the door for her. When she was in earshot, he smiled at her. "You look good," he whispered.

She looked down and cleared her throat. "Uh, thanks."

"I'm glad you decided to stop avoiding me tonight."

"I'm not avoiding you. I told you that I think we should stay friends, you just refuse to listen."

"I have no problem with being friends, but first I'd like you to admit that you've been dodging me. I've tried calling and texting you, and you haven't answered. Every time I walk into the bakery, you're conveniently nowhere to be found or you disappear before I get a chance to talk to you."

"I've been busy." Her voice shook. She knew he saw right through that load of crap she'd just dished out.

Danny glared at her. "It's been months. We need to talk about…"

She sighed and looked up at him and Danny could see the uncertainty in her eyes. "Danny..."

"Come on, let's get downstairs." He gestured for her to go down the stairs ahead of him. As much as he didn't want to drop the subject, he knew that pressing the issue right now wasn't a good idea so he left it alone.

Watching the guys set up the beer pong table always felt like being in some sort of time warp. Tess instantly remembered them all in high school hanging out, playing drinking games, and hoping not to get caught. Now that they didn't have to worry about getting caught, it was just a fun thing to do. She put the cupcake box on the table by the couches where Charlie and Kate were sitting and flopped down next to her best friend.

"I had such a craving for your cupcakes this morning. I'm so glad you brought them," Charlie said, reaching over to grab the box and flipping it open with a giant smile on her face.

Tess gave her a wink. "I aim to please."

"Those look amazing. We loved everything you made for the wedding. Those mini cupcakes were such a hit!" Kate remarked.

"I loved doing it. Plus I know what a sweet tooth Jason has." She laughed.

"Tess, I could've eaten that entire table of cupcakes myself!" Jason yelled over to her.

"Thanks, Jay." She turned and gave Jason a big smile and inadvertently noticed Danny looking at her. She quickly turned back around, hoping she wasn't blushing too much.

Charlie picked up the lemon cupcake and grinned before taking a big bite. "Heaven."

"Can I cut one in half, or is that not allowed? I want to pace myself since there's a lot of deliciousness in that box." Kate laughed.

"Of course it's allowed," Tess said. "That's why I brought down a knife." She slid the knife to Kate, who cut the Oreo cupcake right down the middle.

Kate picked up the cupcake and took a bite. "Oh man, that's good."

Tess grabbed the other half and took a big bite. She had to admit, she knew how to make a good cupcake.

"Are you ladies actually going to play or are you just going to sit there and eat cupcakes?" Nick asked.

"There really isn't much of a contest between Tess's cupcakes and playing beer pong. Clearly the three of us chose correctly, but you guys can play first and then Tess and I will come over and wipe the floor with you," Charlie replied.

"Oh please!" they groaned.

"Tess and I are the reigning champs, are we not?"

"Nick and I almost won that last game!"

"You still lost, Danno, and we have a better record than all you guys anyway."

"Hang on, you beat Danny and Nick?" Will asked, looking confused.

"Yep! And Danny and Jason and Nick and JJ." Charlie smirked while pumping her fist in the air in victory.

"That's just…" Will was at a loss for words. He turned to the guys for some kind of explanation, but no one said anything.

"Surprising?" Charlie laughed. "It's okay, Will, most people would expect that someone like me, who spent more time studying than partying, wouldn't be really good at something like beer pong. But as it turns out, I have excellent hand-eye coordination." She shrugged nonchalantly.

"I just get lucky, so we're quite a pair," Tess said.

"Sounds like it," Will said, rubbing the back of his neck. He still looked baffled.

The guys started playing and the girls turned their attention back to their conversation. "I can't remember the last time I played beer pong," Kate said.

"Well, you know we never miss out on a chance for a little competition."

"Yes, I'm well aware of the Moreau competitive spirit. I wouldn't have figured you were as competitive as your brothers though."

Tess let out a laugh. "Now that's hilarious. She's always been right there with them. If they climbed a tree, she was trying to climb it faster."

Kate chuckled. "I could definitely see that. Ya'll have such a special closeness. It's really nice. Growing up as an only child was kind of lonely, and we moved around a lot so making friends was tough. I missed out on a lot of the stuff you do with your friends when you're younger."

Tess knew that Kate had never lived in one place for very long because her father was in the military, but she had never realized how difficult that must've been for her as a kid, not having any real friends to make memories with. She wouldn't have traded her childhood for the world; she had a good relationship with her younger sister and she'd spent a lot of time around the Moreaus, which had always been fun.

"Well, now you have us so you can catch up on the things you missed." Charlie smiled.

"Thank you. So any idea when you and Nick are going to start looking at places to live?"

"I'm hoping to look at places when we come home for Christmas just to get an idea of what's out there. I don't want to have to pack up everything in New York and have no idea where we're going."

"I'm just glad you're gonna be back," Tess told her.

Charlie nodded and looked down at her hands. "If someone would've told me that I would end up back here and with Nick Russo, I would've called them absolutely crazy, but I couldn't be happier. It's weird, but a good weird."

"Any talk of marriage?"

Charlie shook her head. "I'd marry Nick tomorrow, but I'm okay with things the way they are. There's going to be so much going on over the next seven months between Nick's fellowship finishing up and moving that the thought of planning a wedding on top of that would be very overwhelming. I would never want Nick to feel like I needed more, like the life we have isn't enough," she told Kate.

"I don't think he'd ever think that you were being selfish because you wanted to get married. I was dead set on never getting married. Your brother had to convince me that I was being absolutely ridiculous, if you remember."

Charlie chuckled. "Oh yes, I remember. Jason finally found the woman he wanted to marry and she didn't want to ever get married."

Tess blinked a few times, feeling somewhat confused. "Wait a minute, you didn't want to get married?"

Kate shook her head. "I didn't. I was very happy with my life, my job, and my friends, and then I met Jason at that charity gala that the hospital was throwing. I thought he was just another hotshot athlete, trying to add another notch in his bedpost by being all sweet to me, but I learned pretty fast that he was not that kind of guy. He wanted to get to know me, he wanted to take me out on real dates, and even after I realized that he wasn't looking for some kind of fling, I still didn't think he wanted long-term."

"It's kind of funny because I don't think he ever knew he wanted it either. Growing up, he was so focused on football and making it to the NFL, he never really talked about settling down when the time came or anything like that, but I'm pretty sure when he met you, he just knew that's what he wanted." Charlie gave her a smile.

Kate blushed a little bit. "Jason wanted to be my husband, but I told him that I didn't need a ring or a wedding to know that we were committed. He had shown me over and over that he was completely committed to me, but Jason wanted it all. He wanted to build a life with me, have a family, and he wanted me to be his wife. When he put it like that, everything I thought I wanted just went right out the window. I was so afraid of things changing for the worse that I never considered how good they could be. That's why I'm saying Charlie, if you want to get married, don't brush it aside because you're worried about everyone else and their needs."

Tess gave Charlie a small nod. Charlie had always been incredibly selfless, worrying about everyone else's needs, but Kate was right: if she wanted to get married, Nick needed to hear it.

Groans and cheers erupted from the beer pong table, making them all turn around. "Who's playing the winners?" Danny called over to them.

"We are!" Charlie yelled as she tugged on Tess's arm.

Tess let out a sigh and pulled herself off of the couch. The girls would be playing against Nick and Danny, since they'd beaten JJ and Jason. Tess had played beer pong against Danny more times than she could count, but suddenly her stomach twisted into a giant knot. When she looked at him from across the table, her eyes landed on his lips. All she could think about was how they felt pressed against hers or how they felt on other places of her body. This was not good.

Charlie nudged her as she cracked open a beer and started filling their Solo cups. "Are you okay?"

"Yeah, I'm good." They finished arranging the cups on their side and waited for Danny and Nick to get set up.

"Winners shoot first?"

"Sure, Danno, if you think you need that kind of edge." Charlie smirked.

"I feel like I should pull up a chair and watch," Will said with a grin.

"You won't be disappointed, man. Get your drink and settle in," JJ told him.

Charlie turned to Tess and grinned.

"I swear I feel seventeen again." Tess laughed, shaking her head.

"We're so much better now than we were back then."

"Good point," Tess replied.

"We've got this," Charlie said to her. They bumped hips and fists, their customary pre-game ritual.

"We've got this," Tess repeated. She took a step back and waited for Danny and Nick to take their first shot.

Nick shot first, and his ball bounced off one of the front cups. Danny squared up and released his shot, which bounced off of a cup near Tess. She scooped up the ball and took her position behind the table. Charlie nodded at her to shoot first so Tess took aim and then released the small white sphere, which took a loud bounce off of the first cup. Charlie was already in position, eyeing up her shot. She released the ball and sank it. "Drink up, boys!"

Jason and JJ snickered while Will nodded in an almost approving way.

"Wow," Kate said.

"I'm not even warmed up yet."

Tess laughed. She couldn't remember the last time she'd done something like this. It felt good to let loose and have fun with people she loved. They went on to beat Danny and Nick, JJ and Will, and finally Jason and Kate. Danny and Nick called for a rematch so they agreed to one last game.

There were two cups left in front of Tess and Charlie and one left in front of Nick and Danny, meaning the girls were one shot away from keeping their title. Charlie shot first and missed.

"Oh! Is someone losing her touch?"

Charlie glared at Danny. "You are still losing, big brother, and I've been drinking most of the beer on this side."

Tess shot and also missed. She stepped back as the boys got

ready to take their turns. Nick went first and his ball bounced to the right. Danny wasted no time and took his shot, which landed in the cup right in front of Tess. "Oh yeah! Now we're tied!" He slapped hands with Nick and Tess passed the cup to Charlie. Charlie drank down the beer and put it to the side of the table.

"Okay, enough messing around. Let's end this," Charlie announced as she took her ball in her hand.

Tess let out a deep breath, took aim, and then watched as her ball sailed right over the cup. "Ugh!"

Charlie looked completely focused as she squared up to take her shot. The whole room was silent. Tess watched as her best friend released the ball and it dropped into the final cup. "Boom!"

"Oh!" JJ yelled

"We still get our turn!" Danny said, fishing the ball out of the cup and drinking the beer.

"Go on then." Tess gestured to the cup. She looked over and saw Charlie leaning over with her hands on the table, baring her cleavage right at Nick.

"Yeah, Nick, go ahead. Shoot."

He rolled his eyes. "Are you kidding me, Moreau? How am I supposed to concentrate with you like that?"

"I don't know what you mean." She smirked as she leaned over more.

"Gross! Brothers and cousin in the room!" Danny said, shaking his head.

Tess couldn't hold back her laugh, especially when Nick's ball completely missed the cup. "Damn it! I'm calling a foul!"

"No fouls in beer pong, babe," Charlie said, stepping back so Danny could shoot.

Tess watched him eyeball the cup before releasing the ball. She actually held her breath as she watched the ball bounce right off the cup.

"Yeah! Still the champs!" Charlie pulled her into a hug and then they slapped hands. Danny and Nick shook their heads at their defeat.

"That was impressive," Will told them.

"You should see us play darts," Charlie said, which made the guys grumble. "Ya'll put up a good fight."

Everyone cleaned up the mess in the basement and then made

their way back upstairs. The parents were in the family room sitting around the TV, chatting and having their night caps. "We're gonna hit the road," Jason said. "I've got early practice tomorrow."

They all decided to pack it in for the night, said their goodbyes, and headed out to the driveway. Charlie looped her arm with Tess's as they walked down the driveway. "I'm so glad you made it tonight. I know you've had a long day."

"I couldn't miss this. It's tradition. Besides, I can sleep past six thirty tomorrow, so that's huge."

Charlie turned, looking at her with slightly unfocused eyes, and pulled her in for a hug. "I am forever thankful for you, Tess Marie Carmichael. Have a happy Thanksgiving."

Tess squeezed her back. "I'm forever thankful for you too, Charlie Rose Moreau. Happy Thanksgiving to you too." Charlie kissed her cheek and then hurried to grab Nick from behind. He was talking to Danny by his truck, but he stopped as soon as Charlie's arms were around him and pulled her right up against himself. Tess watched the exchange, and it made her feel incredibly happy that Charlie had found her Prince Charming. She grabbed her keys from her purse and turned to get into her Jeep.

"Sneaking off again?"

Tess turned around and saw Danny walking toward her. "No, I wasn't sneaking. Everyone is going, so I am too."

"Are you okay to drive?"

"Yeah, Charlie drank most of the beer so I'm okay."

"Okay, just making sure."

She looked down. "Well... I should go. Good night."

"How long are you gonna do this?"

She looked at him confused. "Do what?"

"Avoid me."

Exasperated, she ran a hand over her face. "Danny, we've been over this..."

"And it still doesn't make any sense to me. As I recall, after the wedding you showed up at my door at three in the morning."

Tess felt her cheeks grow hot and shifted where she stood. "That was a mistake. That's all."

Danny shook his head and took a step closer to her. "You forget, I've known you since we were kids. I can tell when you're lying. What are you so afraid of? Charlie is completely on board, so it can't be that."

She straightened her spine and put her shoulders back before she spoke. "It has nothing to do with Charlie. Well maybe it has a little to do with her, but more importantly I don't need any complications in my life. I need to stay focused on my bakery."

He took another step toward her and Tess realized she was backed up against her car door. She swallowed hard at his close proximity.

"Your work ethic is one of the things I like most about you. I find it very sexy. I own my own business too, and I understand being devoted to it, but there's more to life than just work, Tess. Are you going to tell me that you don't think about that night?"

Her throat went bone dry. "I... No, there's nothing to think about."

He smirked at her. "Really? Nothing? Do you need me to remind you of it?"

Tess's stomach dropped as her mind flashed back to that night.

Jason and Kate's wedding had been beautiful. The reception was in full swing and Tess had watched as the bride and groom cut it up on the dance floor surrounded by Charlie, Danny, and the rest of the bridal party as well as several others. Sometimes she wished she had an easier time cutting loose, but she spent so much time focused on work. She didn't have time for much else.

Tess made her way over to the bar to get a better view of everyone, and she must've gotten so lost in thought that she never even saw Danny approach her. He slid a glass of bourbon to her and told her how gorgeous she looked. Never one for accepting compliments well, she blushed and took a sip of the bourbon. Before she knew it, he was grabbing her by the hand and asking her to dance. Tess tried to refuse, but it was hard to say no to him when he looked so devastatingly handsome.

Danny had held her close and it reminded her that she hadn't been held that way by a man in a long time, if ever. When their eyes locked at the end of the dance, it was like something changed between them. He led her away from the crowd and inside, where he abruptly kissed her. Tess's first instinct was to push him away, but the feel of his lips on hers was too good and instead she pulled him in for more.

"Come upstairs with me," he'd whispered against her mouth.

That was when she pulled away. She was overwhelmed with fear that she'd made a huge mistake and ran back out to the reception before anything more could happen.

Tess made a point of staying clear of Danny for the rest of the reception and the after party, but when she got up to her hotel room much later, she'd spent what felt like hours tossing and turning. And in the end she'd done what any woman who needed to end her sleeplessness would do: she'd showed up at Danny's hotel room in her pajamas and practically jumped him at the door.

It had been the most brazen thing Tess had ever done, but there was a part of her that liked being the one to take action. They hadn't done much talking; it was as if there was an unspoken understanding as to why Tess had shown up. Their lips met and their tongues tangled as they removed what little they had on before making their way to the bed. At first, Danny had just looked at Tess and then a smile lifted at the corners of his mouth before he kissed her.

He'd touched her everywhere, like he was trying to memorize her, and then his lips made their way down her neck and to her breast. Danny sucked one nipple into his mouth while his hand massaged her other breast. He switched it up to give them both equal attention and Tess could already feel herself starting to come undone. With one hand still on her breast, his other hand traveled down to her center where he slipped two fingers inside her. Tess's head snapped back on the bed, but Danny kept thrusting his fingers inside her while squeezing her breast. All she could do was moan as he moved his fingers faster. When he circled her clit with his thumb, Tess saw stars and screamed Danny's name. He crawled back up her body and took her mouth in a hard kiss as she came down from the wave of her orgasm.

Before she could try to move, Danny was covering himself with a condom and leaning over her on his hands and knees. He looked into her eyes and grazed her cheek with his hand.

"Are you sure?"

"Yeah, very sure." She pulled his mouth down to hers and as their bodies rubbed up against each other, Tess could feel the wetness between her legs again. Danny positioned himself at her entrance and entered her with one swift motion, and Tess's eyes practically rolled back in her head. He filled her completely and while it hurt a little at first, with each thrust she adjusted to him. Danny gripped her hips to keep her in place as he slid in and out of her and Tess hooked her ankles around his waist to pull him closer. He rolled his hips and she fisted the sheets in her hands. The tension was building in her and she wanted a release so badly.

"Harder, Danny. You're not going to break me."

He looked up at her and smirked as he pounded into her harder. She didn't even see him snake his hand between them and circle her clit but as soon as his finger landed on her, an explosion went off inside Tess's body and she let out a sound she didn't even know she was capable of making. Danny thrust into her a few more times and then his own orgasm hit him before he collapsed on top of her.

When he looked down at her, she had a hand over her eyes and was trying to catch her breath. He peeled her hand away from her eyes. "No hiding, you're gorgeous, there's nothing to cover up." Danny pressed a kiss to her lips and then rolled out of bed to go dispose of the condom. He came back to bed and wrapped his arms around her and covered them both with the blanket. Tess's head was flooded with thoughts, but before she could say anything, she heard the sound of Danny's even breathing.

Sleep never came to her. Her mind was racing with what this could mean for them and all the reasons why it was a terrible idea. When the sun came up, Tess knew there was only one thing she could do. She rolled out of Danny's arms and left without a word.

And for the last several months, she'd been trying to forget that night despite all of Danny's efforts to remind her.

Tess cleared her throat. "Nope. Nothing I need to remember."

"I remember it very well. You in my room, peeling off the few clothes you had on. I remember every curve and line of your gorgeous body, I remember what it felt like to have you wrapped around me and to watch you lose yourself as you came."

She swallowed hard and tried to breathe but was having difficulty.

"I remember what it felt like being buried deep inside you and being so connected that we instinctively knew what the other one wanted. I also remember how it felt waking up to an empty bed, to you just being gone."

Tess looked away from him and shook her head. "Danny, I couldn't stay."

"You're scared," he said smugly.

Her head snapped up. "Excuse me?"

"You're scared and I can understand that, but you can't tell me that there's nothing between us. I know you felt it." He leaned in closer and she could almost taste his scent on her lips.

She'd felt it all right. Tess had never felt anything so strong before in her life, which was why she'd run from it so fast.

"I don't like distractions, I'm happy focusing on my bakery."

He raised his eyebrows at her. "You think I'm going to monopolize all of your time and your bakery will suffer. While I would be more than happy to distract you at any given time, I know how much you love your bakery and I'd never interfere with that. I also have my own business to run so I understand what that takes. I'd still like to take you out on a real date and spend time with you. I guarantee that your bakery won't crumble if you go out with me." Danny sighed and ran a hand through his hair in frustration.

Tess tried to gather herself up against her car door. She wanted to say yes. She wanted to believe that she could spend time with Danny and not get distracted, but she didn't trust herself. He made her do unpredictable things.

"Look, I appreciate what you're saying. You're a really good guy, but I have my priorities and I don't plan on changing them."

He looked at her like he was trying to look through her. She hoped that she was putting up enough of a front because she needed him to believe that she was serious.

"We'll see about that. I can be patient."

"There's nothing to be patient about, I'm not going to change my mind," she said, squaring her shoulders and looking him straight in the eye.

"Whatever you say. Have a happy Thanksgiving, Tess." He backed away from her, grinning from ear to ear.

Danny headed for his truck and Tess quickly climbed into her Jeep. She needed to get away from him and into a cold shower.

Three

Tess was so accustomed to waking up with the sun that having a morning with no alarm was a rare treat. When she rolled over, she saw that her clock read a little after eight. After getting in from the Moreaus, she had thought she would be wide awake, especially after her encounter with Danny, but she fell asleep almost as soon as her head hit the pillow.

She used the bathroom, washed her face, and brushed her teeth before padding down the hall to her kitchen. Tess threw her hair up in a messy bun and went straight for the coffee pot. She had three pies to make, and she was going to need some caffeine to get them done. Luckily, yesterday morning she'd gotten up extra early to make the pie crusts so that would be one less thing to do today. She sighed, looking around at her small workspace; she did most of her baking at the bakery due to the big kitchen and multiple ovens. Despite wishing for a bigger home kitchen, her apartment was perfectly practical and that was really all that mattered.

Tess got to work on the pumpkin pie and then poured herself a big cup of coffee. Most people who baked as much as she did would probably never do it once they were home, but baking always relaxed her, made her happy. As she put the pie in the oven, there was a knock at the door. She wiped her hands on the nearest dishtowel and when she got to the door, she was greeted with a familiar smile.

"Happy Thanksgiving, sis."

"Hi! Happy Thanksgiving, Amy."

Her sister stepped through the door and wrapped her in a hug, letting the door close behind her. "I knew you'd be awake, and I got off my shift a little while ago so I come bearing gifts." She held up a paper bag and jiggled it.

"That smells like—"

"Bacon, egg, and cheese on a biscuit from the diner? That's

because it is." Amy smiled and walked toward the kitchen. She removed her coat and put it over one of Tess's chairs before placing her bag on the counter. "Please tell me there's coffee in that pot."

"Of course, help yourself."

Amy went into the kitchen and got herself a cup of coffee while Tess unpacked the bag.

"This smells like heaven and is exactly what I needed," Tess said as she grabbed two plates from the cabinet, grinning from ear to ear.

"Hungover this morning?"

"No. I ended up playing four rounds of beer pong with Charlie last night, but she was on drinking duty."

Amy brushed a piece of her long blonde bob off of her face. "Oh yes, pre-Thanksgiving dinner. I'm sorry I missed it. Did you two kick ass?"

"We did." She laughed. "It was a lot of fun." She refilled her coffee cup and took her plate over to the couch. "The parade is gonna start soon." Tess turned the TV on and sat down.

Amy followed after her and plopped down on the couch next to her. They had always loved watching the Macy's Thanksgiving Day Parade because it got them in the holiday spirit.

"How was seeing Danny?"

"It was fine, why wouldn't it be?" Tess shrugged.

"Ever since the wedding you've been keeping your distance from him," Amy told her.

"No, I haven't."

Her sister's hazel eyes glared at her over her coffee cup.

"He wants to be more than friends and I don't."

"Well explain that again because I still don't understand. Do you know how rare it is for a guy to actually tell you how he feels about you?"

She knew. Most guys were anything but direct and more time was usually spent trying to figure out what they wanted.

Tess slammed her hand down on the couch. "I'm focused on my work. That's not a bad thing."

"No, it's not but in case you haven't noticed, it's the twenty-first century and women everywhere have careers and run successful businesses, and there's no rule that says that they have to stay single in order to do that."

"I got my dream with the bakery and it deserves all of my

attention."

"This is because of that asshole Dean, isn't it?"

Tess almost choked on her coffee at the mention of his name. "What are you talking about?" She placed her cup down on the coffee table, still sputtering.

Amy grabbed her sister's hand and gave it a squeeze. "He broke your heart, shattered it really, and somehow you think you deserved how he treated you, which is crazy but it would explain why you run from any man who's interested in you."

Tess pulled her hand away and reached for her coffee. "That's ridiculous, and it's not like I have men lined up around the block."

Amy rolled her eyes and turned toward her. "You wouldn't notice if you did. I could kick his ass for making you think you're less than amazing. You changed your whole life for him, and not only did he never appreciate you but then he had the nerve to cheat on you."

Tess felt a pain in her chest as the memories began flooding back to her. She'd met Dean at UNC-Charlotte her freshman year of college. They had a class together and for some unknown reason, he made Tess his focal point. He was good looking, funny, and popular on campus. She always considered herself fairly average and more on the shy side, which put her very much out of someone like Dean's league. When she was with him, people noticed her and as much as she hated to admit it, Tess liked the recognition. Had she known then what staying with someone like him would cost her she would've run as fast as her legs would've carried her. She shuddered, thinking back on that time in her life.

"Personally, I think you would benefit from spending some time with Danny. When was the last time you had your engine revved up anyway?"

Tess almost choked on her coffee again. "Jesus, Amy! I swear you've been spending way too much time with Elena."

Her sister laughed as she took a bite of her sandwich. Amy had been best friends with Elena Russo, Nick and Will's younger sister, since they were five. Elena was definitely a bit of a wild one; she was known for doing things her way and she had no filter. Amy was the more laid-back one in their friendship, but Elena had rubbed off on her a bit over the years.

"Oh, come on! Danny is hot, and I think you'd benefit from letting him help you unwind." Amy nudged her arm.

Tess gripped her coffee cup tightly and tried not to look affected by Amy's comments. She knew firsthand how hot he was and what he could do to her body.

"You're one to talk. You don't exactly date either."

"I may not date but you better believe I take care of my engine." Amy grinned and finished off her sandwich.

Tess groaned and covered her face with her hand.

"You need to understand that it doesn't have to be one way. You can be a badass boss lady *and* you can spend time with a guy and the world won't stop. Your bakery won't fall apart. You won't fall victim to a man like Dean again. That's done and over with. You never do anything for you. When was the last time you even took a vacation?"

Tess stared up at the ceiling for a second, trying to remember. "Last summer when we went down to Atlanta for Mara's wedding."

"Two days away for our cousin's wedding doesn't count. Stop being such a scaredy-cat and live your life. Have a little fun."

Tess knew her sister meant well. She knew that she only wanted Tess to be happy, but it felt like no one understood her point of view. "Look, it's the Grinch balloon."

Amy glared at her and then returned her attention to the TV. Tess finished her breakfast and then leaned back on the couch, grateful that her sister didn't bring up her lack of a love life again.

Thanksgiving came and went and then all the focus in the Moreau household was on getting ready for the Pulled Pork and Whiskey Festival. Alice had everything handled and just needed some help with setup. Alice and the chief had left earlier to start setting up, so Danny picked up Nick and Charlie at Nick's mom's house, where they were staying for the weekend, and they drove over to the festival together. When they arrived, the tables and booths were just starting to get set up so it wasn't too hectic yet. On the ride over, Danny noticed that something was off with Nick. He'd been unusually quiet and he was as white as a sheet.

"Oh good, you're here!" Alice said as they walked up to her station. "I have four more containers of things in my trunk that I could use a hand with."

"Sure thing, Momma. We're on it," Danny told her as he guided

Nick back toward the car. Once they were out of earshot of everyone else, he nudged Nick's shoulder. "Okay, what's up with you?"

"What?"

"You've barely said two words since I picked you guys up, and you look like you're gonna puke any second. Are you sick?"

Nick shook his head. "No, I'm not sick."

"Did you and Charlie get into a fight?"

"No, we're fine. Really great."

"Okay, then what?" Danny popped open the trunk to his mom's SUV and waited.

Nick scrubbed a hand over his face. "I'm gonna ask Charlie to marry me."

"Today?"

"No! Not today! I need to ask the chief's permission before I do anything so I figured while we were here I'd ask him in person, but I haven't had the chance yet." Nick ran a hand through his hair and couldn't stand still.

"Holy shit, man, you had me nervous for a second. I thought something was wrong. You need to relax. The chief loves you."

Nick raised his eyebrows. "It's one thing to like someone as their son's best friend, and it's another thing to give them permission to marry their only daughter."

"Good point." They grabbed the containers, shut the trunk, and locked the car. "Seriously though, you've got nothing to worry about. You make my sister happy and that's all that really matters to him, to all of us."

Nick gave a small smile. "Thanks. I don't know what I did to deserve her, but if she'll have me, I'm gonna spend the rest of my life trying to be worthy of her."

Danny let out a laugh. "You sound like such a sap right now." They started walking back toward his mother's station.

"I know I do, but it's how I feel. Sometimes I still have nightmares of her rolling into the emergency room on that gurney, unconscious and bleeding and her heart stopping. I wake up sweating because I honestly don't know how I'd breathe without her. In the blink of an eye it became that simple. She's my reason for everything."

Danny nodded in understanding. Nick had been the orthopedic resident on call the night that Charlie had been brought to the hospital after being in a near fatal car accident. To complicate things further, Nick and Charlie had had a huge falling out at that time and weren't speaking so when she showed up to the ER in such bad shape, he'd been struck with a fear like he'd never had before. Once Charlie had woken up, they both realized the mistakes they'd made and knew they didn't want to spend any more time apart. Danny had never seen either of them as happy as they were together.

"You two have been through the wringer. You deserve to be happy."

Nick grinned. "I'll feel better once the asking is over."

They reached Alice's station and everyone was busy with setup.

"What took ya'll so long?" Charlie asked.

"We forgot a container and had to go back," Danny told her.

She nodded and went back to what she was doing. Danny bumped Nick's shoulder and the two friends shared a smile before getting out of the way.

By five forty-five, everything was ready at Alice's station even though the festival didn't start until six. The smell of all the food was making Danny very hungry, but he didn't dare touch one of his mother's plates before he was allowed to.

"Oh, here comes Tess," Alice said.

Danny looked up and saw Tess, Leanne, and Penny walking toward them carrying containers of what he assumed were the cupcakes his mother had asked her to make. He hurried over to her. "Hey, let me help you with that."

"Oh, thanks." She handed him the containers in her hand. Nick and the chief came and took the rest of the containers from the other ladies and put them down on the empty table next to where Alice was set up.

Danny couldn't help but notice how cute Tess looked in her chef's jacket and her hair in a side braid. She said her hellos and then went to start setting up her cupcakes.

"Honey, I can't thank you enough for doing this."

"Are you kidding? I'm honored you asked me, Mrs. M." Tess gave her a quick hug and then went back to setting up.

"What kind did you make?" Charlie asked, staring at the containers.

"Chocolate cupcakes with a whipped whiskey icing. Penny came up with the idea."

"Partially," Penny chimed in.

"We thought it was a perfect complement to the pulled pork."

"See, this is why you're the best," Charlie told her. "You can't go wrong with a chocolate whiskey cupcake."

"She certainly is the best," Danny said, looking right at her. Tess quickly looked away and busied herself with opening the containers.

People were starting to make their way into the festival and Danny could see the excitement on his mother's face. Ella, Nick's mother, was right beside her, ready to serve their food. He was glad that Ella had decided to join Alice's team. They'd always been good friends and now they had a chance to do something they loved together.

"Where's the best pulled pork ever?" Jason yelled as he walked up to the table with Kate.

"You don't have to say that," Alice said as her oldest son kissed her hello.

"Why not? It's true and I'm starving."

"You're always starving." She laughed.

"Do we have to wait for everyone else to try it or do we get first dibs?"

"Ya'll can start eating but that doesn't mean you can have one of your eating competitions, do you hear me? I need other people to eat this," Alice told her children.

They all nodded in understanding and grabbed a sandwich before the crowds showed up. "Home run, Momma," Charlie told her.

"This might be your best ever," Danny added. Jason nodded in agreement in between bites.

"Go put those stomachs of yours to use and scope out the competition."

"You certainly don't need to tell us twice! We'll be back," Jason replied.

Jason, Kate, Danny, Nick, and Charlie made their way through the festival and started hitting various stands to try out the samples. Charlie snapped some pictures, no doubt for her blog, and made notes in her phone. After they'd had their fill of pulled pork, they decided they couldn't skip out on the whiskey portion of the festival.

They headed back over to Alice's station with as many whiskey samples as they could carry. There was quite a long line in front of her station, and Danny noticed Nick's older sister, Laura, her husband, Pete, and their daughter, Ava, had shown up as well as Tess's parents.

"Well, how's it looking out there?" Alice asked as she plated more sandwiches.

"It wasn't easy, suffering through all that pulled pork."

"Yeah, we had to hold Jason down to do it." Charlie laughed, jabbing her brother in the side with her elbow.

"Yours is definitely the best, no question."

"Danny, that's sweet, but—"

He held up his hand to cut her off. "I'm not just saying it. It's true."

"He's right. Yours is the best," Kate told her.

Alice seemed satisfied that her daughter-in-law wouldn't try to sweet-talk her. She grinned, happy with that answer, and returned to making more samples to feed the long line of people.

"We come bearing gifts," Danny said, offering the sample cups to their family and friends. He walked behind the table where Tess was stationed and held up the plastic cup. "Whiskey?"

"I'm working."

"It's not a bottle. It's barely one finger's worth of a pour. Besides, this is a pulled pork *and* whiskey festival, so I'm pretty sure you're supposed to try the whiskey."

She shook her head and laughed, accepting the cup from him. "You're a terrible influence."

"That's not true. I think you'll find that I'm a very good influence in reminding you of the things you should indulge in." He smiled slyly at her.

She shifted where she stood, clearly uncomfortable.

"Tell you what, I'll trade you that whiskey for a cupcake and then it'll be an even trade. No influence at all." He grabbed a cupcake from a nearby tray and stuffed it in his mouth. Immediately, he was overwhelmed with the delicious flavors, which made him groan. "Oh wow, that's amazing."

Tess looked at him over the top of her cup and then drank down the whiskey. "Happy?"

"I am. That's a great cupcake."

"Thanks."

He noticed the blush on her cheeks and liked that he'd made her react like that.

"Did I miss all the pulled pork?"

Danny looked up and saw JJ, dressed in his uniform, walking toward them.

"No, honey, I saved you a plate," Alice said, gesturing behind her.

"You're the best, Aunt Alice," he replied, reaching for the plate and then taking a bite out of the sandwich. "Amazing."

"Aren't you supposed to be working?" the chief asked.

"I am. Williams and I are making the rounds to make sure everything is secure, and Aunt Alice's stand was on my route." He shoved the last bite in his mouth and grinned. "Back to work! See ya'll later!"

"Belmont's finest," the chief chuckled as JJ hurried off.

Pete walked over to Danny, still holding one of the whiskey samples in his hand. "How's work going? I heard you landed that condo project in downtown Charlotte."

"Yeah, we signed all the paperwork before the holiday and now everything will start moving along."

"Wow, that's great. Congratulations."

Danny sighed. "Thanks. I'm starting to feel like I'm designing the same kinds of things all the time. I want to do something different. I don't know what though. "

Pete tipped back his whiskey and nodded in understanding. He owned his own contracting company so he understood the problems that came with choosing projects. "Sometimes you just need a little bit of a change. I'd be happy to collaborate anytime you're looking to do something. Give me a call and I'm sure we can come up with something."

"That would be great, man. Thanks."

They shook hands and Danny felt good about the possibility of working with Pete. It might just provide that diversity he was craving.

"Is this where the best pulled pork ever is being served?" Elena Russo yelled out as she, Amy, and Will made their way toward the group.

"Your sister's got some pretty amazing cupcakes over there too," Danny told Amy, gesturing to Tess's table.

Amy smiled. "No surprise there. I'm sure you've already had a taste."

He choked a little bit at her suggestive comment. "Best I've ever had."

"Smart man, Danny Moreau. Smart man."

Danny laughed as he watched Amy and Elena head over to Tess. He wanted nothing more than another taste of her, but he could be patient. Although it was definitely proving to be more and more difficult.

After all the votes were in, Alice's Kitchen ended up winning first place in the festival. The excitement over by the booth was booming, and Tess couldn't help but feel excited that she'd been a part of it. There were still some people by her station and she was happy that the cupcakes were such a success.

"I hope I didn't miss all the cupcakes?"

She looked up and saw Cooper standing at her station. "Hey, Cooper. No, not at all." She smiled and handed him a plate.

"This looks delicious. What did you whip up?" He looked at the cupcake closely before peeling off the wrapper.

"It's a chocolate cupcake with whiskey icing."

He took a bite and a large smile painted his face. "Wow, that's incredible." He finished off the rest of the cupcake and didn't stop smiling the entire time. "I'm not surprised. Everything you make is amazing."

"That's sweet of you to say."

He shrugged. "It's just the truth. How was your Thanksgiving?"

"Really nice, I went to my parents' house. How about you?"

His eyes dropped to the ground and then he looked back up at her. "Oh, it was fine. I just hung out at home."

"By yourself?"

Cooper shrugged. "Yeah, I'm still the new guy so…"

"Cooper, I wish I would have known. I would have invited you to have dinner with us."

"That's okay. You couldn't have known, but I appreciate the thought. You know maybe…"

"Hey, Tess, they're gonna start breaking the tables down in a few minutes," Danny said, inserting himself into their conversation.

"Oh, okay."

There was silence for a moment. Danny looked at Cooper and Cooper looked him over. Tess looked between them and could feel the tension.

"I'm Danny, by the way. Danny Moreau." He extended his hand.

"Hi. Cooper Witter. It's nice to meet you." He shook Danny's hand and gave a small smile.

"Cooper owns the new sandwich shop a few doors over from my bakery, the North Main Street Café."

"Oh yes, I've driven past it a few times," Danny replied.

"You should stop in some time, grab some lunch."

"I just might do that." He took a step closer to Tess and when she looked up at Cooper, he stared at her as if he was waiting for her to say something.

"Well, I should be going. It was nice to meet you, Danny. Tess, I'll see you during the week." He smiled at her and started backing away from the booth.

"Nice meeting you too," Danny said with a forced smile.

"Good night, Cooper." Tess watched him walk away and then turned back to Danny, who was still watching Cooper disappear into the crowd. "What's with you?"

"Nothing. How long have you known him?"

"Since he opened his store about six months ago." Tess frowned. "Why?"

"I'm curious if he's aware of your no dating rule because he was eyeing you up like he wanted to devour you."

"What are you talking about? Cooper and I are friends. We're work neighbors; there's nothing going on with us," she said, lowering her voice. Their family and friends were a few feet away outside of the booth, thankfully distracted by their own conversations because Tess certainly didn't want this becoming a public forum.

He bent down and picked up one of the garbage bags for her. "I don't think he knows that."

She rolled her eyes and started cleaning up the table. "You're being ridiculous."

"You're being stubborn. Just because you want to pretend like you don't need a romantic relationship in your life doesn't mean that men aren't going to be interested in you. Cooper is interested in you."

She tossed a bunch of used plates into the garbage bag and

crossed her arms over her chest. "So what, you thought you'd barge over here and assert yourself?"

"I have absolutely no problem saying that I want you."

There was that honesty again. She swallowed hard. "Keep your voice down. You need to stop saying things like that."

Danny dropped the bag and crossed his arms over his chest. "Why? One of us needs to be honest."

She dropped her hands to her hips and glared at him. "What is that supposed to mean?"

"You are so afraid to admit that you feel something for me so you try to deny it. I won't do that."

"I am not afraid. I have been very honest in saying that I want us to stay friends and I don't want to date anyone. I don't know what else you want me to say."

He stepped closer to her and her breath caught in her chest. "This notion you have that you can only have a professional life and not a personal life is crazy. You're a fool if you think this is how it's supposed to be."

Tess felt her blood start to boil. She was suddenly transported back to a time when she was always put down for what she thought or how she felt about things. She took a step back and looked up at him so he could get a good look at the anger in her eyes. "I'm not sure who the hell you think you are, but you don't get to speak to me like that. It's my life and I will make decisions how I see fit. You don't get to act like a damn caveman because another man is talking to me. I don't belong to you. I don't belong to anyone. If I was wrong about anything maybe it was about us being friends." She was no longer whispering and by now all of their family and friends were staring at them with wide eyes, eager to know what was going on. She pushed past Danny and resumed cleaning up her station, hoping everyone would mind their own business. Tess refused to turn around to see if he was still standing there. It wasn't until a few minutes later when she looked that she saw that Danny was nowhere in sight.

Four

I t had been a few days since Tess said goodbye to Charlie before she'd returned to New York. With her best friend gone and the holiday over, Tess knew the next week or so would be less hectic at the bakery, but Tess also knew that wouldn't last with Christmas on the horizon. It wasn't often that she got a mid-morning break, but when she did, she usually headed down the street to Carmichael Auto Repair Shop. When she opened the door, the sound of loud machines humming and the smell of oil filled the air. She made her way through the shop and then stopped in front of a familiar pair of work boots poking out from under a car.

"See anything cool under there?"

"More like a mess, but not for long." The board rolled out from underneath the car and Keith Carmichael smiled up at his daughter. "This is a surprise." He got to his feet and wiped his hands on a nearby rag before he kissed her cheek, the stubble on his face gently scratching her cheek.

"I had some time so I come bearing coffee."

He took a coffee from the tray. "Thanks honey. What's in the box?"

"Just some cinnamon rolls."

Her father's bright green eyes lit up. She slid one out of the box and handed it to him. He took a bite and then let out a moan. "Just as delicious as ever."

Tess hopped up on a nearby workbench and placed the coffee and the box down. "Where's Momma?"

"She's in the office doing some paperwork."

Marion Carmichael managed the shop so that it ran like a well-oiled machine. She was extremely organized, great with numbers, and no-nonsense when it came to work, which allowed Tess's father to focus on fixing cars. Tess always admired the way her parents were able to work together and then come home and be a couple.

When she looked up, she saw one of her favorite people walking toward her. "Is that the prettiest baker I know?"

"Hi, Uncle Wyatt." She leaned down and placed a kiss on his cheek. Wyatt Robinson was one of the shop's best mechanics and her father's best friend. He was the head mechanic next to Keith and he was responsible for keeping an eye on the other two mechanics in the shop. When the shop first opened, her father was the only mechanic. One day Wyatt, who had just moved to town with his wife, wandered in to see if there were any openings for mechanics. Keith was happy to have some help and it wasn't long before the two became fast friends. For as long as Tess could remember, Wyatt had been a part of their lives.

"This is a nice surprise."

"Just popped in for a coffee break."

"What's in the box?" He jerked his chin in the direction of the box resting on the workbench.

"Nothing you need to concern yourself with," Keith told him.

"If you're getting that protective there must be cinnamon rolls in that box. You get crazed over those things."

"I do not."

Tess couldn't help but laugh. She'd always enjoyed their banter.

"Your cupcakes were quite the hit at the festival. Your Aunt Faye wouldn't stop going on about them. You should really sell them at the bakery," Wyatt told her.

"Thank you. I think they're going to end up in the display case soon. We had a really good response to them."

"Well, look who's here!"

Tess turned her head to see her mother walking toward them. "Hi, Momma. I just stopped in for a quick visit," she said, handing her mother a cup of coffee.

"Mmhmm and no doubt feeding your daddy's sweet tooth." She flicked her gaze to the box and then over to her husband.

"I'm just drinking my coffee. That box is for Wyatt," he said, handing it over to him.

Wyatt let out a laugh as he took the box.

She placed her hands on her hips and cocked her head to the side. She may have been petite compared to her husband, but that had never made much difference. "Keith Carmichael, don't you even try it. You think after thirty-two years, I don't know your moves? You polished off that thing in three bites."

Tess couldn't stifle her laugh; her mother had her father pegged. He just shrugged and sipped his coffee.

"Mrs. Benson called. I told her that her car would be ready at three," Marion said, tucking a piece of her chin length blonde hair behind her ear.

"Well then, I best get back to work. Thanks for the treat, Tess."

"Anytime, Uncle Wyatt."

He smiled, clutching the box as he walked back to his station.

"I spoke with Mrs. Williams earlier and she was chewing my ear off about your cupcakes at the festival. She really liked them. She said she'll likely stop by the bakery later this week and order all the desserts for her daughter's bridal shower next month."

"That was nice of her. I'm glad that so many people liked the cupcakes. I was really surprised when Mrs. M asked me to join up with her at the booth, but it turned out really great."

"Why? You know Alice is happy to do anything to help you and the bakery," her mother told her.

Tess nodded in agreement. Alice Moreau was a constant support to her and it meant a lot to not only have someone that she cared about but someone who was also in the food business in her corner. It wasn't that Alice didn't bake; she was actually a really good baker, but Tess knew that Alice gave her any baking job she could so that Tess could showcase her desserts.

"I also noticed you and Danny Moreau having what looked like a rather heated conversation at the end of the festival." Her mother raised her eyebrows as she took a sip of her coffee.

"He was being a stubborn ass, Momma."

"We are talking about the same Danny Moreau, right?" Her father chuckled.

Marion nodded. "I find it hard to believe that he was giving you trouble."

"He practically stalked over to the table while I was talking to Cooper Witter, the owner of the sandwich shop near the bakery. Danny got all territorial over me and he started saying that Cooper was flirting with me. When I told him that he was wrong, he kept bringing up how I refuse to go out with him. No matter how many times I tell him that I want us to just be friends, he doesn't believe me. He told me I was being foolish so I snapped."

"You can't knock the boy's persistence."

Tess threw her arms up in the air and let out a groan. "Daddy, it's like talking to a brick wall. He doesn't understand that I don't have time for a relationship."

"Why is that?" her mother asked.

Tess rolled her eyes. "I'm running a business."

"And? He runs a business too. What does that have to do with dating?" Her mother gave her a perplexed look.

"It's complicated, Momma, and I'd rather not go down that road."

"Honey, just because you've been burned once doesn't mean you stay away from the fire for good. You can't run forever."

Tess looked up and shook her head, knowing all too well just who her mother was referring to.

"What your momma means is that there's never really a right time for a relationship. When it comes along, you just have to go with it. Danny is a good man, and he's obviously got excellent taste if he wants to date you." He smiled warmly at her.

Tess put her hand over her father's and smiled back at him. She appreciated that he was trying to mediate the situation, but she knew how she felt. She hopped off the bench and grabbed her coffee. "I appreciate you two saying your piece but I'm happy with the way things are, okay?"

"Are you really?"

"Marion…"

"Don't Marion me—I'm just speaking the truth. In case you haven't noticed, your father and I have been in a relationship for quite some time, and we also run a business. We make it work. Danny is a hard worker, he's kind, and he's certainly easy on the eyes. Why wouldn't you want someone like that?"

"I don't want anyone right now. I have a business that needs my full attention."

"Do you plan on being single forever? If you're going to have that bakery for the foreseeable future, which I have no doubt that you will, does that mean you have to be alone?"

"I haven't thought that far ahead, Momma."

Her mother blew out a breath. "Keith, please talk some sense into your daughter."

"There's no question that running a business takes focus," he said, gesturing to the shop. "But life is about more than business, honey bun. What's the point of working so hard if you have no one to share it with?"

Tess blew out a deep breath. Everything her father said was right; there was more to life than work but she didn't trust herself to be able to balance the two. She'd gotten lost in a guy before and it almost ruined her. There was no way she could take that chance again, not when she had so much more to lose.

"I think you're choosing to believe that you're happy, but that's because you haven't experienced real happiness yet."

"Maybe not but I'm okay with the way things are."

"Honey, what happened with Dean shouldn't scare you off from every man. They aren't all like him. I'm only saying this because I worry."

"Totally unnecessary, Momma, but greatly appreciated."

Tess hugged both of her parents and her father placed a kiss on her cheek. "Thanks for the coffee."

She waved to them and headed back to work. It didn't surprise her that her parents thought she should give dating a shot, especially dating Danny. He was a great catch, but if things went wrong and she unraveled, then what? She had a lot of responsibility now and she couldn't afford that happening. Yes, her plan of staying friends was the right thing, although convincing herself of that was getting harder and harder.

———

Danny sat in his office in Charlotte looking over some of the plans for the condos. He wanted to get the designs finalized as soon as possible.

Just then, Zack, a very talented architect who happened to work for him and Tom, a real estate agent that frequently worked with them stopped in the doorway. "Is it okay if we come in?" Zack asked.

"Come on in," Danny told them.

Zack and Tom sat down opposite of Danny and stared at him for a second.

"So, what's going on?"

"I know the condo project is going to take up a majority of your time, but I've also been looking at a building in Raleigh and the developer is looking to put in some luxury condos. It's in a great area that's really been spruced up with restaurants and shops over the past couple years. The building is empty so they want to make some useful space out of it," Tom said.

Danny tried not to roll his eyes. More luxury condos. Raleigh was over two hours away from Charlotte, not far by any means, but not the easiest work location either.

"The building is going to have twenty-two floors plus a penthouse, but they're looking for some unique designs and I really think you guys are perfect for the job."

"It is in a great location so I'm sure the real estate would sell well," Zack added.

Tom nodded in agreement.

Danny leaned back in his chair and sighed. "When do they want to start meeting with potential architects?"

"After the new year."

"We're just going to be starting this project then."

"I know, but there are two of you. I'm sure you could leave Zack here for a day and go meet with them in Raleigh. You haven't even been given a meeting yet. I'm just talking about putting your hat in the ring for consideration. When they hear you're the architect on this job, I can't imagine they'll not at least take a meeting with you," Tom told him.

Danny leaned back in his chair and considered what Tom had just said to him. He was right; there was no reason he couldn't leave Zack for a day and go take a meeting if this developer even wanted to meet with him. The truth was, he was looking for excuses not to go because it wasn't something he was looking to do. Still, he knew it was important to keep himself open to any opportunities.

"Give Natalie the information, and she'll reach out to them to see if they're interested in a meeting."

Tom stood up. "I'll keep you posted." With that, he walked out of Danny's office, leaving Zack still sitting there.

"Was there anything else?"

"I had a few ideas for the condos, but we can talk about them later."

"I'm sure you have them on your computer, so send them to me and I'll take a look."

Zack smiled as he got up from the chair. Before he left, he

turned back to Danny. "Is something the matter?"

"No, nothing is wrong. Why?"

"You're usually really excited when we have new projects, and you look pretty miserable to be quite honest."

"I don't know what it is." Danny let out a sigh. "I know getting this job is a big deal and I like that we're not going to have a lot of restrictions on us, but while the money is nice, I didn't get into this business for the money."

"Neither did I. I got into it because I like being able to create homes and spaces for people, and if there happens to be a nice fat check that goes along with that so be it."

Danny laughed a little. "I know the building is going to be beautiful and the units are going to be too, but I feel like I should be doing something else, something more. Designing schools or housing for people who have lost their homes to natural disasters. I did an internship while I was still in college and we rebuilt homes for people who'd lost theirs in a hurricane. It was really fulfilling."

"Who said you can't do that now?"

"No one. It's just I've been so busy focusing on building up the business that I kind of got stuck in a cycle of doing the same stuff." Danny ran his hand through his hair in frustration.

"I totally understand that. I don't think this is like anything we've ever done before. It's the entire building. Is it giving an underprivileged kid a state-of-the-art school to go to? No. But I think it's a great opportunity. If you don't want to do another round of luxury condos, then don't even try to get a meeting in Raleigh. After this job, we are done solidifying ourselves and there's not going to be pressure to take any job that you don't want." Zack shrugged.

Zack was right. Getting the job on this building was a big opportunity and it would help open doors for the company. There was no reason that he had to take on a project that he didn't want just because it was what he'd always done. "Thanks, man. I needed to hear that."

"Anytime." Zack turned and left Danny's office.

It was nice to be reminded that they didn't have their backs up against any kind of wall. Danny had worked hard to make sure his company was successful and now he was starting to see all the fruits of those labors. His mind drifted to Tess. He hated the way he'd left things with her at the festival. He needed to apologize, but he had a feeling it was going to take a little more than an "I'm sorry."

———————————

It was almost closing time and Tess was wiping down the counters when she heard the door chime. She looked up and was surprised to see Danny walking toward her.

"Hi."

"Hi," she said, straightening up.

"I saw your lights were still on so…"

"Yeah, we're still open for a few more minutes."

He nodded. "I was hoping you could tell me what to get for someone when you owe them a big apology?"

She put her rag down and stared at him. "I don't think we have what you're looking for."

"I'll buy out every dessert in your cases."

"That seems a little over the top."

"Well I acted like a big jackass. Will you please let me apologize?"

She crossed her arms over her chest and waited for him to speak.

"Look, I'm sorry for the way I acted at the festival. I had no right to come over there while you were talking to Cooper and be such a jerk. You can talk to whomever you want."

"Thank you."

"I still say that Cooper is interested in you more than just as a friend or neighbor."

She pursed her lips. "Danny…"

"I'm just saying. What you choose to do about that is completely up to you. Let me make it up to you for how I acted."

"You don't need to do that."

"I want to. I thought we could do something fun." He looked at her eagerly.

She studied him, looking uncertain.

"I promise it will be strictly platonic."

"What did you have in mind?"

"I'll pick you up tomorrow night at eight o'clock."

"That's awfully short notice. I can't just… I have to make sure someone is available to close up for me."

"Okay, that's not a problem." He grinned.

"That's all you're going to tell me? You're not even going to let me know where you plan on taking me?" She crossed her arms over her chest.

"If you can get someone to close up for you, I promise you'll like where we're going and I'll have you home before you turn into a pumpkin. I know you wake up early."

Tess thought for a minute and looked up at him. He looked completely genuine, and she had to admit, she was curious to see what he had planned. Besides, she had said she wanted them to be friends and this is what friends did, right? They spent time together platonically.

"Okay but just as long as you understand this is me letting you apologize, this isn't a date. That's *if* I can make it."

"Understood. I'll see you tomorrow at eight." He turned and walked out.

"I didn't say yes," she said to the empty bakery. Tess let out a sigh, wondering what she'd just gotten herself into.

Five

anny pulled up to Tess's apartment a few minutes before eight o'clock. She lived in a small garden apartment complex right in Belmont. He couldn't remember the last time he'd been to her apartment and he suddenly felt his palms start to sweat. As he walked to her door, he reminded himself that tonight was just two friends hanging out. He needed to show her that he could stick to his word, despite how much he did *not* want their evening to be two friends hanging out.

Danny rang the bell and Tess answered it within seconds. She looked incredible in a pair of jeans, a teal-colored blouse that showed just a little bit of cleavage, and knee-high brown boots. Her hair was loose, and he could see she had on a bit of makeup. He knew his mouth was hanging open, but there didn't seem to be anything he could do to stop it.

"Wow—you look great."

"Thanks. Is this okay for where we're going?" she asked, gesturing to her outfit.

"Yeah, it's perfect."

Tess reached up on the coat rack for her coat and purse and then closed and locked the door behind her. "You're really not going to tell me where we're going?"

He opened the passenger door for her and smirked. "Nope, but I promise we're going to have fun."

She gave him a look that said she was intrigued before getting in the car. He shut the door and walked around to his side of the truck. Yup, tonight was going to be fun.

A few minutes later, they pulled up to 820, a bar in Charlotte. Danny watched as Tess's eyes lit up. "Is this... is this a karaoke bar?"

"It might be." He smirked. "Shall we?"

She nodded and got out of the truck. Danny opened the door to the bar and followed her inside. It wasn't overly crowded, so they were able to get a spot at the bar fairly easily. Tess removed her coat and then turned to face the small stage toward the back of the bar. Two middle-aged women were singing "Love Is A Battlefield" by Pat Benatar.

"They're pretty good," Tess said.

"Yeah, they are. So, what'll it be?" Danny asked, jerking his head toward the bar.

"I'll have a Blue Moon."

He nodded and ordered two beers. "You've never been here before?"

"No, but I've heard great things about the karaoke."

He watched her watching the women singing and could almost see the longing in her eyes. Their beers arrived and Tess turned around to face the bar. Danny raised his glass to her. "Thanks for letting me apologize."

"Thank you for apologizing so well." She chuckled as she clanked glasses with him and they sipped of their beers.

"So how come you don't sing anymore?"

Tess froze at his question. "Um... I just lost interest in it I guess."

"I find that very hard to believe. You were always singing, whether it was in the car along to the radio, at school, in church, or when you would ride your bike over to our house. That's a love that runs deep. It doesn't just go away." He looked at her, hoping her face would give away some clue but she refused to meet his eyes.

"Well, I got involved in other things. I grew up."

"You can grow up and still love something like singing, especially when you have a voice as incredible as yours."

She didn't respond and he decided not to press things any further at that moment. A guy in his early twenties was currently on stage belting out "She Thinks My Tractor's Sexy" by Kenny Chesney and it was obvious he had more than a few drinks in him. She spun her stool so she was facing the stage. "Poor thing," Tess said. "It's good that he likely won't remember this."

Danny took another sip of his beer and looked her over. Something or someone had made her stop singing and he needed to do something about it. "I left my phone in the car. I'm gonna go grab it. I'll be right back." He jumped off the stool and headed for the front door. He looked back over his shoulder and made sure that Tess wasn't facing the stage. He crept over toward where the DJ was on the side of the stage and filled out a slip of paper and handed it to him. Feeling pleased with himself, Danny slipped back toward the front door and walked out and back in, before walking back to the bar. He grabbed his phone out of his pocket and then placed it on the bar as he took his seat. "Sorry about that."

"It's okay. This guy right now might take the cake for the worst attempt at karaoke," she said, taking a sip of her beer.

"The night is still young." The guy was butchering "Truck Yeah" by Tim McGraw so badly it was practically unrecognizable.

"You like Tim McGraw, don't you?"

He was surprised that she remembered that. "I do, but I'm more of an Eric Church man."

Her eyes went wide. "Me too! Well, not the man part but you know what I mean. I love his music."

"He's very honest and he does his own thing. Plus, he's from North Carolina, so I feel like he gets extra points for that."

Tess giggled. "And he can rock a pair of aviators like no one else."

"You don't say?" He smirked at her, intrigued by her omission.

The guy on stage finally finished singing and Danny turned to face the stage. He watched the DJ grab a piece of paper and pick up his mic. "Now let's give a big hand to Tess Carmichael!"

Danny turned back around and saw the shocked look on Tess's face. "Go on, get up there!"

"I can't... no."

"Yes, you can."

She looked so uncertain, and that gutted him. "Stand up, Tess. I promise you'll be okay. Just go up there."

"Is there a Tess Carmichael out there?" the DJ asked.

"Trust me, you've got this."

She sucked down the rest of her beer and stood up. She turned to look at him. "You're in big trouble for this, Danny Moreau."

He waved her off and grinned. "We'll talk about it later... now go sing!"

She slowly walked up to the stage and took the mic from the DJ. Danny hoped that once she heard the music she would relax. She stood near the monitor and waited. When the music for "Before He

Cheats" by Carrie Underwood started, he could see a smile form on her lips. Tess was swaying nervously back and forth and then wiped her palm on her jeans.

She closed her eyes, took a deep breath, cleared her throat, and opened her eyes right before she started singing. Danny felt like his heart stopped; she sounded even better than he remembered. It was as if the whole place perked up once Tess started singing. All eyes were on her. As the song went on, she got more comfortable and she started to move around the small stage. Danny snapped a few pictures on his phone to show her later. When she hit the big note at the end, people started cheering and he couldn't help but let out a yell. Tess finished the song and the whole place erupted in clapping and whistling. She smiled and handed the mic back to the DJ before walking offstage. Danny didn't take his eyes off of her as she walked back over to him. She was absolutely glowing.

"You were incredible! The place went crazy over you!"

She took her seat and nodded as if she needed to process what had just happened.

He ordered them another round and gave her a chance to catch her breath.

She finally turned and leveled him with a look. "You really shouldn't have done that. I should be so mad at you right now."

"But you aren't, are you?"

She took a big sip of her beer as soon as it was placed in front of her and glared at him from over the top of her glass. "I want to be, really I do. I was terrified! I haven't sung in front of people in... a long time."

"You killed it. Everyone in here stopped what they were doing to listen to you. I don't think they expected that big ole voice to come out of someone so tiny."

"How did you know... that song... why did you pick it?"

Danny chuckled. "Seriously? After Carrie Underwood won Idol you and Charlie were all about her. When she put out her first album, you two were always playing it and singing along to it, especially this song."

"Charlie used to say it was like Carrie wrote it for me." She looked away again and he knew she was hiding something else.

He put his hand on top of hers. "Please don't be mad. Watching you watch everyone else sing was kind of heartbreaking. I wanted you to feel happy. You lit up that stage, Tess."

Danny could see the blush hit her cheeks but he could also see how overwhelmed she felt by whatever it was that she wasn't saying.

"I'm not mad. Thank you." She gave him a small smile and he took that as a small victory for now.

They got back to Tess's apartment before eleven. The car ride home had been mostly silent, which she was thankful for. She was trying to process the night; Tess hadn't expected to be thrown back into the past but that was exactly what had happened. She half expected Danny to press her about why she'd stopped singing, but he hadn't. It amazed her how he always seemed to know what she needed and when she needed it. The answer to that question was long and complicated and not one that she was particularly proud of. One thing was for certain: when she took that microphone in her hand and started to sing, a familiar happiness filled her chest. Tess had forgotten how much she'd missed that feeling.

They walked to her apartment and then paused at the door.

"See, I got you home well before it got late."

"Yes, I'm not going to turn into a pumpkin."

Danny looked down and then back up at her. Just the way he looked at her made her want to forget all of her fears and launch herself into his arms.

"Well, I guess I'll see you around." He started to turn away but she reached for his arm to stop him.

"Wait—Danny, thank you for tonight. Thank you for pushing me to get onstage and sing. I never would have been brave enough to do it on my own."

"You're plenty brave Tess. You just needed to be reminded of what you're capable of. Getting to hear you sing was the icing on the cake for me." Danny smiled at her and suddenly the air around them felt so thick that Tess couldn't breathe. She needed space.

"I should get inside. Good night."

"Night, Tess."

She walked into her apartment and locked the door behind her. She squeezed her eyes shut and took a deep breath. Tess felt like Danny could see right through her and that scared the hell out of her. For so long she had hidden away the things that she was most ashamed of. Most of the time she tried to act like it never had happened because she hated that she'd allowed someone to blindside her and control her for so long. Tess had loved Dean, but she'd used that as an excuse for longer than she'd care to admit. Of course Charlie knew the basics; he'd cheated on her and she'd returned home to Belmont to open up a bakery, but there was so much more to it than that. If Danny knew the whole truth, he'd never look at her the same way and that was a disappointment she didn't think she could handle.

———————

"Ace! No! Come back!" Danny jolted up and when he opened his eyes, he realized he was in his bed. The clock read 3:30 a.m. Sweat covered his face and neck and he was breathing heavily. He ran a hand over his face in an effort to try and get his breathing to slow down. He pulled the covers back, got out of bed, walked into his bathroom, and splashed some cold water on his face.

Looking in the mirror, he saw he was soaked with sweat. Danny pulled off his T-shirt and tossed it on the floor. He looked in the mirror and let out a sigh. It was the same nightmare he'd been having on and off for months: Danny showing up to the scene of Charlie's car accident and finding her slumped over at the wheel, the door to his truck refusing to open. He tried yelling for help but the next thing he knew he was standing in the middle of the ER with people rushing all around him. The sound of his mother's scream grabbed his attention, and when he ran over to where he thought Charlie might be, he saw a lifeless hand fall over the side of a gurney. Slowly Danny approached and when he got closer he saw that it was his sister. He yelled for someone to help her, to do something, but no one could hear him. He shook Charlie to try and get her to wake up but nothing happened. He kept looking around for someone who could help all while he kept shaking her to try and get her back.

And that was when he would wake up.

It always ended the same way: Danny was left looking at Charlie's lifeless body, helpless to fix the situation. Once he woke up, he knew that she was okay. He knew she'd survived the accident and had made a full recovery, but almost a year later it still ate at him that he hadn't been there to protect her. If he'd gone after her when she'd stormed out of their parents' house she wouldn't have been driving and that drunk, Tommy, wouldn't have run her off the road and almost killed her. Danny had always been the even-tempered one of his siblings, but when he found out that Charlie almost died because of that reckless asshole, something in him had snapped. When Tommy got hauled into the police station shortly after the hit and run, Danny and Jason had walked in there ready to hand out their own kind of justice. Their father hadn't let them have that opportunity and even though, months later, Tommy was still sitting in jail for a few DUIs and attempted vehicular manslaughter, it still didn't seem like he was suffering enough. Danny was the peacekeeper, the fixer, and even though his sister had come out on the other side of her accident, the fact that he hadn't been able to fix things before they went sideways was clearly affecting his subconscious.

He exited the bathroom and headed back to bed. He thought of Tess and how great it had been to see her up onstage singing. She'd lit up the whole room, and he couldn't believe she hadn't sung in God knew how long. Danny couldn't understand why she would want to hide a talent like that, deny herself the joy she obviously got from it. He knew she was keeping things from him, and maybe if he could get her to realize that she could trust him, really trust him, she would start to embrace all the things she'd been denying herself.

Like a relationship with him.

Six

Tess sat in the kitchen at the bakery looking over some orders. Even though Christmas was more than three weeks away, they already had orders for holiday parties and catering events. She hadn't seen or spoken to Danny since he'd dropped her off after karaoke. She was thankful for the space because being around him made her feel all kinds of confused. Baking, on the other hand, always got her mind right.

She spotted an order for lemon almond cupcakes and decided to get started on those. Tess grabbed her apron and turned the volume on the radio higher as she got out the ingredients she needed. Within a few minutes she had the batter going. While she worked she sang along to the radio. She was so immersed in what she was doing that she didn't even notice Leanne walk into the kitchen.

"Oh hey, sorry. What's going on?"

Leanne was looking at her with a funny grin on her face. "It can wait. Why didn't I know you can sing like that?"

"Like what?"

Leanne waved her hands in an all-encompassing gesture. "Like a freaking professional. Where did that voice come from?"

Tess shrugged. "I've always had it."

"Holy hell, woman! I only heard a little bit but damn!"

Tess smiled. "Thanks. So what's going on?"

"Right... so we just got an order for enough gingerbread for ten people to make their own gingerbread houses. I'm not exactly sure how much gingerbread that is, but I'm sure you can figure it out."

"Wow, that's a lot of gingerbread. Yeah, I'll have Betty help me, and we'll figure it out when I'm done here."

"What are you making?" She peered into the bowl to try and get a look.

"Two dozen lemon almond cupcakes for Mrs. Mason. It won't

take me too long."

Leanne nodded and put her order book on the counter. "You never told me where you went with Danny the other night?"

"Oh, we went to 820 in Charlotte. It's actually a karaoke bar."

"How appropriate." She grinned.

"I had no intention of singing but Danny snuck my name in, and all of a sudden they were calling me up to the stage. I was so nervous." She reached for her spatula and cleaned the batter off the sides of the bowl.

"What? Why? Given what I just heard you sound like you could be on the radio."

Tess shook her head and put the spatula down. "Not even close, and I haven't sung in front of anyone in a long time."

"I'm sure there's a story behind that but we can get into that another time. Did you have fun?"

"I did. Danny is easy to have fun with."

"Why am I sensing a 'but'?" She crossed her arms over her chest, waiting for an answer.

Tess let out a sigh. "There's no 'but.' It's just awkward—maybe that's the wrong word. It's intense between us because he wants more and I don't."

"Intense can be good." Leanne smirked.

Tess groaned. "It's complicated. Charlie is my best friend and we all hang out together as a group."

Leanne rolled her eyes. "You and Danny are adults. I'm sure you could find a way to see each other without it affecting the group."

Tess turned to grab the cupcake tins and started lining them with paper holders. "When things go wrong, I wouldn't be able to be around him and I'd hate that. Especially now that Charlie and Nick are moving back. There will be more opportunities for us to all be together, and I don't want to ruin that."

"Why wouldn't it work out? Honey, that man looks at you like you're the only woman in the world. Do you know how rare that is? Take it from someone who was married to the worst kind of man, when a good one comes along you scoop him up. My ex was a liar and a lazy cheat. He was very happy to let me bust my ass working while he pretended to be a rock star. He never paid for anything, and he would get angry when I would get on him about getting his drunk ass off the couch."

Tess knew Leanne had been married to a pretty awful guy. Leanne had told her the last straw had been coming home at two thirty in the morning after working a double shift at the bar and finding two women, likely groupies, "servicing" her husband right in the middle of their living room. She kicked them all out and then served his ass with divorce papers before the end of the week. Then she packed her things and left him and Texas for good. Despite everything she'd been through, Leanne wasn't bitter; she had a pretty good outlook on things.

"I know you got mixed up with a rotten asshole a while back, but that doesn't mean they're all like that."

Leanne only knew the very basics of what happened between her and Dean, so much as she tried to understand Tess's decision, she couldn't. Not completely. "I just think I'm better off staying away from a relationship."

"I get it. You don't trust yourself to make the decision but being practical all the time won't warm your bed at night."

Tess shook her head. It had been way too long since her bed had been warmed.

"I think you owe it to yourself to open up to the possibility that something good can happen. I promise you everything won't come tumbling down if you do something for yourself but in the event it does, you've got lots of people that will help you back up."

"I don't know that I can. This thing with Danny, it's not like anything I've ever experienced with anyone else. He knows me in ways that no one else could and it freaks me out."

Leanne chuckled. "I'd be worried if you weren't scared. Being that transparent to someone else is scary but think of all the time you'll save not having to explain things because he already knows you. You'll still learn things about each other but you already know he thinks you hung the moon which is much better than having to try and figure that out. You need to lock that up before someone else does!"

Tess laughed a little. She hadn't considered the positive angle of how different things would be since they already knew each other, and more intimately than anyone else realized. There would be none of the "getting to know you" awkwardness. She knew Danny was a good man and that he cared about her. Maybe she was being silly trying to fight it.

"Thanks for listening, Lee."

"Anytime. I'll let you get back to it. Let me know about that gingerbread."

"I will."

Leanne left the kitchen and Tess was left with her cupcakes and a lot to think about.

When Tess got home later that night, she was exhausted. She'd gotten through most of the orders, but there were still a lot she needed to complete tomorrow. All she wanted was a bath and her bed.

As she approached her door, she startled when she saw someone waiting for her. "Good Lord, Danny! What are you doing here?"

He was holding a pizza box and a bottle of wine. The delicious smell coming from the box made her stomach growl.

"I thought you might be hungry." He shrugged, looking down at the box.

"How did you know what time I'd be home?"

"I called the bakery and Leanne said you would be finishing up around eight thirty, so here I am."

Tess rolled her eyes. "I'm glad my staff just gives out my whereabouts."

"It was for a good reason. I'm willing to bet you didn't eat dinner?"

"I had a protein bar a few hours ago."

"That doesn't count. This may not be gourmet but it's food." He smiled.

"Did you get pepperoni?"

It was his turn to roll his eyes. "Is that even a question? Come on, before it gets cold," he said, gesturing to her door. Tess opened the door and let them in. She tried not to act flustered, but it was definitely unexpected for Danny to show up like that. Tess dropped her keys and purse on a small table near the door while Danny put the pizza and wine down on the counter. She noticed he was still in his work clothes, which meant he'd come straight to her apartment.

"Why don't you go change or shower and I'll open the wine and have everything ready when you get back?" he asked.

"I don't need to. We can just eat."

Danny shook his head. "You've been on your feet all day. You'll feel better once you get out of those clothes."

She glared at him and he smirked. "I meant that in a completely non-sexual way... sort of."

Tess laughed. "Okay then I'm going to go take a quick shower."

"Sure, take your time."

She retreated to her bedroom and quickly stripped out of her clothes and turned the shower on. Before stepping in, she pulled her hair up in a messy bun and then stepped into the hot spray. It was amazing how good the hot water felt, especially after a long day on her feet.

True to her word, Tess showered and changed into leggings and a T-shirt in less than ten minutes. When she got back into the living room, Danny had poured them each a glass of wine and had pizza on plates on the coffee table. She took the seat next to him on the couch and smiled.

"Thank you for all of this," she said, gesturing to the pizza and wine.

"It's no big deal," he replied, handing her a glass of wine.

"Sure it is. I was planning on taking a bath and going straight to bed."

"Bad day?"

Tess shook her head and took a sip of wine. "Not a bad day, just long. We have lots of holiday orders that need to get filled, so I'm just trying to make sure we don't fall behind."

"Do you bring in more staff at this time of year?"

"I don't usually, but I may need to start thinking about it. Today I was trying to get through any non-holiday orders we have so we can start focusing on the holiday ones. They're already starting to pile up."

"Needing more help is a sign that you're expanding, so that's a good thing."

"It is... but sometimes it's a bit overwhelming."

"I can imagine, but I know it has to feel good for you to be such a success, especially right in our hometown."

Tess smiled at the compliment but said nothing else, not wanting to dwell on it. She was happy that she was able to come back home and start something that was doing well, but she still felt like she had a long way to go. "So are we gonna eat that pizza or just look at it?"

Danny leaned forward and handed Tess her plate. The smell made her stomach growl again. She took a big bite and moaned. "I'm really glad I didn't skip dinner."

Danny chuckled. "Me too." He took a bite of his slice and also looked content to be eating.

"How's work going for you?" she asked.

"Um… it's going."

"That sounds like it's not going well."

Danny took a sip of wine. "It's not that. It's just trying to decide what to do next. A big development group just bought property in downtown Raleigh and we may be a good fit for them. Zack and Tom both think it's a huge opportunity and they're right, it is, but it's just so much of the same thing. I feel a little lost at the moment, I guess."

This surprised her; Danny had always known what he wanted to do and to hear him sounding unsure was not something she was used to. "Maybe you need to spend some time thinking about what you really want to do. It can't be all about just taking a job. Take the time to really consider what you're doing."

He nodded in agreement. "I've been trying to think about it, and I keep hoping that the next thing that comes across my desk will wow me and it hasn't happened. A while back there was the possibility of an opportunity to design buildings in Jersey City, New Jersey, for people who couldn't return to their apartments after Hurricane Sandy, but nothing ever came of that. Designing something like that for people who had been forced out of their homes and needed a better place to live, that was something I felt I could really get behind."

"You would've had to leave if you took a job like that."

"Not forever, but for a few months, yeah."

She shuddered at the thought of him being gone for a long stretch of time. "I don't think I could do that."

"You up and left Belmont if I remember correctly," he said, tipping his wine glass toward his mouth.

Tess looked down at her plate. "Yeah, well, I thought I was in love." She stuffed the rest of her pizza in her mouth so she wouldn't have to say anything else.

"You were. He wasn't, which is crazy to me."

"I thought I was being an adult, compromising but…"

"Compromising means you get something in return. Seems like you were doing all the sacrificing and not getting anything in return," he told her between bites of his pizza.

No one had ever said it to her like that before. Dean had made her a lot of promises but she had been the one to give up everything for him.

"Then I guess I'll have to chalk it up to being young and dumb." She reached for another slice of pizza.

Danny shook his head. "There's one dumb person in that scenario and it isn't you. Honestly, I think you got lucky."

"Lucky? How do you figure that?"

"If you hadn't caught him cheating, you probably would have stayed in that relationship even longer, wasting more years than he deserved. You're loyal, Tess, and if he didn't give you a reason to walk out the door, you wouldn't have—even if he wasn't the right guy for you."

She couldn't look at him. He had no idea how much she hated herself for not leaving sooner, for not seeing what Dean was doing to her. "What about you?"

"What about me?"

"You certainly have a lot of opinions for a guy who doesn't seem to date a lot."

"I haven't dated anyone in a while, but we're not talking about dating experience. I'm just pointing out who you are and why you deserve so much better than some fool who obviously didn't realize he had an incredible woman right in front of him."

Tess leaned back on the couch and looked at Danny. Hearing him say what she deserved made her heart swell. She couldn't help but smile.

"What's that smile for?" he asked, cocking his head to the side.

"It's just nice… the way you see me."

Danny leaned back against the couch and grinned.

"I really need to thank you. What you did for me the other night…"

He held up his hand. "I didn't do anything, I was apologizing."

She turned to face him. "You pushed me on that stage, and I didn't realize how much I needed that. No one's ever done anything like that for me."

He shook his head. "Well that's all kinds of wrong because you deserve that and more."

She looked away and reached for her wine glass. "No…"

"You do, and I wish you could see that. I meant what I said the other night: just getting to see you on that stage and the way your face lit up, that was something I won't forget. I was happy I was lucky enough to be in the room."

Tess picked her eyes up to meet his, and she could see the truth in what he was saying. She was so used to lies and being told she wasn't enough, it was hard for her to believe someone could feel that way about her.

"It meant a lot to me, and I want you to know that."

He smiled at her and that nervous feeling hit her in the stomach again. They finished their pizza and soon the wine bottle was empty too. Tess was going to clear their plates but Danny got up with their plates before she could. She told herself she'd sit there for just five minutes and then she'd take over cleanup. Tess leaned back and relaxed into the couch. Whatever plan she'd had to only sit for five minutes was shot to hell; as soon as she leaned back, she was fast asleep.

———————

Tess awoke with a start and realized she was on her couch. It had to be early because the light was just starting to creep through the blinds. She sat up and looked around for Danny but there was no sign of him. It looked like everything from the night before had been cleaned up and put away. She must've been really tired because she slept through the sounds of cleanup and him leaving. Tess caught a glimpse of the clock on her wall and saw that it was almost five thirty. She needed to get moving so she could get to the bakery because it was going to be another busy day. As she stood up, she noticed a note on the coffee table.

T,

You looked so peaceful I didn't want to wake you. Thanks for sharing that pizza with me, but next time we eat together it's not coming out of a box.

Danny

She couldn't help but smile. He really was unlike anyone else. Tess didn't know what to do with that because no man had ever been that considerate of her needs. It scared her because relationships always started out good, but what if after all that compromise and opening herself up to someone else, she was left in the same place she always seemed to find herself? Caring too much for someone, only to be left on the losing end/

Danny got back to his apartment by five thirty. He hadn't planned on spending the night on Tess's couch but once she fell asleep, he ending up dozing off too. When he woke up and saw her asleep on the opposite end of the couch, he was happy. Danny liked spending time with her. He hoped that by taking things slow he was showing Tess that something could happen between them without it turning into a disaster.

Danny hit the gym for an early workout and by eight thirty he was showered and dressed for the office. He read through and replied to emails while he sipped his coffee. Zack came walking in, carrying his iPad and a cup of coffee.

"Morning."

"Good morning. What brings you in here so early?"

"I was just looking at some projects I have on my desk. Small stuff: kitchen redesigns, office space redesigns, and then I was looking over the building space for downtown Charlotte and I started thinking."

Danny sat back in his chair to give him his full attention.

He looked over the basic design of the building and the specs that they would have to work with. Zack had come up with some really great designs for the units. He'd drawn up a lot of open concept designs, which were very popular. Danny really liked his designs for some of the larger units; they had larger kitchens and more than one bedroom and bathroom so Zack had a little more room to be creative. "These look really great."

"Thanks. It's all in the very early stages right now, but I like that the developers don't want every unit on each floor to be the same. I feel like a little more variety will make the units easier to sell. They can be similar, but they don't need to be identical."

Danny nodded. "Right. Plus I think a lot of people will like having a one-of-a-kind unit."

"Exactly. Especially if they're paying the kind of prices Tom seems to think they're going to be paying."

Danny handed the designs back to him. "I think this is a really good start. They liked the preliminary designs a lot, and I think they'll really like these too."

Zack stood up and smiled. "Thanks. I've got some ideas for the gym area and the pool deck but I haven't gotten those down yet. Once I do, I'll send them to you."

"Okay. I'm gonna get working on the lounge area on the seventh floor."

He nodded and started to make his way out of Danny's office. "Hey, Zack. Thanks for all of your hard work on this. I'm sorry I haven't been my normal self."

"Don't worry about it, man. We're a team. We'll get it done." Zack left his office and Danny felt a little twinge of guilt for not being as hands on as he normally was. At the same time, he also felt incredibly lucky that he had someone like Zack, who not only did great work but whom Danny could trust to step in when he wasn't at the top of his game. Still, it was his business and he took pride in the jobs he did. It was time to get fully on board with this project.

Seven

It had been a few days since Tess had seen Danny. Work had kept them both busy but they had traded texts. He said he'd be passing through Belmont on Friday after work and needed her help with something. At first she was going to tell him she couldn't but then she decided not to. Tess actually felt excited about whatever it was he needed her help with, and considering she couldn't remember the last time she'd felt like that, it seemed like the right choice.

Tess asked Penny and Leanne if they would close up while she went into her office to change out of her baking clothes. She slipped into a pair of skinny jeans, a cream-colored sweater, and brown knee-high boots and pulled her hair from its ponytail. She gave herself a quick once-over in the mirror and reapplied some mascara before she heard a knock at the back door. Tess hurried to open the door and Danny was standing there, his hands in his pockets. He wore black jeans, boots, and a blue pullover sweater that seemed to bring out his dark hair and blue eyes even more. "Hey, I'll be ready in a sec."

"No rush." He smiled as he followed her inside.

She grabbed her coat and purse and turned off the light in her office. "What's the big mystery that you couldn't tell me where we're going?"

Danny let out a laugh. "You'll see soon enough."

She pulled on her coat and noticed he was checking her out, which immediately made her cheeks flush. "Well, I'm ready when you are."

Danny gestured for her to lead the way so Tess made her way out the door and into the parking lot.

"We're only going a few blocks so we can come back for your car later."

"Sure, that's fine."

Danny opened the door of his truck for her and she climbed up.

He got back around to his side and started up the engine. "Are you going to tell me where we're going?"

"You can't wait a few blocks?" he asked with a laugh.

She sighed and put her seatbelt on. Tess watched him as he drove and she couldn't help but notice he had a smirk on his face. True to his word, Danny stopped a few blocks away but Tess was confused when she saw they pulled up to Ferguson's Tree Lot.

"What are we doing here?"

"When I was over the other night, I noticed that you didn't have your Christmas tree yet, so I thought we could get you your tree and pick out one for me. I know how much you love Christmas trees, so I thought you'd be the perfect person to get a tree with."

They got out of the truck and started walking toward the lot. "You remember that I love Christmas trees?"

"Uh, yeah." He chuckled. "You never made it a secret."

Tess couldn't deny that. For as long as she could remember she loved coming to Ferguson's and picking out a Christmas tree with her family. She loved the smell of the trees, the way they looked standing in rows waiting for people to come and take them home, and she especially loved seeing them all decorated. She always wanted a tree that was too tall or too fat. When it was time to get rid of the tree at the end of the holiday season, Tess always felt sad. It had been years since she had her own tree. When things at the bakery took off, the holidays became one of her busiest seasons, and she was never home to really enjoy a tree so she settled for a small tabletop fake tree instead.

"I was surprised you didn't have your tree up the other night when I was over. I would've imagined you'd come pick yours out the day after Thanksgiving."

"It's been awhile since I've had a tree."

Danny turned to face her, shock coloring his face. "Are you kidding me?"

She sighed. "No. I'm always at the bakery during the holidays so I'm never home to enjoy it."

"I can't believe it! The girl who loves Christmas trees doesn't get a tree? Well, that's getting fixed." He turned on his heel and started down the row of trees.

"Danny, it's fine. I don't need a tree."

"Yes, you do."

"Don't tell me what I need."

Danny stopped suddenly and Tess almost crashed right into him. "That's the one."

She turned to look and in front of them was a beautiful tree that was probably just about five feet tall with a full bottom. She reached her hand out to touch the branches. They were strong. "It is beautiful."

"Hey, guys! Nice to see you."

Tim Ferguson, the oldest of the Fergusons' three kids stood in front of them.

"Tim, how's it going?" Danny said, shaking his hand.

"It's going," he said with a laugh.

"Hi, Tim. How are Kelly and Shane?" Tess asked.

"Doing well, thanks. What can I help you with?"

"Would you believe that Tess has been without a Christmas tree for years?"

Tim scratched the back of his head. "Are you pulling my leg? You love Christmas trees, Tess."

"That's exactly what I said. I think this one right here will make up for her neglect toward Christmas trees," Danny said as he jerked his head at the tree next to him.

Tim looked up at the tree. "Well, that one sure is a beauty."

"It sure is," Danny replied smugly.

"Tim, need I remind you who made all of your wife's pregnancy craving sweets and had them on hand to save you trips to the grocery store?" Tess said, placing her hands on her hips.

Tim sighed. "No, I will forever be in your debt for that. I'll stay neutral in this."

Tess looked at the tree and knew it was meant for her. "It really is a beautiful tree, and I suppose since we're already here and we're standing in front of it, I should just take it."

His face lit up. "Excellent. I'll take this one down and have it up by the register while you look for Danny's tree."

They nodded and continued walking through the rows of trees. "You realize you almost gave poor Tim a heart attack when you said you didn't plan on getting a tree? Everyone knows how much you love Christmas trees," he called over his shoulder.

"I didn't think you'd remember that."

"I remember lots of things about you."

She quickened her pace so she was right alongside of him. "Like what?"

"Your favorite color is green, you were afraid of the dark until you were seven, you broke your wrist jumping off the swings when you and Charlie were nine, the first time you shared your baking with the public was for the ninth grade bake sale, you made brownies, and the first guy you went on a date with was Michael Simmons in tenth grade."

Tess was practically stunned into silence. She couldn't believe he remembered all those things about her. Apparently Danny had been paying attention all along. "Wow, those are things I haven't thought about in a long time. Michael Simmons, I haven't seen him since graduation."

"He was a complete loser."

"He was not!"

Danny glared at her. "The kid was lazy. He copied off of other people because he couldn't be bothered to actually do the work. How many weekends did you spend sitting on the couch in his parents' basement because he'd rather sit on his ass playing video games than actually spend time with his girlfriend?"

"We were fifteen! I didn't think we were supposed to be doing anything else."

Danny shook his head and kept walking.

"You dated some people that weren't exactly so perfect."

"Like who? I didn't date that many people in high school."

"Christy Cullen."

"What was wrong with her?"

Tess scoffed. "I'm pretty sure she would've tattooed your name on her ass. That's how crazy she was for you. She broke into your truck during ninth period so when school was over she was waiting in nothing but your varsity jacket."

"I can't say I minded that." he grinned.

Tess groaned and shook her head.

"Obviously we weren't meant to be. She's married with a kid now and lives in New Orleans."

"Does she send you a Christmas card?"

Danny laughed. "Someone sounds jealous."

Before Tess could respond, she caught sight of a beautiful tree. It was tall, taller than Danny and perfectly full. That was Danny's tree.

"What? No response?"

"Danny, stop walking."

He turned to face her. "You can admit that you were jealous, you know?"

"Danny... look up."

Danny looked up at where she was pointing and smiled. "Wow, that's some tree."

"You would've noticed it sooner if you'd quit blabbing nonsense."

"Oh it definitely wasn't nonsense, but this tree is perfect." He reached out and touched the branches. "I knew you were the girl for the job."

Tess smiled, feeling quite proud with her selection. "It's beautiful, and I was never jealous."

Danny let out a laugh. "Whatever you say."

"Is this it?" Tim asked, appearing out of nowhere.

"Yeah, this is the one. I knew Tess would pick a winner."

"Well, let's get you wrapped up and ready to go," Tim said to the tree as he got it down and started to carry it toward the front of the lot. They followed after him and Tess couldn't stop thinking about Danny calling her jealous. It was so ridiculous that he would even think that. Christy had always been too over the top and that's what Tess had never liked; it didn't matter that she acted that way toward Danny, did it? As she watched Tim wrap up the trees, she tried to clear her head of any romantic thoughts involving Danny but when she looked up at him and he smiled at her that seemed pretty pointless.

After they had their trees, Danny insisted on some real food so they stopped at the diner. Afterward they stopped at the bakery so Tess could get her car and then headed to her apartment to get her tree set up. He could tell she was excited about the tree but that she was trying to keep her emotions in check. When they got the tree up to the apartment, he watched her set up the tree stand and then put the tree in the stand. Once he was sure that the tree was secure, they took a step back to look at it.

"There... that's perfect."

"Are you sure? I've only moved it about five times." He smirked.

"I'm sure." Tess looked up at the tree and then took a deep breath in. She loved the smell of pine trees. The tree had good, strong branches, and there wasn't a sparse place on it. The middle and bottom were nice and full, taking up the corner of her living room perfectly. "Thank you for insisting I get a tree. It's really beautiful."

"No problem. I like seeing you happy."

She cleared her throat. "Your tree is going to look great at your place."

"You should come over and help me decorate. I'd hate to screw up that tree."

"I don't think that's possible."

He turned to face her. "You can just admit that you like hanging out with me."

"Of course I do. That's not the issue."

"Then what's the issue?"

Her eyes dropped down to the floor. "I don't have the best track record when it comes to men and if we were to start something and it went badly, then what? It's not like we'd never see each other again, our lives intersect all the time. If we had trouble being around each other that would be hard, not just for us but everyone in our circle."

He crossed his arms over his chest. "You're already assuming it's going to go badly? What if it doesn't? What if it goes well? Maybe you don't have a good track record with men because you pick the wrong type of men."

Tess couldn't argue with that. Dean had been every kind of wrong and the few before him hadn't been much better. After things fell apart with Dean she'd stopped trusting herself when it came to men, but Danny had proven over and over how different he was. Maybe it was time she stopped assuming the worst would happen.

"All I'm asking for is a chance. I don't want to change you, I just want to spend time with you, see you as happy as you were when you laid eyes on this tree." Danny stepped forward and cupped her cheek. His hand on her skin felt so good. "You're in the driver's seat, Tess."

She let out a deep breath and looked up into his eyes. He looked so certain about her, about them, that she decided she was done fighting it. "Okay. I'm in."

Danny's face lit up and he pulled her to him until their lips met.

He kissed her slowly, deeply, and Tess felt like her whole body woke up. She wrapped her arms around his back and took control of the kiss. She nipped his lip and he slipped his tongue in her mouth. His hands moved to her waist and he started walking them back toward the couch. As Tess's back hit the cushions, they never broke their kiss. Danny lowered himself onto her and she could feel how hard he was for her.

"Have I told you how much I love your mouth?"

"I don't think so," she said between kisses.

"I can't get enough of it." He slid his hand down her sweater and under the hem until his hand was on her bare skin. Just his hands on her made her moan.

"I love the way you feel—so soft and smooth." His hand kept moving up until he cupped her breast. He dragged his thumb across her nipple over her bra and Tess practically shot up off the couch.

"Danny!"

"I've got you Tess," he said against her lips. He lifted her sweater higher and pulled the cups of her bra down so he had full access to her breasts. He kissed his way up her stomach until his mouth was wrapped around one breast and his hand was filled with the other. He squeezed and sucked simultaneously and the sensations were pushing her over the edge. She writhed beneath him and as usual, he sensed what she needed and pressed himself to her center, giving her the friction she desperately needed.

"I'm so close."

He sucked her nipple into his mouth and rotated his hips and Tess's orgasm hit her so hard that she couldn't help the loud cry that escaped her lips. Danny lifted his head and took her mouth while she rode out the wave of her orgasm. Once she started to return to normal, she pulled away from him to catch her breath. She adjusted herself so her clothes were back in place while Danny hovered over her with a big smile on his face.

"I love seeing that satisfied look on your face."

"You're way too good at that, especially since I had most of my clothes on."

"You already know what I can do with all of your clothes off and mine for that matter." He waggled his eyebrows at her.

Tess covered her face and laughed. "Yes, I do. Is this what you had in mind when you said for me to give us a chance?"

"I'm certainly not complaining about it, but no, I meant everything."

"That sounds... pretty great."

"I'm glad you think so. Although right now I'm going to peel myself off of you, even though it's the last thing I want to do, because I want you to know that I'm capable of taking things slowly." He smiled. "I'm going to show you all the things you've been missing out on like someone to take you out on dates, someone to do things for you and with you, someone to go to sleep with and wake up with in the morning, and someone to spend time with you and have fun with you—in addition to worshipping that gorgeous body."

She let out a giggle. There was still that voice in the back of her head that was screaming panic but she decided for once to ignore it. "I think I can get on board with that."

"You won't be sorry." He stood up and then extended his hand to her to help her off the couch.

"Thank you again for convincing me to get a tree."

"Happy to do it. Thanks for helping me pick out mine." They stared at each other for a moment and then Danny finally leaned down and pressed a quick kiss to her lips. "Good night, Tess."

"Night, Danny." She watched him leave and then sank against the door as she closed it. Maybe it was the high she still felt from that orgasm, but for the first time in a long time Tess felt excited about something that had nothing to do with work.

Danny woke up the next morning feeling happier than he had in a long time. Hearing Tess say she wanted to give them a chance felt like something he'd been waiting for for a very long time. Leaving her hadn't been easy, but he'd meant what he said: he wanted to show her all the things she'd been missing.

He got out of bed, hit the gym, showered, and got ready for the office. As he headed out to his car, he started thinking about some of the things he wanted to do with Tess. His tree did need to be decorated so maybe he could invite her over, cook her dinner, and they could enjoy a nice, casual night. That seemed like a good place to start.

Danny approached his truck and noticed that the driver's side tire was flat. He crouched down and saw that the tire had definitely been slashed. He looked down at the back tire and saw that it had also been slashed. The passenger side tires were both untouched. He let out a deep breath and ran a hand over his face. He snapped a few pictures of the tires and made a call.

"Hi, Mrs. C. I know it's early for me to be calling but I've got two flat tires on my truck. I was hoping you could send someone over to change them whenever you have someone free. I only have one spare. I don't know what happened. I walked out to it like this as I was leaving for work. Okay, great, thanks Mrs. C. I really appreciate it." He hung up and unlocked his Mercedes, which thankfully escaped any vandalism. Danny climbed in and made one more call.

"Hey JJ—sorry, I know it's early but I'm going to send you a few pictures. It looks like someone slashed my tires."

Eight

A few days later, Tess was busy going through orders. With Christmas less than three weeks away, orders for holiday parties were starting to roll in fast. The back bell rang and she hopped off her stool to go open it.

"Morning, Tess."

"Good morning, Porter." Porter was Tess's baking supplies deliveryman. He usually came by once a week with her supplies, and given all the orders she had, she was in serious need of a restock.

He walked in with a hand truck holding boxes of supplies and headed for the counter. "It smells delicious in here."

"Thank you. Can I get you anything?"

"Oh, no. The missus is cracking down on my calories," he said, patting his belly.

Tess laughed. "Shirley just wants to keep you healthy."

"She's a cookie scrooge." He unloaded the boxes onto the counter and handed her the invoice.

"Hang on, I ordered three dozen eggs and three pounds of flour and they're not here." She opened up the boxes and sure enough the eggs and flour were missing.

"Are you sure you ordered them?"

"Yeah, I knew I was going to need them." She reached into her binder that held all the supply orders and pulled out her invoice. It listed the three dozen eggs and three pounds of flour.

"Huh. That's odd. I can't understand what happened, Tess. Let me double check the truck to see if maybe I missed them."

She followed him back outside and stood outside the truck while he went searching for her missing items. "This is the strangest thing. I always make sure that everything is correct before I leave the warehouse."

"It's okay, Porter, it happens."

"No, I feel awful. I'm sorry but I still have a few stops to make before I can go back to the warehouse. I can try to send someone over with replacements."

"Thanks. Whatever you can do as soon as you can would be great."

He climbed back into his truck looking as disappointed as she felt. Tess huffed out a sigh as she watched him drive away. She didn't see her day starting off this way.

"Why the long face?"

She looked up and over and saw Cooper standing outside his back door, just two down from hers. "Oh, hey. It's nothing. Just some of my baking supplies didn't come."

"That definitely sounds like something. I'm sure you've got orders up to your eyeballs."

"Yeah, kind of. It's okay, replacement supplies will be here before the end of the day I'm sure. I'll make do with what I have for now."

"Don't be silly. You're welcome to use anything of mine to hold you over until your supplies get here."

"That's really nice of you, but I wouldn't want to put you out."

"Tess, I'm offering. It's not an imposition. Aren't neighbors supposed to help each other?"

She really could use the help. "Okay, if I could borrow some eggs and flour that would be a big help."

"Of course, whatever you want. Come on," he said, waving her over.

Tess walked the short distance over to Cooper's back entrance. He held the door open for her and smiled. "Thank you, I really appreciate this."

"It's my pleasure. Come on in."

His kitchen smelled like bacon and other delicious breakfast food.

"Can I get you anything to eat?" he asked.

"Oh, no. I need to get back."

"Of course. So tell me what do you need?"

"A dozen eggs and a pound of flour would be great if you can spare it."

He went into his refrigerator and pulled out a carton of eggs and placed them on the counter and then went into the cabinet and pulled down a sack of flour. "Are you sure you don't need anything else?"

"No, this is great, I really appreciate it."

"Of course. So I know it's a busy time but I was wondering if you might want to grab dinner? Maybe tonight after work?"

"Oh... I'm... I've gotta work late tonight."

"Oh, sure. I know you're busy. I just thought it would be nice to sit down and catch up."

"Yeah, I appreciate you asking. It's just a really crazy time right now."

He nodded. "I understand. We'll have to do it another time."

"Yeah, some other time. I should head back. Thanks again for this. You're a lifesaver."

He smiled brightly at her. "I'm always happy to help you, Tess."

Tess was grateful that she had Cooper to turn to. It was nice having someone nearby who understood the demands of her job. She gathered up the supplies and he walked her to the back door. She gave him a smile and then walked back to the bakery, eager to get back to work.

———

Danny had texted Tess earlier in the day to invite her over for tree decorating and dinner. She told him she would be working late, until at least eight or nine, but he told her to come by anytime. As he was getting into his car to leave the office, his phone rang. "Hey, JJ."

"Hey, D. Are you home?"

"I'm just leaving the office. Why? What's up?"

"I was gonna head over there and see if we could take a look at the security footage from the parking lot to try and get a visual on who slashed your tires. What's the building manager like?"

"He's a good guy. He'll be happy to help."

"Great! I'll meet you there in fifteen."

Danny disconnected the call and pulled into the parking lot of his complex fifteen minutes later. JJ pulled in right after him and they headed into the building.

"Hey, Wes."

"Hey there, Danny. How's it going?" Wes was a middle-aged man with the patience of a saint and great organizational skills. Danny admired his work ethic.

"Not too bad. This is my cousin, officer JJ Moreau. It seems like my truck was vandalized the other night. We were wondering if we could take a look at the security footage from the parking lot to see if we could possible get a visual on who did it."

JJ extended his hand. "Nice to meet you. Sorry for barging in like this. I'd just like to have a little more evidence."

"Of course. Whatever I can do to help. We keep our footage right through here." He led them through a doorway where several monitors were set up in addition to a computer. Wes sat down at the computer and typed in a few commands. "What night was it?"

"It would've been Tuesday night... any time after ten."

Danny and JJ zoned in on the screen as Wes pulled up the footage. It took a little bit of searching but then, right across the screen, a figure in a black hoodie, jeans, and sneakers walked up to Danny's truck and stared at it for a moment. They reached into their pocket and produced a knife before crouching down and slashing both tires. Unfortunately, whoever it was never showed their face to the camera.

"Well that didn't help very much," Danny said.

"They were smart. They hid their face, wore dark clothes," Wes replied.

"So we're back at square one."

"Not necessarily," JJ told him. "Watch as they walk away from your truck. They get into what looks like a black Bronco. Can you zoom in on that?"

Wes nodded and zoomed in on the Bronco.

"I can only make out a partial plate but it's a good start. Do you know anyone with a Bronco?"

"Can't say that I do."

JJ made notes on the truck and tucked them in his back pocket. "We'll start with this and see where it takes us. I'll let you know if I find out anything."

"Yeah, okay. Wes, thank you for your help."

"My pleasure. Let me know if there's anything else that you need."

Danny shook hands with him and then walked JJ out. "I know you're pissed and frustrated but me and Ethan will dig into it, I promise."

"I'm gonna owe that partner of yours some beers after this is over."

JJ let out a laugh. "What am I? Chopped liver?"

"Considering all the times I bailed you out when we were younger, I feel like I should be the one owed beers."

"Sure, sure. Just try and sit tight and I'll call you as soon as I have something."

"Thanks, man. I really appreciate it."

JJ climbed into his truck and Danny headed back into his building trying to shake off his frustration. Someone had targeted him and he needed to know why.

Tess stood in front of Danny's door feeling incredibly nervous. It was nearly eight when she texted him to say she was finishing up and he told her that dinner was waiting. There was no reason she should feel nervous, yet her palms were sweating and she felt the butterflies turning in her stomach. It had been a strange day. First with her supply order getting so messed up and Cooper coming to her rescue, and now she was at Danny's apartment, where he'd cooked her dinner, like a real date. Her head was spinning, but she raised her hand and knocked on the door. Danny answered, wearing a pair of worn jeans and a Carolina Panthers T-shirt. It was incredible how hot he made casual look.

"Hi."

"Hi." His mouth lifted at the corners as he opened the door wider for her.

She walked in and suddenly wasn't sure what to do. Should she kiss him? Hug him? Just stand there? "I know it's late. I'm sorry to hold things up."

"You're not holding anything up. I would've waited all night." He leaned down and pressed a kiss to her cheek. Danny took her coat and led her into the kitchen.

"It smells really great in here."

"Thanks, but I'm sorry to say I can't take all the credit. My momma gave me a container of her pesto sauce, all I did was cook the pasta."

"Well I certainly don't mind eating Alice's pesto sauce." She noticed he had two places set at the counter for them and a bottle of wine opened. No man had ever cooked her dinner before. "Can I help you with anything?"

"I just need to strain the pasta. You can pour the wine if you want."

"I can definitely do that." She grabbed the bottle and saw that he'd chosen a Chianti, which happened to be one of the red wines she liked a lot. She poured them each a glass and then sat down while he got the pasta ready.

"Did you get a lot of orders done?"

"We did, but we're probably going to work late tomorrow night so that we can get orders done for the weekend plus the baking for the store," Tess told him.

"Everyone wants to make sure they get their holiday dessert from your bakery, makes sense why you're overflowing with orders."

"We're also the only bakery in town."

"Come on, you know your stuff is great."

She felt herself smile. If there was one thing she was absolutely sure of it was that her desserts were good. Still, it was nice to hear it. "Thanks, I'm proud of what we put out."

Danny placed the pasta bowl on the counter and then came around to sit next to her. He scooped a dish for each of them and then raised his wine glass. "Thanks for coming over to help me decorate my tree."

Tess grabbed her glass and lifted it to his. "Looking forward to it." They clinked glasses and drank. "I didn't realize how much I needed that wine until right now."

Danny chuckled as he picked up his fork. "I'm surprised you ladies don't have a secret booze stash in the bakery for nighttime baking sessions."

"Who said we didn't?"

He let out a big laugh. Tess dug into her pasta and sighed when it hit her mouth. "Wow, that's good."

"My momma sure knows what she's doing in the kitchen."

"No one could ever argue against that. I'm so glad her catering business is taking off. She really deserves it."

"She waited until she knew she didn't need to be home for us after school and, little by little, she really turned it into something pretty incredible."

"I admire her so much. Being in the service industry, especially food, is challenging at times but I've learned so much from your mom from how she runs her business and her presentation."

"I'm sure she appreciates that. She's so proud of you and all you've accomplished."

She felt warmth spread in her chest. It meant the world to her that Alice Moreau was proud of her. She was like a second mom to Tess in a lot of ways. "Thank you for saying that."

"I only speak the truth." He shrugged with a grin.

"Today I did not feel very accomplished. If anything, I felt like a big mess for the first half of the day."

"I find that hard to believe."

Tess told him what happened with her supply delivery.

"Oh, man. Well I can see how that would set you off kilter. What did you end up doing?"

"I was able to borrow some things and then by the end of the day the rest of my order showed up." She decided to leave out the part about Cooper lending her supplies. She didn't need Danny making more out of it than it was.

"It was just a strange day. In all the years I've been ordering from Porter that's never happened. The timing was really bad, but we managed."

"Did he say what happened?"

She shrugged. "All of the items were on the invoice but somehow they didn't make it on the truck. Poor guy felt terrible."

"I'm sure. So how's your tree doing?"

"It's good. I haven't decorated it yet, but I like just having it there."

He stared at her for a minute and she rolled her eyes. "Yes, okay, you were right. I missed having a Christmas tree."

"I'm glad you saw reason."

"I need to get my decorations out and then I can get to it. I'm gonna try for some time this weekend."

"I can always come by and help, you know. Repay the favor."

"Thanks, I'll keep that in mind." She smiled. "How's work going for you?"

"It's okay. Everything is finalized for the condo project. The contractor is coming by next week to go over the plans."

They finished eating and Danny insisted they just leave the dishes in the sink so they could get right to the tree decorating. He carried the rest of the wine into the living room where he had his box of decorations.

"That looks like a serious box of decorations," Tess said.

"I don't mess around." He smirked as he bent down to open the box.

They managed to get the lights on fairly quickly and then started with the rest of the ornaments. For some reason, Tess imagined that he would have a bunch of store-bought, generic ornaments, but he actually had more personal ornaments than anything else. He had an ornament for his alma mater, Georgia Tech, as well as ornaments from places he'd visited, like San Francisco, Chicago, New York City, New Orleans, and Atlanta. He even had one that said "#1 Architect," which she knew Charlie had given him when he'd graduated college. However, the ones she loved the most were the wooden ones that looked like they were handmade.

"These are beautiful. I love this one," she said, holding up a wooden train.

"That's the first ornament I ever made."

"You made this?"

Danny nodded. "Yeah, I think I was ten or eleven. The chief had to help me cut it out because him and Momma weren't exactly going to let me use a woodcutter myself."

"It still came out pretty good for your first attempt. I forgot that you used to love trains."

"I still do. Once I learned how to use woodworking tools and could cut things myself, I was able to make the solid wood ones like these."

He lifted a beautiful handcarved train that was painted blue and gold with shiny black wheels, and then showed her another ornament: a cowboy boot. "The boot is probably my favorite."

"These are incredible. Ever think about having a side business?"

"What? Making Christmas ornaments?" He laughed.

Tess grabbed her wine glass off the table and took a sip. "Not necessarily, but even just pieces that people might want. You obviously know what you're doing with wood. People would pay good money to have handmade tables or cabinets. That bookshelf you made Charlie when she graduated high school? She still has it in her room at your parents' house and it's gorgeous."

He grabbed the back of his neck and let out a deep breath. "I honestly never gave it any thought."

"It's something you enjoy doing so it might get you back in touch with that rather than doing things you really don't want to."

"It might. I'll keep it in mind." Danny reached for his wine glass and took a look at the tree. "So what do you think?"

"All the ornaments are on, but it's kind of hard to tell without the lights turned on."

"Good point." He plugged the lights in on the tree and then shut the lights off in the room. They took a step back and admired the tree. The different colors from the lights sparkled around the room and the ornaments hung beautifully on the tree. Tess couldn't help but be filled with warmth. "I thought it was a nice tree before but all decorated, it's really something. You sure know how to pick 'em," he said, bumping her shoulder.

"I guess I can use this as my fallback. If my bakery fails, I can become a professional Christmas tree picker."

"You'd have to charge a lot because you'd only have to work five or six weeks out of the year."

"Part of that doesn't sound so bad." She laughed.

"You'd be so bored."

"I would be. As much as the craziness can be overwhelming, especially during the holidays, I really do love it. I think I was born with flour and sugar under my nails because for as long as I can remember, I've always been at the kitchen counter with my hands in a mixing bowl."

"It's your passion and it shows. That's why you never have to worry about being a professional Christmas tree picker." Danny turned to face her. He grabbed her hands and turned her toward him. "Can I tell you something?"

She nodded while nervously holding her breath.

"I haven't been able to stop thinking about you since I left your apartment the other night. When you walked in here earlier, it took every ounce of self-control to not throw you up against the door and strip you naked."

Tess swallowed hard. "Really?"

"Yes, really. The other night was just a small taste of the things I want to do to you and with you."

She felt her heart pounding in her chest. No one had ever said anything like that to her before. "Oh."

He moved his hands to her waist and pulled her close to him.

Their bodies were flush against each other and Tess felt like she couldn't breathe.

"You're gonna have to tell me. What do you want me to do?"

She looked at him, unsure, but his eyes told her she could say what she wanted. "Kiss me."

He bent his head down to hers and took her mouth. He slid his tongue across her lips and she opened her mouth for him. Their tongues tangled and Danny slid his hand under her shirt so it was on her bare skin. One touch was all it took for her to want his hands everywhere. Her hands went to the hem of his shirt and he pulled away from her so he could reach over his head and remove his shirt. Tess had almost forgotten how incredible his body was. Danny stepped toward her again and kissed her hard. "Bedroom," he said against her mouth.

"What happened to taking things slow?"

"If you want me to slow down, I will." He looked into her eyes, searching for some kind of answer.

"Don't slow down."

Danny smirked and cupped her cheek. "Good. I want a lot of room so I have all the space I need to explore this body." He kept walking them back toward his bedroom while never breaking their kiss. Tess felt her knees hit the mattress and then they both toppled on it. He reached for the hem of her sweater and she sat up so he could quickly get it off her. Danny stared down at her. She loved the hungry look in his eyes. It ignited something in her she didn't even know existed. He trailed kisses down her neck and past her collarbone before hovering over one of her breasts. His mouth came down on her skin again at the same moment that he yanked the cup of her bra down. His tongue swirled her nipple and she fisted her hands in Danny's comforter. He continued licking and sucking before moving on to the other one and Tess actually felt dizzy. She didn't think she could take much more of this foreplay.

"Danny…"

"I know you're close. I can tell by your breathing."

She shook her head and closed her eyes. "I don't think I can take much more."

"Oh, I'm positive you can." His mouth descended on her again and he gripped her other breast with his hand and squeezed. She had no idea what it was about this man's mouth and hands that put her over the edge but she absolutely loved it. He grinded his hips against hers only a few times and soon Tess saw stars before she was crying out Danny's name. How was every orgasm with him more and more intense?

When her breathing finally returned to normal, Tess looked up at Danny and found him smiling down at her. They were both half naked and she decided that she'd definitely had enough of taking things slow. She sat up and unhooked her bra and tossed it on the floor. Danny looked surprised but she wasn't even remotely finished yet. She flipped them so he was on his back and her hand went for the button of his jeans.

"What are you doing?"

"You told me to tell you what I wanted. Right now, I want you inside me. No more messing around. I just want you."

"I can do that." He rolled them so he was on top and quickly pulled her jeans and underwear down her legs and tossed them onto the floor. He removed his jeans next and then hovered over her in nothing but his boxer briefs. Tess pushed them down and he shook out of them. Danny used his knee to part her legs. "Spread those legs wide for me."

She did as he asked and he leaned over to the nightstand and grabbed a condom out of his drawer. He tore open the foil and covered himself with it before settling back between her legs. "You're so goddamn beautiful." He took her mouth in a hard, fast kiss. Tess reached between them and took him in her hands and guided him to her entrance.

"You really are impatient tonight," he said against her lips.

"Yes, and it would be in your best interest to not make me wait anymore."

He entered her with one hard thrust and Tess felt a moan escape her lips. He completely filled her and she loved it.

"Are you okay?" he asked.

"I'll be even better once you start moving."

Danny started moving in and out of her and she could feel her hips lifting to meet him. She grabbed his neck and pulled his mouth down to hers, needing more contact. While their tongues tangled, he continued to thrust in and out of her at a deliciously perfect pace. She ran her hands up and down the muscles of his back and then gripped his ass in her hands. Tess could feel her orgasm starting to build again and she didn't know how much longer she could hold out. "Harder, Danny."

He wasted no time and did exactly as she asked. Tess gripped his shoulders tightly as she wrapped her legs around his waist, doing whatever she could to get closer to him. When he hit her clit, her breath caught. "Yeah, right there!" He pounded in and out of her and she could feel the sparks starting to go off behind her eyes. "I'm coming!" Danny kept pumping his hips and the aftershock of Tess's orgasm hit her almost as hard as her actual orgasm. A few seconds later, she felt him tense as his own orgasm hit. They rode out the wave and then lay together in a tangled mess of limbs and sheets.

"Remind me why I waited so long to do this with you again?"

Danny laughed and kissed the top of her head. "I can't think of one good reason. I hope you won't insist on us waiting so long after this time."

She turned to face him and a devilish smile slid across her lips. "I was thinking somewhere along the lines of five minutes?"

"I'm not sure if I can manage that."

Tess grinned at him. "What? You need more recovery time?"

He rolled over and pinned her to the mattress. "Five minutes might just be too long." He lowered himself to her and kissed her. Tess gripped his cheeks between her hands and pulled him against her. She had a feeling they were in for a long night of making up for lost time and she couldn't wait to get started.

Nine

Danny felt sunlight on his face and reluctantly opened his eyes. He felt like he'd just fallen asleep, but he didn't mind. The whole night had been more than worth it. Having Tess in his bed was something he'd thought about for a long time and the reality had been beyond his expectations. She wasn't shy with him, and she didn't try to hide any part of herself, which he loved. He also loved how she wasn't afraid to initiate things. When she wanted something, she had no problem telling him or just taking it, and that was fine by Danny.

He extended his arm to the other side of the bed and felt empty space. He quickly sat up to find that Tess wasn't there. He looked toward his bathroom and found it completely dark. He glanced at his phone. It was almost 7 a.m. She was usually at work by now. Danny climbed out of bed and walked out into the hallway, where he was met with total silence. "Tess?"

He walked into the kitchen to see if she'd left a note or something but there was nothing there. He ran a hand over his face and let out a deep breath. She ran off *again*. He understood that she'd gotten spooked after they'd slept together at his brother's wedding, but he couldn't understand her running away after the night they'd shared. He knew that they were still figuring things out, but he wanted answers and there was only one way to get them.

Tess stood behind the counter facing the register, staring out into space. To say she was tired was an understatement; if she managed three hours of sleep that would've been a lot. Not that she could complain, it had been fantastic. She was sore in places she'd long forgotten about, but it was worth it. Danny knew all the ways to make her body light up and after a night like that, she knew she could become addicted to him very easily.

What was distracting was how aggressive she'd been. She didn't exactly have a long sexual history, but Tess had always been on the docile side, letting the man take the lead, getting what she could out of it but never taking charge. With Danny, she'd been bold; she woke up around 4 a.m. with his arm wrapped around her stomach and she had the urge to push his hand right down on her sex. So she did. Just a few swipes and she could already feel another orgasm coming, but then he woke up and took over. Not only did he get her off with his hand, but he went back for seconds with his mouth. Tess tried to hide her blush at the thought.

She hadn't meant to leave without telling him, but when she'd woken up it was after five and she didn't want to be late. The last thing she wanted to do was wake him up. He'd looked so peaceful, so she quietly left.

"Hey, Tess, are you going to make the lemon cookies or are you staying up front? I was going to go check the inventory," Leanne asked.

"Inventory?"

"Yes, you know all that stuff we keep in the back that helps us put orders out? I want to make sure we have enough." She laughed. "Did you skip your coffee this morning?"

"Coffee?"

Leanne rolled her eyes. "Lord. You are clearly caffeine deprived."

Tess pinched the bridge of her nose. "Yeah, I probably am."

"How did Danny's tree turn out?"

"Oh, it's really nice. It looks really beautiful."

"Uh-huh. I'll bet you're real tired from all that tree decorating," Leanne said with a smirk. "Good for you, Tess. He's sexy as sin. You deserve it."

Tess could feel herself blushing. "Thanks."

"Who's sexy as sin?" Penny asked, walking over to them to ring up a sale.

"Danny Moreau. Tess was helping him decorate his Christmas tree last night."

Penny's eyes lit up. "Oh! Good for you. He is smoking hot!"

Tess shook her head and laughed. "No argument there."

"Just so you know, the ginger donuts are flying off the shelves."

"Of course they are. They're your recipe," Tess told Penny.

She beamed with pride. "I thought they'd be a nice holiday morning treat."

"They were a good call. Keep those trays stocked."

Penny smiled and gave her a nod.

"Okay, I'm gonna go start on the lemon cookies and then I'll be back up here, Lee, so you can go take care of inventory."

"Uh, you might want to hold off on that."

"What for?" she asked Leanne.

"Good morning, ladies." At the sound of Danny's voice, Tess's stomach dropped. She slowly turned around. He was standing in front of the counter wearing the same jeans from the night before and a long sleeve Henley shirt. He did not look happy.

"Hi... what brings you here so early?" She checked her watch and saw that it was almost seven thirty.

"I would think that would be obvious." He folded his arms across his chest and there was no denying that he was pissed.

"Why don't we step in the back and talk?"

"Great idea," he said through gritted teeth.

She gestured for him to follow her so he walked behind the counter. He gave a nod to Leanne and Penny and then followed her into her office. Tess walked behind her desk and Danny stood directly across from her.

"Look, I know what you're going to say—"

"I doubt that."

"Okay then, go ahead."

"Do you have any idea what it was like waking up and finding you gone again? I'm not sure what it is but it seems like any time we have sex, you run away the next morning."

Tess rushed past him to close her door. She didn't need anyone hearing this conversation. "That's not true."

"Really? Both times we've had sex you haven't stuck around for the next morning. It's a pretty shitty feeling to wake up alone. Especially when I thought we had an amazing night."

"We did have an amazing night," she said, taking a step toward him. "I woke up and saw that it was after five. I needed to get to work. You were asleep and I didn't want to wake you."

He held up his hand to stop her from continuing. "I don't care if

I've been asleep for five minutes. If you have to leave, you wake me up. It's that simple."

Tess didn't know what to say. No one had ever cared enough that they wanted to know that she was leaving unless it directly affected them. She dropped her head and sighed. "I'm really sorry. I'm... I'm really terrible at this, and I don't know what to do in these situations."

"What is it you think you're terrible at?"

She gestured between the two of them. "This... dating... sex. All of it."

He rolled his eyes. "You aren't terrible at any of it, especially not the sex."

"I don't know what came over me last night. I'm not usually like that."

"Okay, you've completely lost me."

Tess sighed and looked down at her feet. "I just mean that I've never been... I've never been so... commanding."

"Do you think there was something wrong with anything you did last night, or anything we did, for that matter?"

"Well... no. I'm just telling you that I've never been like that before. I don't know what happened that made me act like that."

Danny closed the distance between them so that their chests were practically touching. "I would like to think it's because you felt comfortable enough with me to know you could ask or take what you needed. Just so you know, I loved how vocal you were. I have a pretty good idea what gets you going, but it was nice hearing you say what you needed. It was really hot having you take control. I'd be very satisfied waking up every morning with you pushing my hand between your legs."

Tess blushed. She wasn't sure if she'd ever get over doing that. "I'm really sorry that I left without telling you. It's just never really mattered much if I was the one who left."

"It matters. You matter to me. I never want to wake up and wonder where you are."

Her gaze dropped down to her feet as she tried to hide her embarrassment. Danny's index finger came under her chin and lifted it. "Hey. I know we're still trying to figure this out, but I don't want you running off every time you get worried. I'd much rather us figure it out together." He cupped her cheek and touched his nose to hers.

She closed her eyes and breathed him in before looking up into his eyes. She knew that he meant what he was saying. He wasn't trying to tell her what to do or how to be. He just wanted to be with her. Tess almost didn't know how to react to that. "I like the sound of that, us figuring this out together." She ran her hands up his arms and smiled.

"What I'd really like is to throw you on that desk and hear you scream my name again."

Oh sweet Jesus. She clenched her thighs together.

"Don't worry. There's plenty of time for that." He grinned. "I know you've got a busy day, so I'll head out. I've gotta get to the office soon anyway. Why don't you come by when you're finished up for the night?"

"We're working late tonight."

"I don't have a curfew. You can come by whenever you're through here."

"Why does this feel like a booty call?"

"You can call for my booty anytime you want."

She let out a laugh and covered her mouth with her hand.

He gripped her by her waist so she was right up against him. "That being said, I want to take you out on a date Saturday night."

"Is that right?"

"Yes. Are you available?"

Tess grinned up at him. "I'll have to check my calendar but I think I'm free."

"I'm glad to hear it. I'll let you get back to work." Danny leaned down and kissed her.

"Let me walk you out." She led him toward the back door and then watched him walk back out to the street. Tess leaned her head up against the doorframe and let out a sigh. He really was sexy as sin, and for the first time in her life, she planned on enjoying every second of it.

The following week, Tess left the bakery a little early to go meet up with her sister. She and Amy went Christmas shopping every year at a spot not far from town that had a bunch of small shops. They had always preferred that rather than trying to shop at a crowded mall.

Tess pulled into the parking lot and saw Amy leaning against the hood of her car. "Hey, sorry I'm a little late. I was helping Betty with some orders."

"No problem, I just got here. Oh my God! You had sex!" Amy exclaimed.

Tess covered her face with her hand and gasped. "Will you lower your voice? What on earth is the matter with you?"

Amy shrugged at her sister. "Nothing. I just looked at you and you're practically glowing."

"I am not glowing."

"Oh, yes you are. I'm a medical professional. I recognize the glow."

Tess rolled her eyes. "You're ridiculous."

"I'm right though, aren't I? You totally had sex."

"Christ almighty. Yes, okay. Happy, now?"

Amy clapped her hands together in delight. "Give me details."

Tess started walking and Amy followed after her. "Danny and I... it just kind of happened. One night he was helping me put my tree in my apartment and then giving me a killer orgasm right on my couch and then I went to help him decorate his tree and we ended up having sex, a lot of sex."

"Oh, this is fantastic! Who would've ever known that Christmas trees were such an aphrodisiac?"

"They aren't." She laughed. "I don't know what it is but he barely has to touch me and I completely come alive."

"I always liked Danny but I really like him knowing he has those kinds of powers. The world needs more men like that."

Tess couldn't disagree with that; he was incredible.

"What made you actually let your guard down? I've been trying to tell you for years to give Danny or, well, *any man* a chance and you've flat-out refused."

"I know... things started between him and I at Jason and Kate's wedding."

"I knew it!" she gasped, pointing her finger at Tess.

"Are you going to let me fill you in or are you gonna keep interrupting?"

"Continue."

Tess covered her face with her hand and sighed. "The long and short of it is we kissed and I ran away and then after I tossed and turned in bed for what felt like hours, I showed up at his hotel room and practically jumped him right at the door. And then afterward I snuck out before he woke up."

Amy gasped. "I can't believe you kept this to yourself all these months!" She swatted her sister's arm. "Please tell me he was happy about you showing up at his room like that?"

"Oh, he was, but I felt so embarrassed about running out on him that I couldn't face him or talk to him. I was hoping he'd just forget about it, but Danny wasn't willing to do that. He kept insisting that I should give him a chance and that we were good together. He took me to a karaoke bar in Charlotte, and Amy, he got me to go up and sing."

"You haven't done that in forever! Oh man you must've been amazing! That's so sweet that he did that."

"I finally decided to stop fighting it. I figure I owe it to myself to give this a shot." Tess shrugged.

"Yes! Hell yes!" Amy clapped her hands together and smiled.

Tess covered her eyes with her hand. "Will you lower your voice?"

"Sorry, but this is monumental. You have been all business for the past five years and you are finally letting a man into your life. It's cause for some serious celebration. We are having very large cocktails after we shop."

Tess giggled. She couldn't help but love her sister's enthusiasm.

"So, then you two are officially dating?"

"We haven't exactly labeled anything. We've been spending a lot of time together. He took me out on Saturday night for dinner in Charlotte and he planned everything. It was so nice."

Amy raised an eyebrow at her. "What do you mean you haven't exactly labeled anything? Ya'll are going out on dates and you're sleeping together. You're dating."

Tess had made a point of not putting too much thought into it; she was just going to go with it. Overthinking tended to make her panic set in, and Tess was really trying to avoid that.

"I'm just really glad that you're finally embracing life and doing something for yourself. You let that asshat Dean control you for too long."

Tess's stomach lurched at the mention of his name. "This has nothing to do with him."

"It absolutely does. I know there's more to the story than you've ever said. When you came back home after you two broke up, you were so different. You thought no one noticed but I did. You had stopped singing. You used to sing all the time! When you were walking around the house, when you were in the shower, in the car, in church, and you just stopped after you left him. You loved wearing high heels when you went out and you always wore such pretty, bright colors and then it was like the shoes disappeared and you forgot about the clothes you loved."

"People change, Amy. It happens all the time."

"You changed because of someone else. I know he made you think there was something wrong with you so you changed to try and be whatever he thought you should be even if you won't say it." She turned to Tess and gripped her arm, forcing her to stop. "The point is I'm really happy that you let Danny in, that you're actually giving him a chance, because I think he could be really great for you. You deserve to feel special and I'm sorry you didn't feel that way for such a long time. One day, I hope that you'll tell me exactly what happened between you and Dean but for now, seeing you with this glow will suffice."

Amy had been right in so many things that she'd said, but Tess wasn't ready to go into the details of what had happened between her and Dean. She loved how fiercely her sister cared for her; she was incredibly lucky. "Thank you. I'm really happy."

"That's the best thing I've heard in quite some time. Let's get this shopping done so we can go get some cocktails!" They linked arms and were about to walk into a store when a man stepped in front of them.

"Tess, hey."

"Cooper! Hi! What a surprise. What brings you here?"

"Just picking up a few Christmas presents for my parents. One of my customers told me about the stores here and I decided to come check them out."

"Yeah this place is the best. Cooper, this is my sister, Amy. Amy, this is Cooper, he owns the sandwich shop a few doors over from the bakery."

Cooper extended his hand to her. "It's very nice to meet you, Amy."

"You too."

"We just came to do a little Christmas shopping ourselves."

Cooper turned back to Tess. "I'm surprised you left the bakery, I know how busy you've been."

"Yeah, well, this is a tradition for us, so I usually cut out for a few hours and then go back to finish up."

"That's really great. I'm glad to see you doing something for yourself and I have no doubt you have everything under control at the bakery. Oh, don't forget, we said when things slowed down for you we'd go grab a bite or a drink and catch up."

"Right, yeah, I don't expect things to really slow down until after the holidays but we'll figure something out."

Cooper's face lit up. "Great. Well, I don't want to hold you ladies up. Amy, it was a pleasure meeting you. Enjoy your shopping."

"Nice meeting you too."

Cooper walked down the path and in the direction of another store.

"He seems nice."

"He is."

"Why am I detecting a 'but'?"

"There's no 'but.' He is a really nice guy. When my supply delivery got messed up last week, he loaned me some eggs and flour so I could get my orders done. He's fairly new to town and he doesn't seem to have many friends yet."

"He sure seems to like you."

Tess shrugged. "We're just friends."

"He certainly isn't hard on the eyes. I might have to start eating more sandwiches." Amy smirked.

Tess laughed and nudged her sister as they made their way to the first store.

Ten

Danny pulled up to the empty lot and saw that Pete was already there waiting for him. He got out of his truck and grabbed his iPad. "I didn't keep you waiting long, did I?"

"Not at all. I just got here. How's it going?" Pete asked as he extended his hand to Danny.

"Not too bad. I appreciate you taking the time to meet me."

"No problem. You've definitely got me curious as to why we're meeting on an empty lot."

"I figured. Sorry for all the secrecy but I know how news travels round here so I figured I'd tell you in person."

Pete chuckled. "Total understandable."

"This here is mine." He pointed to the empty land in front of them.

"This property?"

"Yeah, all three acres of it."

"Wow. Well, it's a great space," Pete said, walking around the lot. "What do you plan to do with it?"

"Build my house."

Pete cocked his head to the side. "Something happen to that swanky condo you have?"

Danny laughed. "No, it's great. I love living there but I want a space that's all my own. A place my family can come visit and everyone can fit, and I want to have a place for my own family one day."

Pete nodded. "I can certainly understand that. What's got you thinking that way, or should I say who?"

"It's something I've always wanted to do."

"I'm sure, but that's not all that's behind this." Pete crossed his arms over his chest.

Danny dropped his head and sighed. "You're right. I bought the land after Charlie's accident last year. It had been something I'd been holding back on doing because I was waiting for the right time, and when she got hurt I realized that there really is no right time and that I should just go ahead and do it, so I did."

"I can understand finally doing something you've been putting off. Good for you, man. I think it's great. I just thought that maybe Tess had something to do with it?" He grinned.

"What would make you think that?"

"Man, we're practically family and you know how fast word spreads in this crowd. We all saw you two at Jason and Kate's wedding. It looked like there were sparks flying between you."

Danny let out a laugh. "Yeah, there's definitely something going on between us. We haven't exactly figured out what that is yet, but when I picture the house I love the idea of her being in it."

Pete smiled at him. "I get that. When I knew Laura was the one for me that was all I thought about, making a life with her. I wanted nothing more than to build a house that we could call our home and raise our family there."

"Well, you built a beautiful house. I'm hoping you can help me do the same."

"I'd be honored. You have any plans in mind?"

Danny flipped open his iPad and turned it toward Pete. "I sketched out a few things."

"Wow! These look great." Pete looked over what Danny had on the screen and his smile kept growing wider. "I definitely think we can make this work. When you draw up a full set of plans, let's sit down and we can go over everything."

"That sounds perfect. I'll get to work on it and let you know when I have something."

"Great. I look forward to hearing from you." They shook hands and started walking back to their trucks. "Hey, Danny," Pete called. "I'm happy for you about Tess. She's a catch."

"Thanks, man. Me too. I'll talk to you soon." Danny climbed in his truck and glad to finally feel excited about a project—even if it was for himself.

Christmas was less than ten days away and the bakery was overflowing with orders. Tess had been getting in by five every morning for the past week and not leaving before nine or ten every night. She had a huge order of cupcakes for a new client just outside of Belmont that she promised she'd deliver herself. Once all six dozen cupcakes were loaded in her Jeep, she hopped in, hoping for a quick drop off so she could get back and finish by eight. It had been a few nights since she'd seen Danny, and she was missing him something awful. He, of course, had told her that she was always welcome to come by whenever she finished up, and he had even offered to go to her place, but she'd been so exhausted that she was only able to think about sleeping.

Now, all she could think about was finishing up for the day and spending time with him. Tess never thought she could have room for work and a relationship in her head, but so far she was making it work and it felt really good.

She turned her key in the ignition and nothing happened. She tried again. Still nothing. "Ugh! No! Come on, Jesse! Don't do this to me now!" Tess popped her hood and got out of her car. She'd spent enough time around her dad to know what to look for, and she didn't see any major problems. She went to try and start her car, and the ignition still wouldn't turn over. Tess grabbed her phone out of her purse and called her dad's shop.

"Hey, Momma. Jesse won't start. Can you send Dad over? I've gotta go make a delivery, and I really need my car started. He's on a test drive? Can you send someone else over? I know everyone is busy, but I really need my car. Okay, I'll see if I can borrow someone else's. Please send someone over when you can. Thanks." She hung up the phone and sighed. This was definitely not what she needed right now. As she was about to turn to walk back inside, she spotted Cooper walking across the parking lot toward her.

"Everything okay?"

"Oh, no, actually. My car won't start and I've gotta deliver six dozen cupcakes to a client in the next twenty minutes. I was just gonna go see if I could use one of the girls' cars."

"I can take you. My truck is a few spaces over. We can just load everything into there and you don't need to waste time trying to find a replacement car."

"I don't want to impose."

He waved her off. "It's not an imposition. I'm done with work for the day, and you need help. Let me help you."

She really didn't have time to waste and despite hating looking like she was incapable, being late for her client would bother her more. "Okay, that would be really great."

They got everything into Cooper's truck in two trips before climbing in themselves. Tess put the address into her phone and directed him out of Belmont.

"How was your Christmas shopping the other day?" he asked.

"Oh, it was good. Amy and I got gifts for our parents and we usually break off and get our gifts for each other as well. I picked up a few other things while I was there too," Tess told him.

"I was really impressed with how many stores were over there."

"It's so much better than going to a mall."

"Yeah, I really love the small store experience. I picked up a few things for my parents. I'm supposed to go and spend Christmas with them, but they live in Florida now and taking off the day after Christmas is a little rough at the store."

"They can't come here?"

"They don't really like to travel." He shrugged. "I'm not big into the holidays anyway."

"Really? How come?"

He let out a sigh and kept looking straight ahead. "My wife died two years ago, and the holidays always remind me of her."

Tess's jaw dropped. "Cooper... I had no idea. I'm so sorry."

"Thank you. It's hard to believe she's been gone for almost two years. We grew up together, so when she died I felt like a part of me had died too."

She shook her head in shock. "That had to be... I can't even imagine. How come you never mentioned this before?"

He released a shaky breath. "It's really hard for me to talk about. Izzy was incredible. She lit up a whole room when she walked into it. Losing her to leukemia was, well, there just aren't words. That's why I needed to start some place new. I didn't want constant reminders of her."

Tess felt her throat get tight with emotion. "I really am so sorry for your loss. It sounds like you two had a special relationship."

"We did." he smiled. "I was lucky I had her in my life for as long as I did, and I was lucky I was able to start over in a great new place and meet such nice, welcoming people."

"We certainly are a friendly bunch." She chuckled, trying to lighten the mood.

"In case I haven't said it enough, I really appreciate how helpful you've been to me with letting me know all the ins and outs of the town and sending customers my way."

"Oh, that's no problem at all. It's what we all do for each other."

"Yeah, but I'm the new guy. Ya'll didn't have to embrace me so much, and I know you were a big part of it."

"Everyone who works on Main Street is happy to see the businesses flourishing. You've got a great thing going."

"Thank you. That means a lot coming from you." He looked over at her and she gave him a small smile. He was a man who had suffered a terrible loss and was just trying to rebuild his life.

"I was thinking, whenever we decide to go grab that drink, there's this great spot in Charlotte I heard about that I thought would be fun to try."

"Which place? I was in Charlotte recently at a really fun karaoke bar."

"Really? Did you go with the girls?"

Tess shook her head. "No, I actually went with Danny Moreau. We just started seeing each other, I guess you could say. I'm not really sure what to call it, I'm still getting my bearings."

"Oh... well, that's really great, Tess."

"Thanks." She smiled, looking down at her hands. "So, what place were you talking about?"

He turned his eyes back to the road. "Oh, um, I think it's called the Blind Tiger, I'm not one hundred percent sure."

"I've never heard of it but I'm sure it's great. Once things slow down, we can definitely catch up."

He gave her a nod but never looked at her. Maybe everything he'd told her about his wife had upset him? There was an awkward silence and Tess tried to think of something to say as they pulled up to the house. He gave her a small smile right before getting out of his truck, which made her feel slightly relieved. After everything he'd been through, Cooper certainly could use a friend and Tess was more than happy to be that person for him.

Danny could see the smoke coming from a car as he approached what appeared to be a bad accident. As he got closer, he noticed the truck was his and suddenly he was filled with panic knowing his sister had been driving it. He rushed over to the driver's side door and saw her slumped over the wheel, blood streaming down the side of her face. He tried to open the door but it was stuck. "Ace! Wake up! Wake up! I'm gonna get you out of there!" He banged on the window but she didn't stir at all. Danny looked around but there was no one to help him. He could hear sirens in the distance, but they weren't close enough. When he turned back to his truck, Charlie was gone. He blinked a few times and then he was standing in the middle of the emergency room. People were rushing all around him, monitors were beeping and he could barely hear himself think. He looked around frantically for Charlie but he couldn't find her. It wasn't until he heard a scream that he turned around and went running toward a curtain. That was his mother's scream, there was no mistaking it. He heard someone say, "I'm terribly sorry" and then he heard the long beep of a machine. Danny pulled the curtain back and saw Charlie's arm hanging off the gurney, her body completely lifeless and the heart monitor showing a flat line. "No! Ace! Come back! Come back! Ace!"

Danny jolted up in bed and gasped. He was covered in sweat and it took a second for him to realize that he was in his bed and once again it had just been that terrible nightmare.

"Danny, are you okay?"

He turned and saw Tess sitting up, her eyes wide. "Yeah, I'm sorry I woke you."

"Don't worry about that. You were yelling for Charlie. Were you having a nightmare?"

He nodded slowly and blew out a breath. "Yeah, I must have been." He wiped the sweat from his face.

Tess inched closer to him and wrapped her arms around his arm. "Were you dreaming about the accident?"

Danny looked down at her, his lips pursed. "It's nothing. You should go back to sleep."

Tess glared at him like she wasn't taking no for an answer. Danny sighed. "I can't help but think that I should've gone after her that night. She left the house upset after that fight with the chief and I just let her leave. If I was with her, she wouldn't have been driving and Tommy's drunk ass would've never driven her off the road and into that tree."

"There's no way you could've known what was going to happen."

He shook his head. "She almost died. In my nightmare, that's what happens, she dies. I have the same dream over and over."

"That has to be really hard. I know she almost died but you can't blame yourself for what happened. It was an accident. A terrible accident, but Charlie is fine. She's more than fine, in fact. Have you talked to her about this?"

"No, there's no need. It's my shit."

"Okay, but maybe if you talked to her that would help release whatever guilt you're feeling."

Danny wasn't sure if anything would ever relieve his guilt. He felt like he'd failed his sister in the worst way possible. His job as her older brother was to protect her and when she'd needed him the most, he hadn't been there.

"Maybe it would, I don't know. Come on, let's go back to sleep." He lay back down and opened his arms to her. Tess laid her head on his chest and snuggled up against him. He appreciated that she didn't press him further on it. Danny didn't know how to tell Charlie how he felt about this. It had been hard opening up to Tess about it, but when he saw the look in her eyes, he knew he needed to tell her. It felt so good having her in his arms. At least this moment he could forget his guilt and just focus on the present.

Tess paced behind the counter of the bakery kitchen, her phone pressed to her ear. "I don't understand how that could've happened. I checked the order myself. Of course I know it's an important party, Rita." She blew out a deep breath and squeezed the bridge of her nose. "I honestly don't know, but nothing like this has ever happened before. Okay let us run something over to you guys right now. We'll be there in less than ten minutes. Okay, thanks." She tossed her phone down and tried to collect herself before walking up front. When she walked out, the bakery floor was fairly busy. She caught Leanne's eye and she made her way over to her.

"You need something?"

"It seems like I messed up the order for the mayor's Christmas party."

Leanne's eyes went wide. "What do you mean? How did you mess it up?"

"I don't know. I thought I double-checked everything before I sent it out but I guess I didn't realize that I forgot a whole dozen of the vanilla ginger cupcakes."

Leanne's face dropped. "Oh. Well… it happens."

"No, no it doesn't. Rita, the mayor's assistant, just called me and said they were specifically looking for them. I told her we'd run something over to them quickly. I just can't believe I did this. This was a big event that we were lucky to be associated with."

"It's okay. We'll put something together. It'll be fine." Leanne gripped her forearm to reassure her but all Tess felt was panic. She had never messed up something that important at work before. She was always laser-focused. When she went through the order she'd been alone, there hadn't been anyone around to distract her, but the entire time she'd been thinking about Danny's nightmare. To say she'd been shaken by hearing him scream for Charlie was an understatement, but seeing the panic and guilt in his eyes had been gut wrenching. It was still no excuse for her to be unfocused.

"What's going on over here?" Penny asked, walking over to them.

"We're gonna need a dozen of the vanilla ginger cupcakes boxed up as fast as you can."

"I'm not sure if we have a dozen," she told Leanne.

"Well, we're gonna just have to hope that we do."

Penny grabbed a box and hurried down to the counter where the cupcakes were kept. She filled it and then brought it back over to them. "There were ten, so I put in two of the carrot cake ones. They're very popular."

"Okay. That'll have to work." Tess undid her apron and hung it up by the register. "I'm gonna go run these over to the mayor's."

"No problem. We've got everything covered here," Leanne told her.

Tess took the box, grabbed her keys, and got in her Jeep. Her stomach was in knots as she made the short drive over to the mayor's house. She had no idea how she was going to walk in there without wanting to burst into tears, but she sure as hell was going to try.

Eleven

After making the emergency delivery over to the mayor's house, Tess wanted to go home and crawl into bed and stay there for a long while. She managed to sneak in through the back and leave the box with the rest of the dessert without disturbing the party. She'd also left a note on the box saying the entire bill was on the house. The mayor had spent over three hundred dollars on all the desserts he'd ordered and now she was going to eat the cost of everything because she'd messed up.

She didn't make it back to her apartment until after nine and she'd been so distracted by the day that she completely forgot that she'd told Danny to come over after work. He was waiting for her outside her door with a large bag of food. "I hope you're hungry. I picked up burritos from this great place near my office."

Tess tried to look happy but her face always gave her away. "Yeah, I'm not really that hungry."

"What's wrong?" he asked, stepping closer and gripping her arm.

"Nothing. It was just a really long, tough day."

"Why don't you go get comfortable and then you can tell me all about it?"

She nodded and led them into her apartment. She dropped her keys and her purse on the table near the door and then turned back to him. "I'll be right out."

"Take your time."

Tess slipped into her bedroom and let out a deep breath. She'd never had anyone care enough to want to listen to her after she'd had a tough day. She changed into a pair of leggings and a T-shirt, washed her face, and pulled her hair up into a high ponytail. When she walked back out into the living room, Danny had dinner laid out at the counter for them. "I picked up beer too. That seemed to pair better with burritos than wine."

111

"Good call." She sat down on the stool and took a long sip of the beer.

"So tell me what happened." He sat down and turned to face her.

"I told you that we got hired to make the dessert for the mayor's Christmas party, right?"

He nodded and took a sip of his beer.

"Well, somehow I left out a dozen of the cupcakes from the order. I could've sworn I counted them in with everything else but I completely forgot them. The mayor's assistant called me to let me know. I ran a box over there and slipped in unnoticed but that has never happened to me in all the time I've been in business. I was mortified."

Danny leaned forward and placed his hand over hers. "It was an honest mistake."

"I don't make mistakes like that."

"I get that, but it's a really busy time. You have a lot going on, so it's completely understandable that something like this happened."

"I was so embarrassed. Getting this party was a really big deal." She ran a hand over her face and sighed.

"I know it was and I'm sure everything turned out fine. You were able to get another box in there and it was like it never happened."

She shook her head and took another sip of beer. "You don't understand."

"I'm trying to. You didn't purposely leave that box out of the order, you didn't give them something they said they didn't want, and you didn't give them something they were allergic to. I know that you aren't happy that it happened, but my point is you were able to fix it."

"This time I was. What if next time I can't? What if the next time I'm distracted I really screw up?"

"You're being way too hard on yourself. No one is perfect."

"I'm not being too hard on myself."

"What distracted you today?"

Tess looked down at the plate in front of her and immediately felt sick. She didn't know how to tell him that he'd been the thing distracting her. "I didn't say I was distracted."

"You said 'the next time I'm distracted' so that makes it sound like you were distracted this time. Was there something else going on that took your attention away when you were getting the order together?"

She couldn't look at him. She stood up and walked around to the other side of the counter, needing some space. Danny turned and looked at her, the concern etched all over his face. "Will you please tell me what's going on?"

Tess looked up at him, tears stinging her eyes. "I was thinking about your nightmare this morning, all morning actually. I hated seeing how tormented you were by it and that's what was on my mind instead of my orders."

He looked taken aback by what she said, which just made her feel worse.

"I'm sorry that you were thinking about that. I told you, there's nothing to do about it."

"You've been having the same nightmare for almost a year and you don't think it's a big deal?"

He shook her off. "It's just a bad dream, Tess."

"No, it's not just a bad dream, Danny. You were screaming for Charlie. Do you have any idea what it was like to try and wake you up? You just kept screaming for her. Even after you woke up, I was really worried."

"I appreciate that and I'm sorry if I scared you, but you don't need to worry about it."

She threw her hands up in the air and groaned. "I don't need to worry about it? You're clearly not worried about it so someone has to be."

"Why are you making this a thing?"

"It is a thing! It's so much a thing that I couldn't even focus today!"

"Oh, so you want to blame me for that?"

"If I wasn't with you, I would've been kept out of it."

Danny pushed off of his stool and laid his hands down on the counter. "I hate to break it to you, Tess, but that's not how life works. You can't just cut people out whenever it's convenient for you because you can't afford any kind of distraction. Things happen with people you care about, and you can't control how and when it happens but it's pretty unrealistic to think you can just avoid it."

"Maybe I was wrong. Maybe I can't do this."

Danny's eyes widened. "Do what? Us?"

"Yeah, maybe this was a bad idea, like I said."

Danny walked around the counter so that he was right in front of her. "That's not true. This has been nothing short of amazing and you know that. I know you do."

"I just don't think it's going to work."

"Because of one bump in the road?"

"Yeah, it's a pretty big bump. This is interfering with my work."

"You make it sound like it was a life or death situation. You forgot a box of cupcakes, and I know that's not something you want to do, but no one would've died without those cupcakes."

Tess was suddenly filled with anger. She knew it wasn't a life or death situation, but she didn't run her business that way. What was worse was that she felt like Danny was minimalizing what she did and she'd sworn she would never tolerate that again. "They may just be cupcakes but I have my standards and the bottom line is I didn't live up to them today because of you."

"You'd rather blame me for what happened today than just call it what it was, a mistake, and move past it?"

She looked up at him and swallowed the lump in her throat. "There's nothing to move past."

Danny stepped back, shaking his head. "You're talking crazy. Of course we can get past this."

"How else would you like me to say it? This isn't going to work. You need to go."

Danny looked at her for a moment, like he was waiting for her to take back what she'd just said. Instead Tess crossed her arms over her chest and held her ground. He finally walked back around to the other side of the counter and grabbed his car keys off of the coffee table before walking out and slamming the door.

Tess jumped at the noise and the tears she'd been holding finally streamed down her face. Seeing Danny walk out hurt her more than she could say, but she'd done the right thing. Her work had to come first. It was the only thing she could truly depend on.

———

A few days later, Danny sat in front of the airport at the arrival area. It was two days before Christmas and Charlie and Nick were coming in from New York for the holidays. He was really looking forward to seeing his sister and his best friend; he needed some kind of distraction from how he'd been feeling since he'd walked out of Tess's apartment. He'd felt terrible that his nightmare had upset her so much, but it wasn't worth her being that worried. True, it had been going on for a long time, but what could he do? It was just a dream.

It had hurt him that she didn't think they were worth trying to figure out. He really thought he could make her see reason, but hearing her tell him to go felt like a blow to the gut Danny had never seen coming.

A knock on the passenger side window jolted him from his thoughts. Charlie stood at the window, smiling and waving at him. He unlocked the doors and she opened the door. "Hey, Danno. Sorry, baggage claim took a little longer than we thought."

"No problem. Where is Nick?"

"Grabbing the last bag. He'll be along any minute."

Charlie looked toward the airport door and smiled. "Ah, here he comes."

Danny heard his tailgate open and then the bags hit the bed of his truck. Once the tailgate was closed, Nick rounded to Charlie's side of the truck.

"All ready to go. Hey, man. Thanks for the ride," Nick said as he climbed into the back of the truck.

"Good to see you, Doc."

Charlie got in and buckled up, and Danny headed for the exit. "Will didn't fly down with you?"

"No, he's working on a case so he'll be here tomorrow night," Charlie told him. She peeled off her hoodie and smiled as she sat there in just a T-shirt. "December twenty-third and it's fifty-eight degrees."

Danny couldn't help but laugh. As much as Charlie loved living in New York City, she had never quite adjusted to the colder temperatures. "Is it a little chilly up north?"

"It snowed last night. It didn't really stick but it was twenty-five degrees."

"It wasn't that bad, and when we left it was almost forty degrees," Nick said.

"I will take fifty-eight degrees at almost five o'clock in December any day." Charlie declared.

Something sparkly caught Danny's eye. He looked over at

Charlie's hand and saw the sparkle was in fact coming from her hand—her left hand in particular. "Charlotte... what's on your hand?"

"Whoa! Did he just Charlotte me?"

"He definitely did," Nick said from the backseat.

"Oh, you mean this gorgeous, sparkly thing?" she said, holding up her hand in his direction.

"Holy shit! You guys are engaged?"

"We're engaged!" his sister squealed.

"How could you not tell me, either one of you?" He glared at his best friend in the rearview mirror.

"Sorry man, we wanted to tell you, but we knew we were coming home so we thought it would be better to tell you in person."

"When did this happen?"

"Two nights ago. That's why we didn't call you because then we would've had to call everyone and in person is just much easier," Charlie told him.

"What the hell? I'm not everyone. I would've kept it a secret. I knew Nick was gonna propose, and I didn't say anything."

Her face twisted in confusion. "You did?"

"Yeah, he told me at the Pulled Pork and Whiskey Festival."

Charlie turned in her seat to face Nick. "No wonder you were acting so strange when we got back to New York. You looked like you were going to puke every time I asked you something."

Nick laughed a little. "I was so afraid I was going to say something to give myself away."

"I was completely surprised. Teddy asked me to meet him at his store but when I got there all I found was a note that said 'meet me on the rooftop,' which I thought was strange because, again, it was cold out and I couldn't imagine what the hell Teddy would be doing on the roof. When I got up there, Nick had strung up a bunch of lights and was clutching a glass of whiskey so hard it looked like it was going to break into a million pieces," she said, giggling.

"I was trying to be cool, and I was shaking like a leaf. I ended up downing the whiskey and I started rambling. I'm not even sure what I said at first, but then I finally got my shit together and then I got down on my knee and asked her if she would do me the honor of marrying me."

He looked over and could see his sister blushing at the memory.

When he looked in his mirror, he could see his best friend smiling and he felt overwhelmed with happiness. "Wow, that's great. I'm really happy for ya'll."

"Thank you. Now I want to hear about you and Tess," Charlie said, turning toward him.

Danny cleared his throat and shifted in his seat.

"Oh no. What happened?" Charlie asked.

"We're not seeing each other anymore."

"What? What the hell happened? Things were going great when I talked to you both just a few days ago."

"Everything was great until a few days ago," he bit out, tightening his grip on the steering wheel.

"Explain, Danno."

Danny shook his head. "It's the same argument. Tess doesn't think she can give attention to anything other than her bakery. We've been spending a lot of time together over the past few weeks and it's been really great, but yesterday she had an order to fill for a party and she got distracted thinking about something we'd been talking about earlier and the order got messed up. When I tried to tell her it was just a mistake—one she was able to fix, by the way—she completely pushed me away. No one died because they were missing their cupcakes."

"You didn't say that did you?" She cringed.

"Yeah! It's true! She was acting like it was the most horrible mistake and it wasn't."

"You're an idiot."

"I'm an idiot?"

"Do you remember after college Tess moved to South Carolina to live with her boyfriend, Dean?"

"Yes, the asshole that cheated on her."

"The very same. She had always planned to open a bakery, and when he asked her to move back to where he was from, she said 'okay' and figured that she would just start something there. Not right away, but eventually. He was working for his family's financial firm and was being groomed for a big position. Tess isn't the type to sit on her ass and do nothing, so while she tried to learn the ins and outs of buying a bakery, she took a job at a local bakery to earn some money but learn the ropes. Every time we talked, she would tell me her plans for the bakery she wanted to own, and then one day she stopped talking about it. When I asked her about it, she told me the chance of her finding something to buy was slim to none. She'd always been so optimistic about it, it seemed strange to me that she was all of a sudden giving up on it."

Danny shook his head. "Wait, how come I don't remember this?"

"Maybe because I didn't tell you? Best friends keep secrets for each other." She glared at him.

"Why do I feel like there's still more to this story?"

"There is. I went down to visit her one weekend and when I mentioned the bakery, she clammed up. When I called her out on it, Dean looked at me and said there was absolutely no reason that she would ever need to work. He would be making enough money to provide for her. Plus, making dessert in a bakery wasn't a real career; it wasn't like she was a pastry chef at a five-star restaurant."

"Oh, shit. He said that?" Nick asked.

"Yeah, it was awful, but Tess didn't argue. That's when I really saw the change in her, like something inside of her had died. It wasn't long after that that she caught him cheating and luckily didn't stick around for any more of his bullshit."

Danny let out a deep breath. He knew Tess's ex had been awful, but he had no idea he'd been an absolute bastard.

"The point I'm trying to make is that I don't even know all the details of what happened between the two of them but if I had to guess, I'm going to say that he routinely told her that her dreams were stupid, that she wasn't good enough. He wanted her to be a certain way and for some reason she thought she had to be like that. If she hadn't caught him cheating, I don't know how long she would've put up with that. And then you come along promising to be different, which you are, but then you tell her that her cupcakes aren't a matter of life and death, and, again, not wrong but to her that sounds like you're saying what she does doesn't matter."

Danny dropped his head as what his sister said sank in. "That is absolutely not what I meant."

"I know that, but I think she automatically hears him cutting her down when she hears things like that."

"I get that, but she gave up and pushed me away because of one mishap."

"She isn't used to being with a good guy. She isn't used to

anyone who isn't a self-centered prick. You wanting to be with her scares her more than being alone. She knows how to do alone, but the relationship thing? It scares the hell out of her."

"She won't listen to me. No matter what I said last night, Tess was dead set on us not being together."

Charlie turned to face him. "Well then, big brother, it looks like you have quite the challenge on your hands, don't you?"

Danny nodded slowly. He didn't want to give up on Tess, didn't want to give up on them, and now that he realized why she was so quick to push him away, he was determined to make her see he wouldn't walk away that easily.

Twelve

Tess stood in her kitchen finishing a bowl of cereal over the sink. It was after nine o'clock and she'd been on the go all day. She, Penny, and had Betty spent the majority of the day baking sheets of gingerbread for a customer who wanted to make gingerbread houses with her family. They needed enough gingerbread for ten houses—and not small houses either. Since Tess had no idea what that meant in terms of gingerbread, they'd made enough for the construction of all the houses and then some extra in case there were any mishaps.

Being busy had been a good thing because otherwise, she would've had way too much time to think about Danny. Her chest still hurt when she thought of him leaving her apartment, the hurt in his eyes when she told him that they shouldn't be together. She had tried to have both, work and a relationship, and the relationship had compromised her work. She couldn't allow that. She'd worked too long and too hard to get where she was to start making bad choices.

A knock at the door shook her from her thoughts. She placed her bowl in the sink and headed for the door. When she looked through the peephole she squealed with delight and hurried to open the door. Charlie was standing on the other side holding a bottle of whiskey and smiling big.

"I thought you weren't getting in until later tonight?"

"We were able to switch to an earlier flight." Charlie stepped inside and wrapped her in a big hug; she hadn't realized how much she needed that.

"I'm so happy to see you but you didn't have to come over. I would've come to you."

"Honey, I know you're working like a maniac right now and are probably ready to pass out. Besides, Nick is hanging out with Danny so I was more than happy to come over here."

The mention of his name made Tess shift where she stood. "Don't worry, I already know that you two aren't together anymore." Charlie reached out and pinched her arm. "By the way, that was not cool to not tell me."

"Ouch!" Tess laughed. "It just happened."

"I don't care. I'm going to crack open this whiskey, pour us each a glass, and then we're gonna sit down and you're gonna tell me exactly what happened." Charlie made quick work of pouring the whiskey and they flopped on the couch. "First, how are you?"

"I'm okay."

"Liar," she said, taking a sip.

Tess shook her head. When she looked down, she noticed a sparkle coming from the glass. "Hold on, what's that? Are you engaged?" She reached out and grabbed Charlie's left hand.

"I am." Her mouth lifted into a giant smile.

"Ah! Oh my God! When did this happen?"

"A few nights ago."

"And you didn't call me?" She returned the favor and pinched her arm.

Charlie laughed as she swatted at her hand. "I wanted to see the look on your face in person. We can go into specifics about that after. Right now I want to hear about what happened with you and Danny."

Tess took a deep breath and put the glass to her lips, taking a long sip of the whiskey. "I thought I could do it, have my business and have a relationship. Danny and I started spending a lot of time together over the past few weeks. Even when I was working late, I would either go over to his place or he would come to mine. It was great, just spending time with him. We went out on real dates too, so it wasn't like this was just a late night rendezvous kind of thing."

Charlie giggled and covered her mouth with her hand. "Sorry, but the thought of you two having late night rendezvous. Never mind, keep going."

"We were hired to do the dessert for the mayor's Christmas party, and it was a big gig. I didn't realize it at the time but I'd been distracted by something he and I had been talking about earlier that morning while I was trying to put the order together. When the mayor's assistant called me and said there was a box missing from the order, I was so embarrassed. Luckily, I had what they ordered in the case, so I was able to run them over and no one at the party was the wiser, but I don't make mistakes like that. I'm always on top of things, especially big orders."

"Yes, you are. It wasn't like you gave them the wrong thing though."

"I know that and it could've been a lot worse but it really upset me and Danny didn't understand that."

"I already yelled at him for being an idiot," Charlie said, tipping her glass against her lips.

"You did?"

"Of course I did. He's my brother and I love him, but I'll be the first one to tell him when he's being an idiot. First of all, you have to know that when he told you that it wasn't a life and death situation, he didn't mean that what you do isn't important. He was trying to ease your guilt. Danny is a fixer; he always wants to find a way to help the other person, so he thought by telling you that your mistake wasn't as big as you thought it was that he was helping you."

Tess sighed. She could see how he might think that. At the time, it didn't sound like he was trying to help. It sounded like he was criticizing her and that's why she'd put her walls back up.

"You aren't exactly the best when it comes to accepting help, you know."

Tess's eyes bulged as she lowered her glass from her lips. "That's ridiculous!"

Charlie glared at her. "You are always waiting for the other shoe to drop. You have it in your head that good things like being with a good man while running a successful business is something that isn't meant for you."

Tess opened her mouth to speak but then clamped it shut. Charlie's statement was accurate.

"Will you please tell me what He Who Shall Not Be Named did to you? I need to understand."

She almost spit out her drink. "I'm sorry, did you just make a Harry Potter reference?"

"He's a bad guy, so it seems fitting he's referred to as a villain." Charlie shrugged.

"He cheated, and I caught him. You know that."

"That's not what I mean and you know it. When you moved down there, you had your dream of opening a bakery and then one day, it was like that dream had just disappeared. You stopped sounding like yourself. You sounded like someone else wanted you to sound. When I came to visit, all he said was that being a baker wasn't a real career and you were done with that nonsense."

Tess balled her hand in a fist at her side. The memories were all starting to flood back to her and she was feeling overwhelmed by it all. Her throat went dry and she could feel the tears coming. Charlie turned toward her and crossed her legs in front of herself and inched toward Tess so that their knees were touching. "Hey, it's me. There's nothing you can't tell me."

"I can't tell you this."

"Yes, you can." She took her hand and smiled reassuringly at her.

Tess emptied the rest of her glass and looked up at the ceiling before refocusing on Charlie. "Honestly, I don't even remember when it started or how, but it wasn't that long after I moved down to South Carolina. Anytime I would mention my plans for the bakery, Dean would ignore me or try to get me to do something else. He said I also had a business degree and I could use that or go back to school and get my MBA, get a real career. I had no desire to work in an office or go back to school, for that matter, and once he realized that I wasn't going to change my mind, he started attacking my career choice every chance he got. He came from a family with a pedigree and they wanted him to settle into the business, marry someone, and make heirs. They wanted a particular type of someone, and I didn't fit the mold."

"That's absolutely insane."

She shrugged. "I loved him. I thought he loved me so I wanted to at least try to be what he wanted me to be. He told me that my clothes were too bright, so I toned down what I was wearing. He said my hair looked like I belonged on a farm so I stopped wearing a braid. He hated the music I listened to while I baked so I stopped listening to it and he told me that my singing was annoying."

"Asshole. You have a gorgeous voice. He deserves a good, swift kick in the balls."

"Sex was all about him, and I just never felt…"

"Like he wanted you?"

She nodded slowly. "Yeah. If he didn't want me the way that I was then I don't know, I didn't feel good about myself."

"That's completely understandable."

Tears rolled down her cheeks and she quickly wiped them away. "I should've never let it get that far. I should've never listened to what he said."

"It's absolutely not your fault, and it kills me that you think it is. You did nothing to make him treat you like that."

"I should've never let him treat me like that. I gave up everything I loved for him and for what? So that I could feel terrible about myself? I believed everything he said."

Charlie looked her square in the face. "You believed him because you loved him and you couldn't imagine that someone you loved would tell you something that wasn't true. The important thing is that you pulled yourself out of that hole and you rose up stronger than you were before. You did everything you always wanted to do, and you did it on your own, but honey, that doesn't mean that you aren't allowed to be happy."

Tess sniffled and wiped at her cheeks again. "I swore that once things ended with Dean I would never again live for a man. I would never lose myself, and I would keep my focus where it needed to be."

Charlie squeezed her hand. "You should be so proud of your bakery and what you've accomplished. I'm really proud of you. You deserve to have someone who makes you happy and I think Danny makes you happy."

She nodded.

"I almost ruined my chance with Nick. I was so afraid to admit how I felt about him and that I wanted to be with him that I pushed him away because I thought I had to. Then the accident happened and honestly that taught me that life is far too precious to mess around with. Now I'm happier than I ever thought I could be. Nothing is perfect—not work, not family, not relationships. Nothing and that's okay, but you need to stop hiding and start living."

Tess drew in a shaky breath and leaned into, Charlie who wrapped her in a hug. "I'm an idiot."

"No, you most definitely aren't." She pulled Tess back so they could see each other. "I know my brother said a dumb thing, but he's not Dean. He respects you, he cares about you a lot, and I think if you really give him a chance, you'll see that."

"I was really happy with him."

"Good. Then get your head out of your ass and tell him you

made a terrible mistake and make his Christmas would ya? I didn't fly all this way to watch him mope."

Tess laughed. "Thank you."

"No thanks needed."

"I need to be completely honest with you."

"Of course."

"Things with me and Danny… well they didn't just get started. We kind of slept together at Jason and Kate's wedding."

Charlie's eyes grew wide. "I knew it!"

"What do you mean you knew it?"

"You bolted the next morning before brunch and you didn't answer me for hours so I knew something was up. Plus Danny was acting all weird. Please remember, I don't need specific details because this is my brother, so ew, but tell me, was it good?"

Tess covered her face with both hands. "Oh my God, yeah. I don't know what came over me. I just showed up at his room and I couldn't walk away."

Charlie squealed with delight. "I do know the feeling. I take it the sex was finally about you too?"

She nodded. "I didn't know how to handle it at first because it's never been like that for me, but Danny is the furthest thing from selfish."

"That's what you deserve, being treated like the special person you are."

Tess pulled her into a hug. "Thank you for being my best friend."

"Back at you!"

"I can't believe you're getting married!" They giggled and spent the rest of the night polishing off that whiskey bottle and talking. Tess really was lucky to have Charlie in her life and tomorrow she was going to apologize to Danny and hope that would be enough to make things right.

Danny woke up to the sound of someone banging on his door. He looked at the clock and it was barely six. He'd been up late talking with Nick, which had been something he really needed. Nick understood his frustration completely. When Charlie had been unable to admit her true feelings for him, he'd cut her out of his life. It had been a big mistake but everything had worked out. Danny didn't know how things between him and Tess could work out if she refused to give them a real chance.

He pulled a T-shirt over his head as he made his way to the door. When he opened it and saw Tess on the other side, he was taken aback.

"Hi, did I wake you?"

Danny shook his head. "It's fine… is everything okay?"

"Yes… and no. Can I come in?"

He opened the door wider and gestured for her to come inside. Tess walked straight to the kitchen and took a seat at the counter. "I don't have a lot of time, but I needed to come and see you. I couldn't let the whole day go by, and I know it's Christmas Eve and we both have family stuff later."

"Tess—it's okay. Go ahead."

She blew out a breath and looked up at him. "I'm really sorry about the way I reacted the other night. It wasn't fair to you."

"I shouldn't have said what I said. I absolutely didn't mean that what you do isn't important. You have to know how much I respect what you do."

"I do know that and I'm sorry that I interpreted it in the worst way. The truth is, my ex, Dean, well, he did a number on me. I'm really embarrassed to admit it because I can't believe I allowed myself to put up with that, but basically he wanted to change me and I let him. If he didn't like something I wore, I got rid of it. He told me my singing was annoying so I stopped singing. He told me baking wasn't a real career and little by little I believed him. When I finally got out of that nightmare, I focused solely on building my bakery. I promised myself that if I ever got it, I would hold onto it and never let anyone mess that up. I guess I didn't realize that I was hiding behind it."

She looked down at her feet before meeting his eyes again. "I'm still putting myself back together and I don't know how long that will take, but I am trying."

"I'm so sorry that you went through all of that. He's a goddamn fool. He was lucky that he had you in his life for so long."

"The thing is, I don't want to hide behind it anymore. I want to have my work but I also want to be with you."

He turned toward her and felt his mouth lift in a smile. "You do?"

"I was scared. I let everything that happened in the past get in the way of now. I'm done being scared."

He leaned forward and wrapped his arms around her waist and pulled her stool closer to his. "I'm really glad to hear you say that. I've been miserable."

"Me too." She cupped his cheek and pressed her lips to his. Danny grabbed the back of her neck to deepen the kiss, his lips moving fast over hers. Tess pulled back to catch her breath. "I really wish you didn't have to go to work, but I get it. Go kick ass and I'll see you later. I'll be at my parents' for Christmas Eve dinner but you let me know whenever is good for you and I'll meet you back here or your place and we can have our own Christmas Eve and Christmas morning celebration."

She grinned. "That sounds pretty amazing." Tess stood up and started making her way toward the door. Danny grabbed her hand and pulled her against him again.

"Thanks for waking me up."

"Thanks for letting me in."

"Always." He leaned down and kissed her but pulled away quickly, knowing she needed to leave. "I'll see you later."

She smiled and walked out the door, and Danny felt like this might be a Christmas for the books.

Tess woke up Christmas morning wrapped in Danny's arms in his bed. It was the best Christmas morning she could remember in a long time. They exchanged gifts under Danny's gorgeous tree, and he had completely surprised her with tickets to see Eric Church in Charlotte in February . He also got her a spring pan that she'd been talking about. She'd gotten him a beautiful handmade wooden train that he could display all year long since he liked trains so much, in addition to a new Titans sweatshirt because his had seen better days. She also promised him that she'd bake him any dessert that he wanted, which he was particularly excited about.

She felt like her gifts were nothing in comparison to what he'd given her and she started second guessing-herself, but then she remembered the smile on Danny's face as he opened his presents and she knew she'd succeeded.

The following week, Tess got out of her Jeep, ready to start her day when she heard her name from across the parking lot.

"Hey Tess!" Cooper said, tossing a garbage bag into the dumpster.

"Morning, Cooper. How are you?"

He smiled sweetly at her. "I'm good. I never asked you, how's your Jeep been?"

"Oh, it's fine. Something was up with my battery, nothing major."

He nodded. "I'm glad it wasn't anything more serious."

"Yeah, I was lucky you came by when you did."

"I'm always here to help you." He smiled.

"Thank you. Well, I should get in there."

"Okay, have a good day."

She noticed he watched her as she made her way inside to the kitchen.

"Morning, Boss."

Tess jumped at the sound of Leanne's voice. "Christ almighty. You're here early."

"My boss usually likes when I'm here early. What has you so jumpy?"

"I ran into Cooper in the parking lot and he startled me a little. I'm supposed to grab a drink with him and I keep putting it on the back burner. He didn't mention it just now, but I feel like an ass because he's asked a bunch of times."

"A drink?"

"Yeah, he'd asked a few weeks back to grab a drink and catch up, but with the holiday rush I just didn't have the time."

"Does he know you're in a relationship?

"Yeah, he knows I'm seeing Danny. Why?"

Leanne shrugged. "That man has stars in his eyes when he looks at you. I don't think a friendly drink is what he has in mind."

Tess waved her off. "We're just friends. Friends can get a drink together and talk."

"Sure, but that man has more than talking on his mind," she drawled.

Before Tess could respond, Leanne looked down at the notepad in her hand. "We got an order for a sweet sixteen and it's pretty big."

"How big?"

"They want cake, they want cupcakes, they want cookies."

Tess shook her head and smiled as she dropped her bag in her office. "Okay then. It sounds like we better get to work."

———

Danny sat at his desk, going over the revisions to the plans for some of the units for the condos. Zack had come up with some great ideas and the developer was really happy with the design. He was hoping these would be the final revisions to the blueprints so they could get started on production.

He reached for the folder he had on his desk for the Raleigh project. He hadn't taken the meeting yet, but the developers did want to meet with him. It was in a great location and the building looked like it had good bones from what he could tell. Danny just didn't know if he could bring himself to do another round of luxury condos. He needed to make a decision sooner rather than later, but right now he was thinking about getting home early and waiting for Tess.

"Hey Danny, I'm getting ready to head out. Did you need anything else?" Natalie said, poking her head into his office.

"No, thanks, Nat."

"You looking over anything interesting?"

He tossed his pen down and shrugged. "Just reviewing the revisions for the plans for the penthouse units."

"They swore this was the last revision."

Danny let out a laugh. "Famous last words." He pushed the plans aside and stood up. "I'll walk you out. I could use a little air."

He followed Natalie to the elevator and once they were inside, he noticed that she was wearing a little more makeup than she normally did and had traded the flat shoes she usually wore for a nice pair of heels. "Heels?"

"Yeah, I actually have a date," she told him as her mouth lifted into a smile.

"That's great. First date?"

"No, we've been out a few times actually. Would you believe that we met at the grocery store? We both reached for the last pepper jack cheese in the dairy case. I tried to play it cool like I really didn't want it, but I think he knew I did so he let me have it. I did feel kind of bad about it but I needed that cheese for tacos."

"Understandable."

"We met up in the checkout line and he said if he had to lose a block of cheese to anyone, he was glad it was someone as beautiful as me. We both laughed at how corny that was and then he asked for my number."

"Wow, that sounds really great."

"He is. He works for the Department of Transportation, the railroad in particular, and he's actually been working a lot in Belmont."

They reached the lobby and made their way out to the parking garage. Danny walked Natalie over to her car and waited as she opened her driver's side door. "You look really happy."

"I'm trying not to get ahead of myself, but I am happy. For the record, you look really happy too."

He chuckled and nodded. "I am most definitely happy."

"You deserve it, Danny."

"Thanks, Nat. So do you." He leaned on her door as she climbed in and then shut it for her. He waved to her as she drove away and then started to go inside when something caught his eye.

The windshield of his truck had been smashed.

"Shit!" Danny got closer and examined the area. There was nothing else on his windshield so nothing had fallen to cause the break. Someone could've walked into the garage at any time and smashed his windshield. There were cameras in there; they had to have caught something. All Danny could think was that the person who slashed his tires was probably the same person who had done this. What the hell had he done to piss this person off so badly? He took pictures and again sent them to JJ.

So much for getting out early.

Thirteen

anny sat in front of his father's desk at the Belmont police station, something he hadn't done since he was a kid. JJ stood at the side of his desk, going over the information that he'd taken down. Danny couldn't believe his truck had been vandalized twice. Someone clearly had it out for him, but he had no idea who it might be. He'd had to call the Charlotte police and file a report since it had happened at his office, but he knew he needed to loop his dad in too.

"Can we get a look at the security cameras in the parking garage?" the chief asked.

JJ shook his head. "The officer who took the report asked the same thing, but the building manager was already gone."

"I know the building manager, so I'm sure he'll let us see the footage if we want to," Danny added.

"The Charlotte police need to see it first. We don't want to step on their toes," the chief replied.

Danny let out a sigh. "I don't really care who looks at it. I'd just like to know who is damaging my truck."

"I'll call over to the Charlotte PD tomorrow and ask to speak to the officer. Hopefully as a professional courtesy they'll keep us looped in. You can't think of anyone who might want to do this?"

"No. I have a good relationship with my clients and everyone who works for me. It doesn't make any sense."

"Well this is pretty deliberate," JJ said. "Are you sure you don't have any crazy ex-girlfriends out there?"

Danny glared at him. "Yes, I'm sure."

"I'm out of guesses then."

"Let's just wait until we find out what's on that security footage. Until then, just keep your eyes open," the chief told him.

Danny stood up. "I will."

"Hey—we'll get to the bottom of this."

He wanted to believe that, but the last video they'd looked at had given them no clues so he wasn't exactly hopeful about this one. If it was in fact the same person, they would be very careful about not being seen. "Thanks, Dad. I appreciate it."

His father gave him a nod and JJ followed him out. "We'll get a handle on this. Don't worry."

"I know you will. It's just frustrating."

"Wanna grab a beer?"

"Actually, I was hoping you could give me a ride home since my truck is at Mr. C's waiting to be fixed. Tess is coming over soon so I've gotta get there."

JJ laughed. "You guys really are serious?"

"Yeah, we are."

"It's about damn time. You've only been pining for her since grammar school."

Danny rolled his eyes. The thing was, he couldn't deny it. He'd wanted Tess for such a long time, but he'd spent so many years thinking it was impossible that he'd never done anything about it. He hated that he'd wasted all that time.

JJ dropped him off at his place. As he was about to walk into the building, Tess got out of her car. "Hey, is everything okay? How come JJ was dropping you off?"

"I had some car trouble so I needed a lift."

"Did you call my dad?"

He nodded. "My truck is at the shop. He said he'd take a look in the morning."

"What happened?"

"Let's go upstairs and I'll fill you in." He took her hand and they headed for the elevator. Once they were inside his condo, he headed for the kitchen and checked the fridge to see what he had. "Do you wanna order Chinese or would you rather order pizza?"

Tess dropped her purse on the counter and crossed her arms over her chest. "I'd like for you to tell me what happened."

Danny blew out a deep breath. "My windshield was smashed in the parking garage."

Her eyes went wide and her jaw dropped. "Oh my God! That's terrible. No one saw anything?"

"No. The police want to check the security footage, see if they can identify the person who did it, but I'm sure whoever it was was smart enough to stay mostly hidden."

"You don't know who it could be, do you?"

He put his hands on his hips and shook his head. "I wish I did."

"So they just smashed your windshield? They didn't do anything else to the truck?"

"Just the windshield but... a few weeks ago my tires were slashed."

She gave him a puzzled look. "When?"

"The morning after I came to your place with pizza and wine. When I was leaving for work, I saw that they were slashed."

Tess's eyes went wide. "Why didn't you tell me?"

He shrugged. "It didn't seem that important. We couldn't see anything on the security footage, so nothing really came of it."

"It still happened."

"Yeah, I just didn't think it was that big of a deal."

"Except now someone smashed your windshield. That can't be some weird coincidence."

"Probably not. The Charlotte police are going to check the security footage from the parking garage and see if they can find anything, and in the meantime JJ and the chief are in the loop."

"There isn't anyone you might have pissed off? A former client or someone you worked with on a job?"

Danny shook his head. "I've been racking my brain and can't think of anyone. I've always gotten along really well with all my clients and everyone I've worked with."

"What about another architectural firm? Maybe one of your competitors is trying to get back at you?"

Danny let out a sigh. "If they were trying to get back at me, I don't think they'd go after my tires or my windshield, but I suppose anything is possible. I really can't imagine who would have it out for me."

"People are driven by all kinds of things. You have a successful business; it's not hard to imagine that someone might be jealous of you."

"I guess so. The whole thing is just really bizarre. Oh, did something happen to your Jeep? When I brought my truck to your dad's shop he said something about having to make a house call to check it out."

"Oh… yeah it wouldn't start the other day when I had to go make a delivery so I had to have him come look at it. Something with the battery."

"You may have to accept that Jesse is on her last legs."

Tess scowled at him. "Bite your tongue! She's still got plenty left in her. She just happened to pick a horrible time to be temperamental. Luckily, Cooper was walking through the parking lot then and offered me a ride so I wasn't late for the delivery."

"Oh, he just happened to be there?"

"Yeah, but we do share a parking lot behind our businesses. We see each other every day so it's not unusual that he'd be there." Tess shrugged and leaned her hip against the counter.

"It seems a little convenient that the second you have car trouble he's there to swoop in and help you."

"What do you mean 'convenient'?"

"He got to be the one to save you. I'm sure he liked that."

Tess rolled her eyes. "You're being ridiculous."

Danny grabbed the back of his neck and went into the refrigerator. He pulled out a beer and quickly popped the top. He took a long swallow and turned back to Tess. "Why didn't you say anything about your Jeep not starting and getting a ride from him for your delivery?"

"I didn't really think it was that big of a deal."

He let out a frustrated laugh. "You can do better than that."

She threw her hands up in the air, exasperated. "I knew you would overreact. We were just starting to figure things out between us and I knew if I mentioned that he gave me a ride you wouldn't like it, and nothing happened so there was no point for me to mention it."

"I'm telling you, Tess. That guy is into you as more than a friend."

She shook her head and groaned. "You're acting jealous for no reason."

"And you're acting naïve."

She stood up and crossed her arms over her chest. "Why? Because I refuse to believe that a man can just want to be my friend?"

"You can't be so trusting. You of all people should know how people can pretend to be something they're not." As soon as the words were out of his mouth he wanted to take them back.

Tess's eyes went wide and she stepped toward him. "I should know? Because I was cheated on? Oh, that's right. I forgot, nothing has ever gone wrong in your perfect life. You know why? Because you've never had any real kind of relationship, so you have no idea what it feels like to give your heart to someone else and have them rip it out."

Danny blinked a few times. Her words stung, but she was right; he'd dated but he had never been in a long term relationship. He'd never felt any serious heartbreak. "You're right."

"Excuse me?"

"I said you're right. I have never experienced anything like that. I never had a girl break my heart, and I was never cheated on so I have no idea what any of that feels like. I've never fully invested in anyone like that. I'm pretty sure it was because I always had you on my mind."

She stood silent for a moment and he closed the space between them. "I have never felt about anyone the way I feel about you. I'm always excited to see you. You make me nervous, you make me laugh, and you turn me on like no one else ever has."

"I feel the same way," she told him.

Danny placed his hands on her waist and pulled her up against him. "I'm sorry for what I said and if I came off jealous, but I can't shake the fact that Cooper is more interested in you than you think he is. Can you at least try to be open to that idea?"

Tess put her hands on his shoulders and looked up at him. "Okay, I can do that.".

"Thank you." He leaned down and kissed her. It meant a lot to him that she was willing to keep an open mind about Cooper.

"The more important thing is we need to find out who's behind the vandalism. I don't like the idea of someone going around damaging your stuff."

Danny pulled Tess into his chest and took a deep breath. It definitely made him uneasy that someone was targeting him, and he knew he wouldn't shake that feeling until they found the person behind it.

Fourteen

Danny pulled up to the fourth house of the day and killed his engine. Charlie had stayed behind in North Carolina after the holidays to start looking at places for her and Nick, and he, of course, told her he'd go with her. Tom had lined up some great places for them to check out between Belmont and Charlotte. This place they pulled up to was a ranch that had been remodeled to look like a beach house.

"Wow, this is so cute," Charlie said, getting out of the truck.

Danny got out of his truck and took a look at the house. It definitely was a cool looking house. It was a pretty big ranch with what looked like a good-size property. Tom opened the front door as they walked up. "Come on in."

They stepped in and Danny watched his sister's eyes light up. The whole place had an open concept and it was bright with neutral tones and white-and-ocean-color accents. The hardwood floor was beautiful and as Danny walked through the family room, he couldn't help but notice the beautiful fireplace. "Whoever did the work on this place did a fantastic job. The design is really great too."

"It was just updated about six months ago and the owners wanted to give it all the modern touches while still having that coastal vibe," Tom added.

"I'm in love. I think this is a great starter home."

"You like it better than everything else we saw today?" Danny asked her.

"I do. I can't explain it, but there's just something about this house."

"Sometimes the house chooses you," Tom said with a smile.

"Ignore him. What he means is choose the house with the biggest commission for him."

Tom let out a laugh. "Oh, come on, I'm not like that!"

Danny glared at him.

"Okay, I like a commission as much as the next guy, but I wouldn't do that to your sister."

"Smart man."

Charlie shook her head and continued walking through the house. Danny paid close attention to the design of the house, and he had to say it was really well done. All the big windows let lots of natural light into the house, which is exactly how he would've done things. The rooms were all spacious. There were two bedrooms plus an office, two and a half baths, a family room, dining room, a beautiful front porch and a small porch and patio area in the back.

Charlie let out a deep breath and grinned. "I really love this house, Danno."

He chuckled a bit as he crossed his arms over his chest. "You might have mentioned that. You're okay with this being closer to Belmont than Charlotte?"

"I spent the last six years living in a city. It'll be nice to live in a town again. I love Charlotte, but it's a little too cityish for me. We're still close enough for Nick to get to the hospital." She snapped a few pictures on her phone, no doubt to show Nick.

"So, what's the consensus?" Tom asked, walking back over to them.

"I'm going to have to speak to my fiancé, but I really think this is it."

"You're the first person I've showed this house to but there are definitely other people interested in it."

"I'll speak to my fiancé as soon as we leave here and I'm sure once I show him the house, he'll be on board."

"Okay, I emailed you all the other information like taxes and utility fees on the house so you have everything. The sooner you can put in an offer the better." Tom double-checked his cell phone before sticking it back in his pocket.

Charlie nodded. "You'll definitely be hearing from me soon. Thank you so much for setting all this up today."

"Happy to do it." Tom smiled and Danny knew he meant it.

Charlie gave him a hug and Danny shook his hand before they made their way to the front door. "I'll see you next week to talk about the Raleigh project."

Ugh. The Raleigh project. That thing that Danny had been

purposely putting off.

They got in Danny's truck and he tried to shake off that uneasy feeling he had. He looked over at Charlie, who was beaming. "You look like a little kid on Christmas morning."

She let out a laugh and nodded. "I feel like one. It's so perfect. It's just the right amount of space for us. It'll be nice to be able to have a backyard again and real closet space. Part of me doesn't know how I'm going to leave New York, but the other part of me is more than ready. Does that make sense?"

Danny nodded. "Yeah, it does. I didn't think you'd move back here, but I'm really happy about it."

"If we get this house, you'll only be twentyish minutes away."

"More like less than ten."

She turned to him, looking confused. "I'm sorry, did they move your condo building?"

"No, it's still there. I won't be there forever though. Especially once my house is ready."

"Your house? I'm lost."

He laughed. "I bought a piece of land for a house and I spoke to Pete about it a few weeks ago. We're gonna break ground soon."

"I can't believe you didn't tell me!" she said, swatting at his arm.

"You know how fast word travels in this family. I wasn't ready to hear what everyone had to say."

Charlie glared at him. "What did you say to me? 'I'm not everyone'? Neither am I."

"You're right, Ace. You're not. Now you know. I'll bring you by to see it soon."

She seemed satisfied with that answer. He started up the truck and pulled away from the house. "Are you thinking about settling down?"

"Not tomorrow." He laughed. "Eventually though, yeah. I want a space that's my own, big enough for everyone to come and visit and to raise my own family there."

"I think that's a good idea. I like that we'll be close to each other. What does Tess think?"

"She thinks the house plans are great."

Charlie rolled her eyes. "No, knucklehead. What are her thoughts on the future?"

"Honestly, I don't know. I'm trying to go slow so I don't freak her out. We have the Eric Church concert in Charlotte next month and we're staying overnight. I feel like that's a big deal."

"It is a big deal in the sense that Tess never had someone do anything like that for her. It was always about the wants of whoever she was with, not about what they both wanted for their relationship."

"She told me what happened with Dean. I'd like to put him through a wall for making her feel like that."

Charlie let out a sigh. "Get in line, Danno. I can't believe she kept all of that in for so long. No wonder she's kept her head down and focused on work and avoided relationships. I do think that she's really starting to put herself back together and I think you, big brother, have a lot to do with that." She grinned at him.

He gave her a nod and started up his truck. There was nothing that made Danny happier than knowing he was helping Tess get back those special parts of herself. He knew that he couldn't completely erase what had happened, but he was always going to make sure that she knew how much he valued her and that she knew exactly what she deserved.

———

Tess stood at the end of the counter going over an order with a customer when the bell over the door caught her attention. Cooper walked in and she gave him a wave. The customer finished up with her requests and Tess jotted everything down before telling her she could pick it up on Saturday morning. As soon as the customer stepped away, Cooper stepped up to the counter. He placed both forearms on the top of the glass and smiled at her.

"Hey, Cooper. What can I get for you?"

"It's the funniest thing. All day today I had such a craving for carrot cake cupcakes. I was trying to fight the craving but then I thought, why should I when the best cupcakes in the world are just a few doors over?"

"That's awful nice of you to say." Then she realized what he'd asked for. "I'm sorry, did you say carrot cake cupcakes?"

"I did. I hope you still have some left."

She fumbled opening up the case. "Oh... yeah, of course just making sure I heard you right. How many do you want?"

"Just two."

Tess turned around to get a box so that her back was to him and she hoped that would allow the panic to disappear from her face. Carrot cake cupcakes were Danny's favorite. It could've been a weird coincidence; they were a popular cupcake. She quickly put the cupcakes in the box, wrapped them up and slid them over to him. He handed her a ten-dollar bill but she put her hand up. "On the house."

"No, I couldn't."

"Please, I insist. You've brought us food a bunch of times. It's the least I can do."

A smile lit up his face. "Thanks, I really appreciate it." He started to turn to walk out and then turned back to her. "I'm really looking forward to these."

"Enjoy them."

He gave her another smile and then was out the door. She breathed a sigh of relief.

"Are you okay?" Leanne asked her.

"Yeah, yeah. I'm fine."

Leanne raised her eyebrows at her. "You do realize I can smell bullshit a mile away."

Tess laughed a little bit. "Cooper just came in for cupcakes."

"Okay, and? That still doesn't explain the weird look on your face."

"He ordered two carrot cake cupcakes. Those are Danny's favorite."

"Honey, do you think Danny Moreau is the only person who favors carrot cake cupcakes?"

She shrugged. "No, I don't know, it was just a strange coincidence. Danny is convinced Cooper wants to be more than friends with me and I'm trying not to dwell on that thought."

"He's a smart man, that Danny Moreau."

Tess glared at her. "Cooper is a nice guy, he's good looking, and he's running a great business. I have a lot of respect for him, but I'm not interested in him romantically. I told him I was seeing Danny and he seemed okay with it so I really don't think it's an issue."

"What seems and what actually is are usually two very different things. Trust me."

"How do you do it, Lee? After all the bad shit you went through, how do you still have faith that people won't disappoint you?"

Leanne threw her hands up and clapped them down against her

thighs. "I don't know. I guess I'd like to believe that not all people are assholes. I married one but that doesn't mean that there still aren't good people out there. I came here, met you, and you gave me this kickass job that I love. I met Penny and Betty and now I have the family I've been missing. If I wasn't open to that, I would've never met ya'll and that would've been more tragic than what my loser of an ex put me through."

Tess couldn't help but smile. Leanne's outlook gave new perspective to a lot of things. Tess'd spent so much time letting what happened in her past control her decisions in the present that she had missed out on so many things, and she was done with that. Dean hadn't broken her; damaged her, yes, but she wasn't broken. Danny was worth the effort and so was she.

Danny sat on his couch with his sketchpad in his hands and Tess's feet in his lap. They'd fallen into a nice rhythm where they spent a few nights together during the week and then spent the majority of the weekend together. He liked waking up with her at his side, but he also liked sitting in comfortable silence doing their own things while being together. Pete had told him that they should be able to break ground at his house before the end of January, which was only a couple of weeks away. He still needed to finalize a few sketches for Pete so he wanted to get it done as soon as possible. Tess was busy flipping through her iPad for recipes. His mother was catering a Valentine's Day event and she'd asked Tess to provide the dessert. Tess was set on making something fun and different.

She jotted down some notes in a notebook and took a sip of her wine in her free hand. She let out a sigh and shook her head, so he put his sketchbook down. "What's troubling you?"

"Nothing. I'm just not loving what I'm finding."

"What do you have so far?"

She waved him off. "You're sketching. Don't worry about it."

"I put my pencil down. Tell me."

She nodded and looked down at her notebook. "Red velvet sandwich cookies with cream cheese icing in the middle."

"Oh, I'd like that."

"Vanilla cupcakes with a chocolate butter cream icing and Hershey kiss on top."

He wrinkled his nose. "Eh, I think you can do better."

"I could do heart-shaped butter cookies, keep it simple, and then decorate them really pretty. Well, Penny would have to do that. She's got the better hand for decorating."

Danny grinned at her. "I think your hands are just fine."

Tess laughed. "Smooth one. Yeah, my hands are great, but when it comes to decorating Penny is a natural. I was just hoping something would inspire me and it's not happening."

"You have more than enough time to figure something out."

She nodded and looked down at the screen again. "I know, but I don't want to get busy and then forget about it."

"It's important. You won't forget."

She let out a deep breath and put her iPad down on the coffee table. "How are your sketches?"

"Good. I've got the kitchen just about finished."

"Let me see." She sat up and scooted closer to him.

He turned his sketchbook toward her and her eyes went wide. "Wow, it looks incredible."

"I wanted a pretty big island and enough room for cabinet storage as well as a double wall oven and an oven underneath the stove."

"It looks really nice. Very spacious."

"I'm glad you like it. I don't think I've ever seen anyone look sexier taking something out of an oven than you."

She shoved at his shoulder and laughed. "Oh please!"

"Seriously. Babe, you have no idea what you do to me in that apron when you're holding a tray of whatever baked goods you've just made. It's really hot."

"What about when I'm not wearing my apron?" She smiled devilishly at him.

"Still hot. I actually prefer you without any clothes."

Tess let out a laugh. "That's funny because I prefer you without any clothes too."

Danny smirked at her, tossed his sketchbook on the table, and leaned into her until her back was flat on the couch. "I'd certainly hate to disappoint you." He reached over his head and pulled his T-shirt off. Tess licked her lips at the sight of his naked torso.

"I really appreciate you being so thoughtful."

"You're about to appreciate a whole lot more than that." He slid her leggings down her legs and tossed them on the floor before removing his sweatpants. Tess sat up and pulled her T-shirt over her head and threw it on the floor. Danny stared down at her and then ran his hand from the top of her chest straight down her body causing her to shiver. He settled his hand over her center and she was already wet. A smile crept onto his face. "I love that this is for me."

She reached down and cupped him through his boxer briefs and there was no hiding the massive erection he was sporting. "I'm pretty happy that I do this to you too."

He lowered his mouth to hers and swept his tongue across her bottom lip\\ which made her moan. She met him stroke for stroke with her tongue and he never wanted to come up for air. Danny kissed his way from her neck down her body until he hit the waistband of her underwear. In one motion he removed them and settled between her legs. His mouth found the inside of her thighs and he peppered kisses there, climbing higher and higher. Tess kept trying to lift her hips and he couldn't help but smile. "Don't worry, I know exactly what you need."

Danny's mouth descended on her and he wasted no time running his tongue up and down her folds. She reached for his head and ground his mouth against her. He could feel that she was starting to unravel but he wasn't ready to be done with her just yet. He slipped a finger inside her, causing a gasp to escape from her lips. "Please."

Danny knew he could never deny her anything, especially not an orgasm. He found her clit and sucked hard, making her grip his hair. He kept sucking and sliding one finger and then another in and out of her and then he felt her start to quake as she screamed his name. Danny kept lapping at her until there was nothing left and when he finally lifted his head, he saw Tess's flushed cheeks as she caught her breath.

As soon as she locked eyes with him, it was like something overtook her. Tess sat up and pinned Danny to the couch so that she was straddling him. "You once said you liked me saying what I wanted and taking control."

"I do."

"Good." She smirked. She unhooked her bra and threw it on the floor. Before he even had time to react, she removed his boxer briefs and then looked at him like she wasn't sure what she should do next.

Danny reached up and cupped her cheek. "Take what you want. I'm yours."

She leaned down and pressed her lips to his. "Thank you." She reached down between them and grabbed his cock. She positioned it at her entrance and then leaned forward before sliding down until she was flush against him. They both let out a groan.

"You feel amazing, Tess."

"So do you." She lifted up slowly and then came back down. She picked up her pace and they found a perfect rhythm. He reached up and cupped her breasts. That seemed to set her off. He thrust harder and he could feel her starting to come undone again. He gripped her hips to hold her in place as Tess's breathing started to become ragged.

"Danny…"

"Let go, Tess. Come for me now."

"No—together, I want us to go together." She almost lifted off of him and then slammed back down, causing his eyes to roll back in his head. She kept riding him and grinding against him until she threw her head back and he felt the heat traveling up his spine.

"I'm there, Tess. Right there." With one more thrust they both yelled and Danny emptied himself inside of her. No sooner did that happen than Tess's eyes flashed open, the realization of what had just happened hitting her like a ton of bricks.

"Hey, are you okay?"

She didn't answer right away and he lifted his hand to her face to try and bring her back to the present. "Tess? Are you okay?"

"We didn't use a condom."

"Yeah, I know. I'm sorry about that. I know getting caught up in the moment isn't an excuse. You're on the pill though, right?"

She nodded.

"Okay then. I'm clean so you don't have to worry."

"I've never had sex without a condom."

"Neither have I, but I have to say, I definitely liked it." He smiled hoping to lighten the mood, but Tess still looked horrified. "Babe, please don't worry. You take your pill religiously. I don't think there's anything to freak out about here."

Tess climbed off of him, grabbed her T-shirt off the floor, and quickly pulled it over her head. She hurried down the hall to Danny's bedroom and he heard a door close. He ran a hand down his face and let out a sigh. He hated that she was so panicked. What had just happened had been incredible and he wasn't going to let her worry ruin that. He got off the couch and didn't bother retrieving any of his clothes. Danny made his way into his room and saw the light coming from under his closed bathroom door. He raised his hand and knocked and could hear sniffling on the other side. "Tess, open the door, please."

She opened the door and then returned to where she'd been sitting on the toilet seat. Her purse was on the floor and she'd obviously been rummaging through it.

"Talk to me. What's going on?"

"You couldn't have put some clothes on?"

"No… you got up and didn't say anything so I didn't think clothes were all that important. Talk." He crossed his arms over his chest and stared at her.

"I couldn't remember if I took my pill this morning so I needed to check. I took it, but that panic was overwhelming."

He stepped into the bathroom so that he was right in front of her. "I'm really sorry. Like I said, it's just as much my fault for not stopping before things got too heated. You have to know that I would never do anything to put you at any kind of risk."

Tess wiped her cheeks. "I know that and it's not just on you. I got completely lost in the moment too and it just felt so good."

Danny crouched down in front of her and took her hands and covered them with his. "It felt so fucking good, Tess. I don't want you to worry about anything, not with me."

"And if I hadn't taken my pill and I ended up pregnant? Then what?"

"Then I'd still be happy."

Shock painted her face again. "Have you lost your mind?"

"Not that I'm aware of. You being pregnant with my baby would not be bad news. In case you were unaware, I'm falling in love with you, Tess Carmichael, and I want everything with you. I'd still like to take you out on some more dates before any kids come into the picture, but I'm not going anywhere."

Tess lifted her eyes to his and blinked a few times, clearly trying to absorb everything he'd just said. He understood why it would be hard for her to believe, but he meant every word.

"How about you go put some pants on so we can work on

having more of those dates you mentioned?"

The smile had returned to her face and Danny felt relieved. He put his hand out to her and she took it. He helped her up and they walked out of the bathroom together, both feeling like things were going to be okay.

Fifteen

A week had passed since the no-condom incident, the one thing that had come from it was Tess realizing she felt more for Danny than she was prepared to admit. Most guys would have panicked at the word *pregnancy*, but Danny had been the calm one of the two of them. While she wasn't ready for children yet, it was comforting knowing that it didn't scare him.

Work had been a little slow, which was normal after the holidays, but she still needed to come up with a Valentine's dessert for Alice's catering event, not to mention Valentine's Day themed dessert items for the bakery. Still, she was trying to take it all in stride. When Penny suggested that they all go grab drinks and food at Monte's, Tess was happy to go along.

She sat in between Penny and Leanne at the bar, drinking her beer, listening to Penny rattle off ideas for Valentine's Day. "I think we could even do heart-shaped donuts, bite-sized ones. The morning rush would love that. I can make them the night before, cut them, and then I just have to fry them in the morning."

"I'm sure we can make that work."

"I was also thinking about a chocolate cupcake with a strawberry butter cream icing and a chocolate covered strawberry on top."

"Holy shit, that sounds incredible," Leanne said, picking up a forkful of her shrimp and grits.

Penny chuckled and took a sip of her beer. "Chocolate and strawberries are an excellent pair so I thought it was a good idea."

"I think it's a great idea, Penny. Let's do a test run this week."

"Speaking of great pairs, where is Mr. Hot Stuff tonight?"

"Danny has poker night tonight with some of the guys," she told Leanne.

"I can't imagine him having a good poker face, he always looks so sweet," Penny added, taking a bite of her cheeseburger.

"I don't think he looks sweet when he's playing poker with the guys. He's a Moreau. They're competitive by nature, so I have no doubt he's got a killer poker face."

"I just have to say, I love this new side he's brought out in you," Leanne told her, grinning.

"What new side?"

"You're happier. For once, someone is taking care of you and I don't think you realized how badly you needed that until Danny came into your life like this," Leanne said.

It was true. Other than her family and Charlie, she had never had someone think about her the way Danny did. He did things he knew she liked, he paid attention when she talked, he made her feel safe, and he even pushed her out of her comfort zone at times, which had been a really good thing.

"I am very happy. He's really incredible." Tess took a spoonful of her chili and then reached for a hushpuppy from the plate they were all sharing. It was a really good feeling knowing that she could be in a serious relationship and run her business as she always had.

Just then, she felt her phone vibrate on the bar. It was a text message from an unknown number. Tess always had to look because it could've been a customer. In a town as small as Belmont it was never out of the question to think that someone got a hold of her personal cell phone number.

When she opened the text, three pictures popped up and she had to blink a few times to be sure what she was looking at. It was Danny and a very pretty woman. He was helping her get into a car and they were laughing. There was no mistaking that it looked intimate, and Tess felt her stomach turn over. The other pictures showed them close together, their faces only inches apart and Tess immediately flashed back to finding Dean with that woman from his father's office in their bed. Her chest was tight and her hands were sweaty.

"Tess, are you okay?" Penny asked.

She shook her head, unable to speak.

"What happened? What did you just get on your phone?" Leanne didn't even wait for Tess to show her, she took the phone right out of her hand and looked at it. "What the hell is this?"

"I don't know. It's from an unknown number, but it's definitely Danny in the picture."

Penny had gotten out of her chair and was leaning over Leanne's shoulder so she too could see the text. "Okay, it doesn't mean anything. There could be a perfectly reasonable explanation for all of this."

Tess could feel the tears building in her eyes. "If it's nothing, then why would someone make a point of sending it to me? I can't believe this is happening again." She pushed out of her chair and grabbed her phone from Leanne.

"Honey, don't jump to conclusions. Talk to Danny and give him a chance to explain."

"Lee, I swore I'd never go through this again. I'm a fool." She grabbed her purse and her coat and tossed some money on the bar.

"Tess, please don't go. Just stay here and calm down."

"I can't. I need to go. I love you guys for being concerned but I just... I need to go."

"I expect a text when you get home," Leanne told her.

She nodded and made her way out of Monte's. Her heart was racing and her head was spinning as she put her coat on and tried to grab her keys out of her purse. When she looked up, she almost collided with a large body. "Oh, I'm so sorry. I didn't see you."

"Hey, Tess."

She lifted her gaze up and saw Cooper standing directly in front of her. "Hi—I'm sorry. I wasn't paying attention to where I was going."

"It's okay. Leaving so soon?"

"Yeah... I need to get home, long day."

"That's too bad. It would've been nice getting to hang out."

"Next time," she told him with a shrug.

"Are you okay, you look upset?"

"Yup, I'm great." It took everything in her to hold back her tears.

"Are you sure? I can tell something isn't right."

"I'm sure. I appreciate your concern, but it's just been a really long day and I need to go get some sleep. I'll see you around."

He smiled at her. "Okay, I'll see you around."

She backed away from him and walked quickly to her car. It wasn't until she was inside that she let her tears fall. Tess pounded the steering wheel and a sob escaped her lips. Why, when she was so happy, did something have to come along and ruin it? She let out a shaky breath and pulled out of the parking lot.

Danny sat at the table, holding his poker cards, waiting for his friend Jake to decide if he was in or out. Zack and Tom also sat around the table along with Gus, a guy that worked for Jake. They tried to get together once a week for a poker game, and depending on their schedules sometimes once a week stretched out to once a month, so they made the most of it whenever they got together.

"Hey Jake, do you plan on making a decision sometime tonight or should we leave you alone to figure it out?" Tom said, laughing.

"Shut up. I call." He tossed a few chips into the pile.

Danny glanced down at his hand again and then reached for a few chips in front of him. "I raise fifty."

"I'm out," Zack said.

"Me too," Gus replied as he tossed his cards on the table.

Tom looked at his cards and then at his chips. He pursed his lips, grabbed a few chips, and tossed them in the center of the table. "I raise one hundred."

"Fuck, I'm out," Jake said as he leaned back in his chair.

Danny checked his cards again. He knew Tom liked to bluff, but he also knew he was a good poker player so he didn't doubt that he had a good hand if he just raised. Danny was no slouch when it came to poker either. He just wasn't as cocky about it as Tom. He grabbed some of his chips and casually tossed them into the pile. "I'll call."

"Okay boys, let's see em," Jake told them.

"Full house," Tom said, grinning from ear to ear as he scooped up his beer and took a swig.

"That's a good hand man, it really is, but it's too bad it can't beat a straight flush." Danny laid down a ten, jack, queen, king, and ace of hearts.

Tom's face dropped as Danny pulled in the chips toward his pile. The rest of the table erupted in hoots and Danny couldn't help but laugh. "Don't be too upset, man. a full house is great hand."

"Fuck off." He laughed, shaking his head. "I need a refill."

"Grab me another one too," Zack said.

As Danny organized his chips, he felt his phone vibrate in his pocket. He knew Tess was out with the girls and he hoped she was having a good time. He removed his phone from his pocket and grinned when he saw it was a text from Tess, but when he opened it, his stomach dropped.

There were a few pictures of him with Natalie, close up pictures. Danny's eyes went wide. It took him a second to realize what he was looking at, but then he remembered that was the day not that long ago that he had walked her out to her car when she was leaving work. They were talking as she got in her car but the way the pictures were taken, it looked like they were having a very close, intimate conversation. He had no idea why Tess had those pictures or, more importantly, who had sent them to her. She had typed two words under the last picture: *We're over.* He quickly pushed back from the table, clutching his phone in his hand.

"What's the matter?" Jake asked him. "You look like you're about to puke all over Tom's nice living room here."

"I've gotta go."

"Dude, you're seriously freaking me out. What's going on?"

"I'll explain later, I promise, but right now I need to go find Tess."

Jake nodded in understanding. Danny said his goodbyes and ran out to his truck. He was starting to think all of these things that had been happening lately had less to do with him and more to do with him and Tess as a couple. Maybe someone was really unhappy they were together and they were trying to break them up? His mind went to one person, but he tried to shake it off.

The ten-minute drive over to Tess's apartment felt like hours, but as soon as he parked, Danny ran to her apartment. He'd tried calling her on the way over, but his calls went straight to voicemail. She either wasn't hearing his calls, or she'd turned her phone off. His gut told him it was the latter of the two.

He frantically knocked on her door. "Tess! Open up, please!"

There was no answer so he leaned closer to the door to see if he heard anything on the other side. He heard footsteps and he resumed banging on her door. "Tess! Please, just let me explain! I promise, it's not what you think."

"Go away, Danny!"

"Not until you let me explain."

"There's nothing you can say. Just leave."

"I have a lot to say and you need to hear it. Just give me five minutes. If you don't like what I have to say after five minutes, I'll leave. You don't even have to throw me out. Just please let me in so we can talk."

Again, there was silence but then he heard the door unlock and he felt some hope return to his body. When she opened the door, she was still dressed like she must've been when she went out: jeans, a tank top that showed off just a bit of cleavage, an oversized cardigan, and knee-high boots. Her face was puffy and her eyes were red and filled with anger. There was no hiding that she'd been crying and he wanted to reach out and pull her into his arms, but something told him now was not the right time for that. "Thanks for letting me in."

She didn't say anything as she shut the door. Danny took a few steps inside her apartment and waited. "You have five minutes, I suggest you start talking."

"Right. Can we sit down?"

Tess nodded and he followed her over to the couch. "The pictures of me…"

She turned her face away from him.

"It's not what you're thinking."

"I don't think you want to know what I'm thinking, and now you've only got about four minutes and thirty seconds so use your time wisely."

He took a deep breath and looked at her. He grabbed his phone and opened the text message to the pictures. Danny turned it around to face Tess. "These pictures are of me and my assistant, Natalie. I was walking her to her car a couple weeks ago after work. She was telling me about a guy that she's been seeing. Nat has always been focused on work and helping take care of her younger sister. She hasn't dated much in the three years that she's worked for me so I was really happy listening to her talk about this guy. She told me she was happy seeing me happy. I helped her into her car. That was it. What you see here are two people, two friends just talking, that's it. There's nothing inappropriate going on."

"Then why did someone send it to me?" Her eyes were filled with tears.

"I have no idea. Natalie is a good person, but I've never felt anything for her other than respect and friendship. Nothing has happened between us."

"Do you know what it felt like getting that text?"

"Actually, I do."

"Let me rephrase that: do you know what it felt like after you've been cheated on to get that text?"

"No, I can't say that I do, but I know that it must have hurt you, and that killed me. I would never do anything to hurt you. You have to know that."

Tess wiped at her eyes and sniffed. There was no denying she'd had her heart ripped out before, but everything in her was telling her that Danny would never hurt her. She nodded slowly and then lifted her gaze to meet his. "I do know that. I'm sorry, I just snapped back to the past."

He grabbed her hands. "Don't apologize, I understand why you would think that, but I just need to know that you believe me."

"I believe you, Danny."

He dropped his head and let out a sigh. "I can't tell you how happy that makes me."

She squeezed his hand and he looked up at her, relief painted on his face.

"Look, I've been doing some thinking and I think that whoever is behind all the things that happened to my truck, and now this, isn't someone from a rival business or an angry former client. I think this has more to do with us, with someone not liking that we're together."

Her face twisted in confusion. "No, that couldn't be. Who would do something like that?"

Danny bit down on his lip, hesitating to say the thought that crossed his mind.

"Danny, do you know who it is?"

"I don't know for sure, but I think it's Cooper."

Tess's jaw dropped. "How could it be him?"

"The day those pictures were taken was the same day my windshield was smashed. He could've easily showed up at my office parking garage, smashed my windshield, and then saw me walking Natalie to her car and decided to snap the pictures. It would've been the perfect opportunity."

"I just can't believe he would do all of this." She dropped her face in her hands and tried to make sense of it all.

"I know you don't want to believe it, but I think we have to seriously consider the possibility that he's behind this. He may seem like he's fine with you dating someone else, but if he's liked you for a while and you started seeing someone else, he may not take too well to that. You were at Monte's with the girls when you got the text?"

"Yeah, we'd been there for about an hour and then I felt my phone buzz in my pocket. As soon as I saw what it was, I got up and practically ran out of there and then..." Tess looked up at Danny, her eyes getting large.

"And then what?"

"I actually bumped into Cooper on my way out of Monte's. He asked me if I was okay and I said I had to go, but that was all."

Danny shook his head. "There's no way he was accidentally there as you were coming out of Monte's after getting that upsetting text. He's pulling all of these strings. I don't know how to prove it, but we can't act like it didn't happen."

"Okay, what do you think we should do?"

Danny pulled out his phone and dialed JJ. He quickly explained to him what had happened and JJ asked them to come down to the station to give a statement.

"We're going to figure this out together." He took her hands and pressed his lips to them. Danny was determined to get to the bottom of this and get this lunatic out of their lives. Knowing Tess was with him made him feel like he could take on anyone, and he planned on fighting whoever this was with everything he had.

Danny flung open the door to Cooper's sandwich shop the next morning so hard it caused several people sitting nearby to jump. He spotted Cooper behind the counter putting an order together and he marched straight for him. Everyone kept telling him to be calm, to not jump to conclusions, and while he typically had a lot of patience, he was at the end of his rope. Danny needed to look Cooper in the eyes and let him know that he knew exactly what was going on and that he wasn't going to stand for it.

"Cooper..."

He glanced up and smirked at the sight of Danny. "Oh, hey, I'll be right with you."

"No, we're going to talk right now."

Everyone in the shop turned and looked at them. Cooper had a relaxed look on his face as he stepped away from the back counter and walked toward where Danny stood.

"Okay, what seems to be the problem?"

"You, you're the problem," Danny snarled. "I know you sent those pictures to Tess. I know you're trying to break us up, but it's not going to work. We're together and that's not going to change so you better get over it."

Cooper looked at Danny like he had no idea what he was talking about. "Tess is my friend, I want her to be happy."

"No, I'm pretty sure you want her for yourself."

Cooper leaned over the counter. "Are you sure you're not being paranoid?"

Danny fought to keep his fists clenched at his sides and not grab him by the collar of his shirt. "Whatever game you're playing, it's over. I'm onto you."

"I really wish I knew what sparked you to come in here and accuse me of something like this, but you couldn't be more wrong."

"You may think you have everyone fooled, but not me. I wanted to look you in the eyes and let you know that you're not going to win."

Cooper smirked at him again. "You know, you really should be more secure in your relationship instead of imagining that someone is trying to break you and Tess up."

"If anyone here is unstable, it's you."

He could see the cockiness in Cooper's eyes give away to sheer rage. Clearly, that was a button he didn't like pushed. "I think it's time for you to go."

"Stay away from me and Tess." Danny started to walk toward the door.

"Is that a threat?"

He turned around to face him, his jaw hard. "No, it's a warning, my only one." Danny pushed the door open and walked out, feeling mildly satisfied.

Sixteen

The Carolina Panthers had made it to the NFC championship game. If they won this game they were headed to the Super Bowl, and if they lost, the season was over. Danny knew as soon as they'd won the division series and the championship game was going to be played at home that Charlie would make sure she was back in North Carolina for it. He was really glad she was coming back; a big game like that wouldn't be the same without her, plus having her around would be a good distraction for Tess and himself.

After they'd gone to the police station and had given statements about the messages they'd received, Danny pulled JJ aside and asked him to start digging into Cooper. There had to be something from his past that would connect the missing pieces to what was going on now. Everything had been quiet for the past week, but Danny walked around with his guard constantly up, waiting for the next thing to happen.

He picked Charlie up at the airport and then they made their way over to Jason and Kate's house. Jason was on a tight practice schedule and they wanted to spend some time with him before the big game. When they got to the house, they were greeted by Kate, who was still wearing her hospital scrubs. "Come in, come in. I'm really happy you guys came. I got out of work late so I just got home. Jason is in the family room. I'm gonna run up and change but I'll be right down." Kate made her way up the stairs and Danny and Charlie headed for the family room.

"Remind me again how he ended up with someone so fantastic?"

Danny chuckled. "It was definitely luck."

They found Jason seated on the large couch with ESPN playing on his very large TV.

"Hey, big guy," Charlie shouted as she made her way over to her brother.

"Hey, Ace, good to see you," he said, standing up to give her a hug. "Thanks for coming home."

"You really think I'd miss this?" she asked, stepping out of the hug.

"What, it's not good to see me?" Danny asked, gesturing to himself.

Jason let out a laugh. "Shut up, you live here. I saw you two weeks ago. Charlie is still a New Yorker for a few more months." He slapped hands with Danny and they gave each other a man hug.

"Nick felt bad he couldn't make the game, but he's working this weekend."

Jason shrugged, stepping back from Danny. "It's okay. I guess performing surgery and possibly saving lives is kind of important."

"Yeah, just kind of."

Jason grabbed them each a beer and they all settled on the couches.

"How are you feeling about Sunday?" Danny asked him.

"Good. Green Bay is tough, but so are we."

"Not to mention Marcus has been on fire—he scored two touchdowns in the division game and ran for over three hundred yards. Green Bay doesn't have a running back like him," Charlie added before taking a sip of her beer.

"Look who's become a fountain of football knowledge," Jason said with a big grin.

Charlie rolled her eyes. "Here we go. I have an excellent memory. You two wish you could remember things as well as I do."

"I'm really okay with forgetting algebra."

"Did you remember it the first time around, Jay?"

"Oh!" Danny laughed into his beer. With everything that had been going on, it was nice being around his siblings and just laughing.

"Are you any closer to figuring out who is doing all that creepy shit to you?"

"No, and nothing has happened in a while which makes me think something worse is coming," Danny told his brother.

"I wish you could see whoever it is doing those things on the security footage, then at least you'd have the proof you need. A gut feeling unfortunately just isn't enough. You still think Cooper is behind everything?" Charlie added.

"I do. The guy just gives me an uneasy vibe. I went to confront him the other day and all he did was smirk at me like I was talking crazy. Ace, I can't tell you how much it creeps me out that he's two goddamn doors away from Tess all day and there's no proof tying him to this shit."

Charlie gasped. "You confronted him? What if he went completely psycho on you?"

"I had to. I needed him to know that I'm on to him. If he's innocent, then he's got nothing to worry about, but after looking him in the eyes, he's far from innocent."

"Maybe he's going to slip up at some point. He thought the pictures in those text messages would break you guys up and that didn't happen. If his plan is to get you out of the picture, he's definitely going to try to do something else," she said matter-of-factly.

"I've been trying to figure out what his next move is going to be."

Jason shot him a look. "Bro, you can't try to do that. You're dealing with someone who is clearly not in their right mind. You can't figure out that kind of crazy."

Danny took a long sip of his beer. That was exactly what he was afraid of: not being able to figure out whatever Cooper was up to before he hurt someone Danny cared about.

"I wish there was something I could do to help you nail this guy faster. I don't like the idea of some guy vandalizing your truck and doing all this crazy shit because he doesn't like the fact that you're dating Tess."

"I appreciate the offer and if there's anything you can do, I promise I'll let you know," Danny told Jason. The brothers bumped fists.

"I hope I didn't miss anything interesting," Kate said, entering the room.

"Nope, we're just getting started," Charlie replied.

Kate plopped down next to Jason and they spent the rest of the night catching up and enjoying their time together.

Tess woke up to Danny thrashing in his sleep and yelling "No!"

She quickly turned over and tried to shake him awake but it

didn't work. She flipped on the light and tried again.

"Ace, no!" he yelled before he jolted up in bed, gasping for air.

"Danny, it's okay. It was just a nightmare. You're okay, Charlie is okay." She moved closer to him and wrapped her hands around his bicep.

"Shit, I'm sorry. I don't understand why this keeps happening." He let out a sigh and pulled his knees up to his chest.

"Honey, I know you don't want to hear it but you need to deal with this and finally put it to rest. You need to talk to Charlie." She hugged him tighter.

"I don't want to upset her."

Shaking her head, Tess emphasized, "You're not going to upset her. She's tough; she can handle it and she'll be glad that you told her. You'll probably feel better too."

He ran a hand over his face and Tess leaned her cheek against his shoulder. "You have to forgive yourself, none of it was your fault."

With a loud sigh, Danny laid his cheek against her hair. "I wish I could feel that way."

"Until you do, this nightmare isn't going to stop."

Danny turned to her and pressed a quick kiss to her lips. "I'm sorry I woke you up."

"It's okay." She could tell there was no more talking about it, so she leaned over and turned the light off. Danny pulled her into his side and Tess stayed awake until she heard his breathing even out. She wanted him to have some peace of mind, so it was time that she took things into her own hands.

———

Danny needed to clear his head or he was going to have trouble getting through the rest of the weekend, and with Jason's big game tomorrow night he didn't want anything weighing him down. He drove over to the local marina. It was closed up for the winter but it was a clear day, and there was something about looking out at the lake with the mountains in the background that always made him feel calm. Danny parked his truck close to the water and got out. There was a dock nearby, so he made his way down the planks and sat down so he was overlooking the lake. He took a deep breath and inhaled the fresh, cool air as his legs dangled over the dock. He hated seeing the look of worry on Tess's face the night before. He'd had a great night with Jason and Kate and Charlie; there was no reason that nightmare should've surfaced. Then again, in the back of his mind he was also worried about Cooper and whatever he was planning next because there was no doubt in Danny's mind that he *was* planning something.

"Pondering the great mysteries of life over there?"

He looked over his shoulder and saw Charlie walking down the dock in his direction. "You know it."

She took the spot next him and drew a deep breath in, a smile spreading across her face. "Now that's fresh air. I think my lungs have started to forget what that's like after all those years of living in New York."

"It's a good thing you're moving back here then, for the sake of your lungs and all." He nudged her with his shoulder.

Charlie shook her head and laughed.

"What brings you here? I guess more than that, how did you know I was here?"

"For as long as I can remember, whenever you've needed to think or just clear your head, you come here. Tess told me that you haven't been sleeping so well and she's worried about you."

Danny threw his head back and groaned.

"Stop your moaning. You better start talking. What's going on, Danno?"

He shook his head. "It's stupid."

"Obviously it isn't if you're having nightmares."

He blew out a deep breath and looked straight out at the water. "It's the same nightmare every time. The long and short of it is... you die after the accident. I can't get to you in time, I can't save you... I'm just too late." Danny's throat got tight with emotion.

Frowning, Charlie asked, "How long has this been going on?"

"About a year." He shrugged.

"Why didn't you say anything?"

"How exactly was I supposed to start that conversation? Oh, hey, Ace, how's everything? By the way, I've been having these nightmares that you die," he answered sarcastically.

"You could've said that."

"I thought they would've just stopped, but they keep hanging on."

She turned toward him. "You feel guilty, don't you?"

"Did Tess tell you that too?" He scoffed.

She gave him a light punch in the shoulder. "You think I need her to tell me that? You've always been so protective, not to say that Jason hasn't been because he has, but you looked after me in a way that was just different."

"I did a real shit job looking after you that night."

Charlie rolled her eyes. "Were you driving drunk? I'm pretty sure Tommy was the drunk one and he ran me off the road and into that tree, not you."

"I should've never let you leave. You practically ran out of the house, you were so upset with the chief. I shouldn't have let you drive alone. If I had gone after you, I would've been driving and Tommy wouldn't have pulled that shit with me. You would've never driven into that tree and almost died."

Charlie sighed and grabbed his arm. "Danny, there's nothing you could've done. It was an accident."

He got to his feet and started to pace. "You don't understand."

She stood up so she was toe to toe with him. "Then explain it to me."

"Ever since we were old enough to understand it, Dad told me and Jason that you were our responsibility. We were to watch out for you, not let anything happen to you. I always felt in my bones that it was my job to look out for you. I tried to keep the peace between you and Dad all those years when he hated you living in New York, but when it really counted, I failed."

She gripped his shoulders and looked up at him. "Danno, listen to me. You have never failed me, not once. When I wanted to leave Belmont to go to New York City to make my own life, you bought my bus ticket so that I wouldn't chicken out. You gave me the push that I needed so that I could live a life that I wanted when I was scared to take the leap on my own. When I was in trouble at the magazine last year and I was accused of leaking secrets to our rival, you and Jason stepped up for me. You came to New York when I needed you most. Yes, Jason sent me his lawyer, but it was you who tried to talk sense into me about Nick and why I needed to be honest with myself about what I was feeling for him. You've always had my back. Do you think I'm upset with you for not coming after me?"

He placed his hands on his hips and shook his head.

"You and Jason have always taken care of me. I'm really lucky. Stop feeling guilty about something you had no control over. I'm a grown woman. I chose to drive when I was upset. I could've pulled over, but I didn't. I thought I could get away from Tommy and that would be it. In the end, I was very fortunate, and everything that happened brought me and Nick back together." She smiled up at him.

In that moment, Danny realized she was right. He'd always had her best interest at heart and she knew that.

Looking a bit sheepish, Danny replied, "I probably should've talked to you about this sooner."

"That would've been a wise choice."

Danny smiled and wrapped Charlie in a hug. "Thanks for setting me straight, Ace."

"That's what I'm here for, Danno."

Danny breathed a sigh of relief. He hadn't realized how much he'd been holding on to for all this time. He felt like a giant weight had been lifted from his shoulders. Deep down Danny believed that Charlie might be upset with him for not coming after her, but knowing that she didn't blame him for any of what happened made him feel like he could finally put it behind him.

The Panthers and Packers had played one hell of a game. It had been neck and neck almost the entire game, but then with four minutes to go, the Panthers broke open the game and ended up winning thirty-five to twenty-four. The hometown stadium erupted. Their team was headed to the Super Bowl, and the Moreaus, Russos, and everyone else in the family suite were elated.

Tess's bakery was decked out in all things Panthers and Penny had come up with some beautiful decorating for their cupcakes and cakes in honor of the Panthers' trip to the Super Bowl. The bakery was exceptionally busy the two weeks leading up to the Super Bowl, and Tess certainly wasn't complaining. Valentine's Day was around the corner as well and she still needed to get ready for that despite all the Super Bowl excitement.

Tess finished looking over some recipes, changed her clothes, and waited for Danny to pick her up for date night. They headed into Charlotte for dinner, which Tess was very much looking forward to.

Not that she didn't enjoy when they stayed in and cooked or got take out, but she loved how much Danny liked planning date nights for them.

They parked and made their way across the street to the restaurant. As they walked past a bar, Tess stopped in her tracks. "What's the matter?"

"That looks like Cooper sitting at the bar."

Danny came up behind her and looked over her shoulder. "All the way at the end? Talking to the blonde woman?"

"Yeah, that's definitely him. He must be out on a date."

"Just because he's talking to a woman at a bar? That doesn't mean anything."

She turned to look at him and glared at him. "Either way, he's getting out there and he's met someone or he's trying to meet someone, and that's great. He must realize that I'm with you and that isn't going to change."

"I wouldn't be so sure he actually knows that."

"I think he's moved on. I know you think he's been behind everything that's happened, but he's been through a lot. He lost his wife and I can't even imagine what that had to be like."

Danny clasped her shoulders and turned her to face him. "One of the things that I love about you is your endless compassion for people. And sure, maybe Cooper has moved on, but I still don't trust the guy. I just want you to be careful around him."

"I promise I will be."

"Good. Now, can we stop looking like creepy window stalkers and go to dinner?"

Tess pushed up on her toes and kissed him. "I think that sounds like a great idea."

"By the way, I love those high heels you've got on tonight, babe. Very sexy."

Tess glanced down at her shoes and smirked. The black pumps had an almost four-inch heel and a thin ankle strap, but the best feature was the black bow at the back of the shoe. "Oh, thanks."

He grabbed her hand and they continued on their way to dinner. Tess loved that Danny had noticed her shoes, but more than that, she loved the way she felt in them. She was starting to feel like she was getting back parts of herself that she'd lost and that had been more rewarding than she could've ever imagined.

Seventeen

The Panthers met the Houston Texans in the Super Bowl the first Sunday in February, two weeks after the NFC championship game. They played in Atlanta, as it was customary for the Super Bowl to be played in a neutral site. The whole Moreau family along with Nick and Tess went to Atlanta for the big game. Danny loved seeing his big brother play in the Super Bowl; it was something he'd dreamed about since they were kids.

It was a close game almost right up until the end, and then the Panthers broke things open with four minutes to go in the fourth quarter. Jason scored a touchdown and they kicked the extra point, putting the Panthers up thirty-one to twenty-one. Houston managed a field goal and then the Panthers kicked one of their own. The Carolina defense held strong, and as the clock ticked down, Danny, Tess, Charlie, Nick, and Kate stood practically holding their breaths. Danny blinked and suddenly the clock was at zero and the Panthers had won thirty-four to twenty-four. The entire suite erupted in screams and cheers. It was one of the greatest things that Danny had ever experienced. Still, nothing was better than when they got to see Jason on the field after the game and celebrate with him. Danny'd always been proud of Jason, but this was a whole different kind of proud.

A week passed before some of the Super Bowl excitement had started to die down. However, getting to experience the Super Bowl, the win, and then the team parade with the entire family was something Danny wouldn't be forgetting anytime soon.

Things were moving along well for the condo project in Charlotte. They were waiting for the engineer and the contractor to look over the designs they'd sent last week, and Danny was hoping they wouldn't have to make too many changes. He knew the developers wanted work to start on the units as soon as possible.

Danny looked up from his desk and saw Natalie standing in his doorway, looking distraught. "Nat? What's going on?"

"I just got a call from Rowan Dutton's office and they said that they never received the plans you were supposed to send over earlier in the week."

"How is that even possible? We sent them via FedEx—didn't you get the confirmation?"

"I did, but for some reason they didn't get it."

He leaned back in his chair with force. "Shit. They wanted them no later than yesterday."

"I really don't understand how this could've happened. Let's double check the address." Natalie walked over to his desk and they verified the address she had written down was in fact the same one that he had on his computer.

"Okay, so what does Dutton's office want me to do?"

"They want the plans ASAP," she told him.

Danny stood up from his desk. "Okay. Call them back and tell them I'm gonna bring them over within a half hour."

"Are you sure you don't want me to take care of it?"

"No—I appreciate it, but I'd feel better hand delivering it myself at this point."

"Okay, let me go call Dutton's office." Natalie hurried out of Danny's office and he balled his hands into fists at his sides in an effort to stay calm. He'd always had a good reputation with his clients and this certainly wasn't looking good for him. The only thing he could do was get the plans to them as soon as possible and apologize and hope that would be enough.

"So you had to go deliver the plans even though you'd FedExed them days ago?"

"Yeah, and I had to walk into the developer's office with my tail between my legs. Definitely not my finest professional moment. FedEx is doing a search to see what happened to the original documents," Danny told JJ as he took a sip of his bourbon. The two cousins decided to meet up for a drink at Monte's while Danny waited for Tess to finish up with work.

"Are you thinking this is just another time that Cooper is messing with you?"

"The thought definitely crossed my mind, but it seemed a little bit less likely. FedEx tampering has to be pretty difficult to pull off." Danny ran a hand through his hair and blew out a breath.

JJ nodded as he took a sip of his beer. "Yeah, unless he knew when you were sending something out. Not to be super creepy, but it's very possible that he's got your office either bugged or he's got a camera in there so he can see or hear what's going on or both. That would be the only way I could think that he'd be able to intercept that delivery."

Danny leaned back on his chair and shook his head. "Well fuck, man. Thanks for freaking me out."

"Oh, I'm sorry, I didn't realize you were looking for the sugarcoated version."

Chuckling, Danny said, "You know I'm not, but this bastard is not messing around if he's gone to that level. Have you found anything out about his past?"

"Not yet. I can't seem to find any record of a Cooper Witter anywhere near New Orleans, but I'm not giving up. I actually have a buddy who works down in New Orleans, so I'm gonna see what he can help me find out."

Danny drained his glass and nodded. "Thanks, man. I appreciate that. I don't think I'll feel one hundred percent relaxed until we know who we're really dealing with."

"I get it. If there was some creepy dude with eyes for my girlfriend who was likely vandalizing my truck and messing up my shit, I wouldn't feel comfortable until his ass was behind bars." JJ finished off his beer and motioned for a refill. "I'll also sweep your office and your place for any bugs or devices."

He couldn't even believe he was having this conversation, that there was someone who had it out for him and that they would go to these lengths. He checked his phone and still no word from Tess, but he knew she'd be finishing up soon. When he looked up, he saw Cooper walking into the bar. "You've gotta be kidding me."

JJ gripped his arm. "Whoa, whoa. Take it easy, cuz. Don't give him any ammunition."

Danny settled back in his seat and let out a deep breath. He wanted nothing more than to put Cooper up against a wall and shake the answers out of him, but he knew it would never be that simple and then he'd look like the crazy one.

"Danny, hey. Good to see you again."

"Cooper."

"Having a boy's night?"

"No, just grabbing a drink with my cousin, here. JJ, this is Cooper."

JJ extended his hand. "Ah yes, the sandwich guy. I'm on the force, some of the guys have been into your shop, said you make a good sandwich."

"Very kind of you to say. You should come in, all cops get a discount."

"I just might do that."

"I'd invite you to join us, but we're getting ready to head out soon. I've gotta meet Tess."

Danny waited to see if his expression changed at all, but Cooper kept his face the same.

"Thanks, but I'm actually meeting someone for a date. Trying to get back out there, you know?"

"Good for you. I hope it works out."

Cooper gave him a tight smile and a nod. "Good to meet you, JJ. See you around, Danny."

They watched him walk toward the back where a woman with dark hair Danny didn't recognize was waiting in a booth. "Maybe Tess was right. Maybe he has moved on?" JJ said.

"I'd like to believe that but I just can't." Just then, Danny's phone vibrated.

Hey hot stuff—just finished up. Ready when you are.

He smiled at his phone and pushed back from his stool. "Keep me posted."

"Of course. I'll swing by your office first thing tomorrow. Enjoy your night."

Danny tossed some money on the bar and turned to look toward the back of the room to the booth Cooper was in. He didn't know how, but he was going to figure out what the man was up to and put an end to it.

Valentine's Day was quickly approaching. Tess and Penny were spending time after hours working on some new desserts, plus they were trying to finalize what they were making for Alice's catering event on the thirteenth. She was exhausted, but she knew there was a light at the end of the tunnel.

"I really think we should go with the chocolate strawberry mini tarts for Alice's event."

"You think? It's not boring?"

"No, it's not boring," she told Penny. "They're really good and doing them bite size was a really good idea." Tess jotted the tarts down on her list. "I think we're good with everything for the cases in the bakery."

"I'm gonna start on the sugar cookies tomorrow so I have time to decorate them," Penny said, letting out a sigh.

Penny looked just as tired as she felt. "Why don't you head home for the night? We've got another long day tomorrow."

A knock at the back door made Tess look up. She walked over and pushed it open, surprised to see Danny standing on the other side. "Hi, what are you doing here?"

"I wanted to see if you were almost finished?"

"Not quite yet."

"I can finish putting all of this away, Tess." Penny motioned to the cookies that were out on the counter.

"No—that's okay. Can I talk to you for a second?" She motioned outside and he stepped back into the parking lot. "I did say I was working late, didn't I?"

"Yeah, you did. I had a meeting with Pete about some house stuff and it's almost nine, so I just wanted to see if you were finished. What's the problem?"

She put her hands on her hips and sighed. "I don't have a time clock. I'm finished when I'm finished. This is a really busy time; we have a lot of orders and desserts to bake for the store and I don't need to feel pressured about working late."

He held up his hands in defense. "Whoa, whoa. I am not pressuring you in any way. I finished up earlier than I thought so I wanted to see if you were done for the day so we could go home together. If you need to work more, go ahead. I completely understand."

Tess ran a hand over her face. "I'm sorry. I'm just really tired."

He stepped forward and placed his hands on her arms. "I know you are. Finish up whenever and I'll be at my place waiting for you."

"What if I wanted to go to my place?"

"I have a bigger shower." He smirked.

She couldn't help but laugh. How had she gotten so lucky? Tess rose up on her toes and placed a kiss on his lips. "Give me about a half hour and then I'll be there."

"I'll be waiting. Take your time." He turned and walked back out to the street. Tess watched him go and then went back inside to finish up. There was something incredibly nice knowing that after a long day there was someone to go home to. She was sorry it had taken her so long to realize she could handle running a business and a relationship, but at the same time she was glad that it was all happening now. With Danny.

Valentine's Day arrived and the bakery was buzzing with people coming in to pick up their sweet treats for the holiday. Tess was really happy with what she and Penny had come up with for their new items. The chocolate cherry cupcakes were proving to be a big hit as well as the red velvet and white chocolate chip cookies. The night before they'd wowed people at Alice's catering event with their mini chocolate strawberry tarts. It was a really good feeling to see so many people loving what they were baking.

Tess was looking forward to celebrating her first Valentine's Day with Danny. When he'd asked her what she wanted to do, she told him there was nothing she wanted more than to stay home, open a bottle of wine, and relax. The past couple of weeks had been so busy the last thing she wanted to do was go to a crowded restaurant. No, she much preferred to be on the couch in her comfy clothes with just Danny.

Leanne walked past her to ring up a sale. "Let me tell you, those red velvet cookies are going out of here faster than I can blink! Ya'll really killed it this year."

"Thanks! I'm really happy with the way everything turned out too." Tess stacked two empty trays on top of each other and removed them from the counter.

Just then, Mrs. Perry sauntered in and squeezed her way through the people in the bakery. "Lord almighty, it's too early in the day for that woman," Leanne whispered, putting the money in the register.

"Hi there, Mrs. Perry. Happy Valentine's Day! How can I help you?"

"Happy Valentine's Day to you too, dear. Oh my, I didn't realize it would be quite so crowded."

"Well, it is Valentine's Day," Leanne replied with a smirk.

Tess gave her the eye and Leanne smirked as she made her way down the other end of the counter to help a customer. "So, what can I get for you?"

"I was hoping for a dozen of the red velvet cupcakes. I'm also going to need a chocolate cream pie."

"Okay, let me check on the cupcakes." She looked down and saw that thankfully she still had a dozen in the case so she boxed them up and then went to grab the pie. "Is there anything else I can get you?"

She tapped her chin. "Maybe a half dozen of those pecan cookies?"

Tess put the cookies in a small box and stacked it on top of the other boxes. "Is that all?"

"Yes, yes. I think that'll do."

She put all of the boxes in a bag before turning to the register to total up the purchase. "That'll be forty-four dollars."

Mrs. Perry reached into her purse and pulled out a fifty from her wallet to hand to Tess. Just as Tess was about to give Mrs. Perry her change, Tess caught sight of a delivery man walking toward the counter carrying a vase of flowers.

"Excuse me, I'm looking for a Tess Carmichael?"

"You found her," Tess said, taking the vase from him. "Thank you very much."

"Happy Valentine's Day." He turned and headed back out the door.

Tess looked at the vase and she was stunned. There had to be a dozen and a half white roses in there. She set the vase down on the back counter and proceeded to give Mrs. Perry her change. When she turned around, she noticed that Mrs. Perry was eyeballing the flowers.

"That is quite a bouquet you have there."

"Yes, it is."

"I take it that things between you and Danny Moreau are going well?" Mrs. Perry looked at her, lips pursed like she already knew the answer to that question.

At first, Tess wanted to be surprised but then she remembered that in Belmont nothing stayed secret for long. "Yes, ma'am, they are."

"Mr. Perry used to bring me flowers every week when we were dating. That's a sign of good breeding."

"Danny does lots of things that make me feel special."

"I'm sure, but when a man takes the time to do something like pick up or order flowers, it truly shows a lot about his character."

Tess looked back at the flowers. As beautiful as they were, they weren't her favorite and she was a little surprised that Danny didn't know that. He paid attention to details so this seemed strange for him. She handed Mrs. Perry her change. "Do you need help carrying that out to your car?"

"Oh no, I can manage. I hope you're making Danny Moreau make an effort for your time. Too many girls from your generation give everything away for free and men get bored. They need to feel challenged," she said, tapping her index finger on the counter to emphasize her point.

Tess forced a smile. "I'll keep that in mind. Have a nice day."

Mrs. Perry grabbed her bag and gave a wave. Tess couldn't help but turn and roll her eyes once she left. It was absolutely infuriating that Mrs. Perry actually believed that it was the woman's job to keep the man from getting bored. It was so incredibly backwards, but then again, given the generation that Anita Perry came from, it made sense why she would think that. Still, Tess wished someone had made an effort to correct her at some point.

She noticed the card attached to the vase and opened it.

"What gorgeous flowers!" Penny said, coming up from behind her.

"I will let Danny know that you said so."

When she turned the card over, she saw that it was a typed message on a generic Valentine's Day card that said: *You deserve only the best.*

It wasn't signed or anything, just the short message. While the flower selection had seemed strange to her, the lack of signature on the card was even stranger.

"Everything okay?"

"Yeah—it's just I'm a little surprised he didn't pick my favorite flower, but maybe he was just trying to do something different?" she told Penny.

"That could be. Either way, your man sent you some beautiful flowers."

Tess smiled at the vase and nodded. She couldn't wait to get home and thank Danny properly for being so thoughtful.

Eighteen

Danny sat on the couch looking over the latest email the developer had sent regarding the plans for the condos. They'd seemed really impressed with Zack's designs for some of the units. They wanted a few changes to the lobby, but it wasn't anything major. Danny had already started working on it earlier at the office so he didn't have much left to do. He checked his watch and saw it was almost eight. Tess said she'd be there no later than eight thirty. He had lemon chicken, crispy potatoes, and green beans all on the stove ready for when she got there. The wine was open on the counter next to the flowers he'd picked up for her along with a card.

He was glad that Tess had wanted to spend the night in instead of going out. He would've taken her anywhere she wanted to go, but he liked the idea of them having the whole night to themselves.

Just then, the door opened and Tess came in looking breathtakingly beautiful. She'd taken her hair out of her braid and it fell loose around her shoulders. Her lips were red and he could see some red lace peeking out from the v of her black sweater. He put his laptop down on the coffee table and stood up. "Hi. Happy Valentine's Day."

Tess gave him a sexy smile, dropped her bag and coat by the door, and walked toward him. "Happy Valentine's Day." She gripped the back of his neck and lowered his mouth to hers. The kiss quickly turned heated and Tess was digging her nails into Danny's biceps. He pulled back and looked at her lust filled eyes.

"That was one hell of a greeting."

"I wasn't finished."

"Oh, well. By all means, don't let me interrupt."

She took a step back and pulled the sweater up over her head revealing a very sexy, red, lacy bra. "Shirt, off," she told him.

He pulled his T-shirt off over his head and tossed it on the floor.

He watched her lick her bottom lip and his cock actually twitched. She stepped out of her shoes and then pulled her jeans down her legs almost at an almost torturously slow pace until she stood before him in just her bra and a matching scrap of red lace.

"Wow. I think you should say hello like this all the time."

Tess smirked and moved toward him. She slid her hands onto his hips and then reached for the waistband of his sweatpants and pulled them and his boxer briefs down in one motion. He kicked them away and never took his eyes off of her. "For once I actually have on more clothes than you."

Danny laughed and moved so their bodies were touching. "That's something that can be fixed really quickly you know."

"By all means then, fix it."

Danny reached behind her and unhooked her bra and pushed it off her shoulders. He knelt down in front of her and pressed his mouth to her center. She gasped and gripped his head. "These are nice, but I much prefer you bare." He slid them down her legs and she quickly stepped out of them. Danny stood up so they were face to face and he backed her up against the living room wall.

He slid his hand between her legs and parted her with his fingers. She gripped his shaft and squeezed making his head snap back.

"I need to thank you."

"Thank me? For what?"

"For the flowers. Let me thank you, Danny."

She started sliding her hand up and down his length before Danny had a chance to answer. As much as he loved the feel of her lips around him, her hand felt incredible right now. She leaned forward so that her breasts were rubbing up against his chest and then took his mouth in an all-consuming kiss. She pumped harder and Danny groaned into her mouth. Between the feel of her body and what she was doing with her hand, he wasn't going to last much longer. "Tess, I'm gonna come," he said against her mouth.

She didn't slow down and Danny felt his orgasm creeping up his spine. He tried to hold back, but before he knew it, he came all over her hand. He pulled back from her, a very satisfied smile on her face as he tried to catch his breath. "That was so hot."

"I had a feeling you'd say that."

"Be right back." He walked into the bathroom to grab a

washcloth to clean up and another one to give to Tess. He also retrieved a condom from his room and quickly covered himself with it. He handed Tess the washcloth and she cleaned her hand and then tossed it on the floor with the rest of their clothes.

"I like where your head is at."

"I had a feeling you'd say that," he replied as he stepped up to her and pinned her arms to the wall before lowering his mouth to hers.

Their tongues slid against each other and their teeth nipped and then Danny moved his mouth down to her collarbone and up to her neck. Tess was rubbing her pelvis up against his and then she hooked her leg around his waist. "You're not playing around tonight, are you?"

"I want you now," she told him, grinding against him harder.

Danny gripped her hips and hoisted her up so she could wrap both legs around his waist. He positioned himself at her entrance and then thrust into her. Tess's grip tightened on his shoulders and he continued sliding in and out of her while he took her mouth in a hard kiss. He hit her clit and she groaned, which made him smile. Danny lifted her up a little higher for a different angle and he could feel her starting to squeeze around him. "You feel so good," he told her. He picked up his pace and Tess threw her head back against the wall.

"Harder, Danny."

He did as she asked and thrust harder which made her tighten her grip around his waist to bring him even closer to her. "I know you're close, Tess."

"So close."

Danny reached between them and pressed on her clit and that's when he saw her orgasm tear through her. He kept pumping his hips until he felt his release hit him and then he slumped against her and the wall as he tried to catch his breath.

"I really think we should start off every night like this—with one of us thanking each other for something."

Tess chuckled. "Of course you do."

"Do you have any complaints?"

"None." She smiled.

He kissed the tip of her nose and then stepped away to go dispose of the condom. "I can't believe you noticed the flowers on the kitchen counter as soon as you walked in. I don't even recall seeing you glance in that direction," he called from the hall bathroom.

Tess paused as she pulled Danny's T-shirt over her head and then he came back in the room to pull his sweatpants on. "I didn't. I was thanking you for the flowers you sent to the bakery."

His face twisted in confusion. "I didn't send flowers to the bakery."

"Yes, you did."

"No, I didn't."

Tess's face dropped. "What are my favorite flowers?"

"What?"

"Please just answer the question."

He turned and walked into the kitchen and grabbed the bouquet of flowers off the counter. Danny presented the beautifully wrapped bouquet to her. "Calla lilies are your favorite. That's why I got you a dozen of them from June's shop this afternoon. She did an order special for me."

Tess blinked a few times and then looked down at the flowers in her hands. "They're gorgeous. I knew you'd know my favorite flowers."

"They've always been your favorite. Now what flowers came to the bakery?"

Tess told him about the white roses that came to the bakery along with the unsigned card. Danny gripped the back of his neck and shook his head. "I would never send you white roses, and I'd never not sign a card."

She nodded slowly. "I know, I thought it was strange, but I don't know, I thought maybe I was overthinking it."

"This has to be him. Cooper is determined to try and fuck with us. Where did those flowers come from?"

Tess stepped toward him and placed her hands on his arms. "I don't know where they came from, but it wasn't anywhere I recognized. Listen, let's not let this ruin our night. Tomorrow we'll look at everything and figure it out."

As much as he wanted to figure this out now and catch this bastard, he wanted to be with Tess more. "Okay, you're right. How about we eat this dinner I cooked, have some wine and forget all about Cooper and this nonsense?"

Tess wrapped her arms around his neck and smiled. "I think that sounds like a great plan." She placed a kiss on his lips and then turned toward the counter. Danny was really starting to get sick of all of this. Something had to give. He needed something that would get Cooper out of their lives for good.

Tess knew that Danny had agreed to put aside the issue of the mystery flowers so they could finish celebrating Valentine's Day, but she could also tell he was uneasy about the whole thing. Truth be told, so was she. The card attached to the flowers was definitely not from June's shop or any other one she'd ever heard of before. She sent Danny a screen shot of the card so he could show it to JJ and they could try and track down who sent the flowers. In the meantime, she couldn't sit by and do nothing, so Tess decided the best way to get information was to go straight to the possible source.

———————————

The next day, Tess walked over to Cooper's shop later in the morning when she hoped it wouldn't be as busy. She thought maybe if she could get him talking that he would give something away that would tell her once and for all if he was behind all of these things. He spotted her as soon as she walked in and his face lit up into a giant smile.

"Tess. To what do I owe the pleasure?"

"I was actually a little hungry. I was hoping I could get a bacon, egg, and cheese on a biscuit?"

"Of course, coming right up." He motioned to one of his guys, who started working on the order. Cooper leaned his forearms on the counter so he was closer to her. "I'm really glad you came by."

"It's been really crazy, but now that the Valentine's rush is over, we can breathe a bit."

"How was your Valentine's Day? Did you like the flowers?"

Her stomach dropped. "The flowers?"

"Yeah, the roses."

Tess's eyes went wide. "You sent the roses?"

"Did you not like them? I thought they were really beautiful."

"Why would you send me flowers?"

He looked at her confused. "It was Valentine's Day and you deserve flowers from someone who cares about you."

She crossed her arms over her chest and gave him a hard look. "I thought I told you that I was seeing Danny Moreau?"

"Yeah, but I saw you two arguing the other night outside of your bakery. He clearly doesn't respect your work. You don't deserve that."

He'd heard them talking the other night outside of the bakery? It wasn't even an argument; it was her being pissy because she was tired. "I don't know what you think you heard, but there was no argument. Danny and I are very much together."

"Tess, you don't have to pretend with me. He doesn't understand you the way that I do. It's okay for you to want better for yourself," he told her sweetly.

She couldn't believe how delusional he was. She'd been hoping this whole time that Danny was just overreacting but it was clear that he wasn't. "Cooper, I'm going to say this once. I think you're a good guy and I want you to be happy, but it's not going to be with me. I'm in a relationship and I'm happy. I'm sorry if that's not what you want to hear, but you need to accept that."

His jaw went hard and she could see his whole stance tensed. "You don't know what you're saying. He's not right for you."

She straightened her spine. "He is the best man I've ever known."

"You're making a mistake."

One of the guys handed her what she ordered. She placed her money on the counter and left without another word. Her heart was pounding in her chest. It was as if he'd heard nothing she'd said. He seemed set on him being right for her and Danny being wrong for her. It was disconcerting. She grabbed her cell phone out of her apron pocket and pressed a saved number.

"Hi—yeah, I'm fine. I just... you were right, Danny. Cooper sent me the flowers." She bit her lower lip as she walked back to her bakery and listened to Danny talk. The last time she felt this powerless over her own life she told herself it was because she was in love. Now it was because she'd misread the signs. Back then it took her far too long to take back control, but now there was no way in hell that Tess was going to let anyone have that kind of control over her again.

Nineteen

A few weeks later, Danny and Tess went over to Charlotte for their weekend getaway. They had dinner at a new restaurant that belonged to Danny's buddy, Jake, before heading over to the arena for the Eric Church concert, which was incredible. Danny had gotten floor seats for the show and Tess couldn't believe how close they were to the stage. He loved seeing the way she lit up during the concert, but what he loved even more was hearing her sing to herself when she was getting ready for bed and thought he couldn't hear her.

Things were moving along on the condo project after he did damage control with the developers. He and Zack had finalized a bunch of plans for several of the units just today, and now he was ready to relax and spend the rest of the night with Tess. He climbed into his truck and quickly dialed her. "Hey, baby. How's it going over there?"

"We're just finishing up. I should be at my apartment in about twenty minutes."

"Great. I'll order us some takeout. Chinese or Thai?"

"Thai."

"Okay. I'll see you soon." He hung up and made his way out of the parking garage. Not even five minutes after he left, his phone rang. "Did you change your mind? Would you rather have Chinese?"

"Danny, it's Kate."

The sound of his sister-in-law's voice surprised him. "Hi Kate. Sorry, I thought you were Tess. What's—"

"I'm calling because I'm at work and... well... your assistant, Natalie, she was in a car accident. She's okay, just a few bumps and bruises. She was lucky. I asked her if it was okay if I called you an she said it was."

Kate was an ER nurse at Charlotte General and she never got

185

panicked about anything, but Danny could tell she sounded concerned about the whole situation.

"What happened?"

"I'm not one hundred percent sure, but one of the paramedics who brought her in said he heard the officers at the scene talking and it looks like her brakes were cut."

Danny's grip tightened on the steering wheel as a knot in his stomach formed. "Thanks for calling, Kate. I'll be right there." He made a giant U-turn and headed back toward Charlotte. As he drove, he called Tess to let her know he wasn't coming straight home and then he made one more phone call. "Hey, Dad. I need you to meet me at Charlotte General. I'm fine, so are Jason and Kate, and Charlie is in New York and she's safe. Tess is fine too. Yeah, now, I'm afraid. Okay… thanks." He disconnected the call and slammed his hand against the steering wheel. There was no doubt in his mind that Cooper had been behind this. It made sense; he seemed to like to go after vehicles. Danny felt his chest tighten. Now Cooper was going after people that were important to him and he still had no proof to tie him to any of it. Something had to give and he hoped it would happen before someone ended up seriously hurt or worse.

Danny rushed into the emergency room and headed for the desk to find Natalie. A curtain opened and when he looked up, he saw Kate step out. "Danny, hey. She's over here."

He approached the curtain area and saw Natalie sitting up on the gurney with a gauze strip across her forehead near her right eyebrow. Her wrist was wrapped with an ace bandage, and there were some smaller cuts on her forearms, hands, and cheeks. Danny leaned down and placed a kiss on his sister-in-law's cheek. "Thank you for calling me."

"Of course. I knew you'd want to know. I'll give you guys some time to talk."

"Thanks." He stepped past Kate toward Natalie. She gave him a small smile. "Hey, Nat, how are you feeling?"

"Like I slammed into a concrete divider. Oh wait, I did." She laughed and then winced.

"I'm so sorry. Your car was fine this morning?"

She nodded. "I was on my way home and the brakes were just gone. I tried to swerve so I didn't hit anyone. Thankfully I just hit into one of those road dividers and the airbags went off."

Danny dropped his head in his hands and sighed. "I'm so sorry this happened, Nat."

"It's okay. Well, it wasn't a whole lot of fun, but it's not your fault."

He looked up at her, a pained expression on his face. The curtain pulled back and his father stood there, clad in his uniform.

Her face twisted in confusion. "Chief, what are you doing here?"

"I needed to see Danny about something and I heard what happened. I wanted to look in on you, make sure you were alright," he told Natalie.

"Oh, thank you. I'm okay. I was really lucky."

"I need to talk to my dad, but I'll check back on you later. I'm really glad you're okay." He gently touched her hand and then stepped away from the bed.

Natalie gave a small smile and Danny followed his father away from the curtain area. Kate met them by the desk. "I'm sure you two need to talk?"

They nodded. "Come on, follow me." She led them to what looked like a private lounge. "You can have a few minutes in here."

"Thanks Kate," the chief said. She closed the door behind her and Danny started pacing the room.

"I take it you think Cooper is behind this?"

Danny glared at him. "This screams him, Dad. Natalie's brakes go out, she's my assistant, he's trying to hurt the people close to me."

"That would certainly make sense, but it's a hard thing to make stick because—"

"I know we have no solid proof that he's the one doing these things, but what the hell am I supposed to do? My office and my condo were clear of any bugs, but I still can't shake the feeling like this guy knows what's going on in my life. It was one thing when he was just going after me, but now this. What next? Is he gonna try to go after you and Momma, or Jason or Kate or Charlie? How am I supposed to stop him?" He threw his hands up in frustration.

The chief let out a deep breath. "I wish I had an easy answer for you. You're just going to have to be patient and wait until we get some concrete proof or until he messes up. There's a good chance that he'll get sloppy."

"So I have to just wait around until he hurts someone even worse than he hurt Natalie or until he kills someone. That sounds like a great idea."

His father placed his hands on his shoulders. "Hey, listen, I know you're upset."

Danny shook his head. "I'm pissed, Dad. This son of a bitch is making a mess of my life like it's a big game."

"I get it. I do, but you need to be smart about this."

"What I need is to stop him."

The chief took a step back from him and smiled. "You've always been the one who wanted to make things better, fix what was broken. If one of your toys broke, you wanted to put it back together. When Charlie broke her leg on that tire swing, you never left her side. You wanted to make sure that she got better. Anytime anyone got into an argument, you always jumped in to try and mediate. I've always admired that about you. Sometimes you have to accept that it's out of your hands, at least for the time being, son. That's probably one of the hardest things to accept, but the sooner you do, the better off you'll be."

Danny placed his hands on his hips and nodded. His father was right; he was the type who got involved and did what he could to make the situation better. He was just starting to make peace with the fact that he hadn't been able to prevent Charlie's accident, but now all of this was happening because some guy had it out for him. "This has to stop. It just has to."

The chief stepped forward and placed his hand on Danny's shoulder and gave it a squeeze. "Everything will be okay. You need to have a little faith. We're doing everything we can. Your cousin is on his way to Louisiana right now."

Danny's head shot up. "He is?"

"Yeah, he's gonna see what he can find out so we can bury this bastard for good." The chief gave a confident smirk.

He breathed a small sigh of relief. Danny knew that there was no guarantee JJ would find anything that would help them, but it was the best shot they had.

"Come on. I'm gonna go check on the information the police gathered from the crash and then we'll see if Natalie is ready to leave and we'll escort her home. You don't have to fix everything by yourself, Son."

As tough as his dad could be, Danny knew he was lucky to have a father who truly had his back. He wasn't alone in any of this and that was one of the many things that separated him from Cooper. He looked up and nodded and then followed his father back out into the emergency room, feeling slightly more hopeful than when he walked in.

Twenty

The next few weeks, Tess kept busy with work. To say what happened to Natalie scared her was an understatement. Every day she wondered what was going to happen next and the worry was starting to eat away at her. She hadn't said much to Leanne, Penny, or Betty about what had been going on because she didn't want to frighten them, but she knew for their own safety she needed to fill them in.

That morning, she had let Betty know what had been happening, but she still needed to tell Leanne and Penny. They were finishing up for the night, and Tess asked them if they could stay a few minutes late. Penny hopped up on the counter, her long, dark braid hanging over her shoulder, and Leanne pulled up a stool at the counter, leaning on her elbows. Tess removed her apron, ran a hand over her face, and let out a sigh.

"Everything okay, Boss? You look like someone stole your dog," Leanne said."

"It's nothing like that. I need to tell ya'll something." She explained what had been going on between Danny's slashed tires, smashed windshield, his plans getting stolen, and then Natalie's accident. She told them they suspected Cooper but they had no proof.

Leanne threw her hands up in the air. "Lord almighty, why do people have to be so creepy? He couldn't just accept that you're with Danny?"

Tess shrugged. "You should've seen his face when I told him that Danny and I are together and there was no chance for him and me. He looked so angry, and he just kept telling me that I didn't know what I was saying," she told Leanne.

"That's just a whole other level of crazy." Penny shook her head but then looked up at Tess. "Don't worry, we'll keep our eyes open."

"The last thing I want to do is frighten either one of you, but your safety means everything to me so I'd rather ya'll be aware."

Leanne gave her a sympathetic look. "You should've told us when it started. You wouldn't have frightened us. Penny and I are a couple of tough chicks."

Tess chuckled. "You're right. I should have and I'm sorry. I just can't believe that Cooper, who has been nothing but nice to me and all of us would do these kinds of things."

Leanne shrugged. "People can always surprise you, and sometimes it's not in the best way."

Tess knew that for sure. Dean had surprised her in the worst way possible and now it looked like Cooper, someone she considered a friend, a work neighbor, was doing the same thing. Danny, however, had surprised her in all the best ways. He made her see that she had not really been living her life. That was worth all the bad she'd experienced.

"I'm glad I didn't scare ya'll. Hopefully this is resolved soon and then we won't have to worry anymore."

"Do you think it will be?" Penny asked, looking concerned.

"I wish I knew but they're trying to find solid proof to link Cooper to everything. That hasn't been easy."

Leanne leaned back on her stool. "It's better that they're sure they have solid evidence they can hang him with. You want to make sure there are no loose ends."

Tess nodded in agreement. "I just really hope this is all over with soon. I know it's gnawing at Danny."

"Of course it is. Your man wants nothing more than to protect you," Leanne told her as she lightly elbowed her in the side.

Tess couldn't hide her smile. She knew there was no question about that, but she'd be lying if she said she wasn't worried about something happening to him.

"Come on, let's end this night on a good note. Let's go grab a drink at Monte's. I'm buying," Penny told them.

"Uh-oh, we better jump on this! This one hardly ever offers to buy!" Leanne laughed.

"Hey! I bought when we got drinks for your birthday."

"That was six months ago."

They all laughed. It felt good to laugh with everything that had been going on. Tess was lucky that she had such an amazing staff and even luckier that she had such amazing friends. They grabbed their stuff and headed out.

———

Danny met up with Pete after work a few nights later. They were ready to break ground for the house within a few weeks, and Danny was anxious to hear what Pete had to tell him. They met at Grand Main Station, a casual restaurant in Belmont. Pete was already seated at the bar when Danny walked in.

"Hey, man. Sorry I'm a little late, hit some traffic getting out of Charlotte." Danny extended his hand to him.

"I just got here myself," Pete said, shaking his hand.

Danny took a seat on the barstool and they ordered some beers. Pete opened up his iPad and flipped to his notes. "I emailed your plans to the engineer I always work with and he has just a few minor issues, but otherwise he doesn't see any major problems with your plans. I put in for all of the permits and they should be ready in the next ten days or so. Once we have those, we can break ground. Are you okay with me using my crew and various subcontractors I know for all the work that has to be done?"

"Absolutely, I know you only work with good people."

Pete nodded and tapped his iPad. "Good then I think we're in good shape. Things should be underway before the end of March."

Their beers arrived and Danny breathed a sigh of relief. He was happy at least that everything going on with his house was going well. "Sounds great. I really appreciate it." Danny raised his beer to him and they tapped bottles before taking a sip.

"How's everything going on that condo project?"

Danny moved his head from side to side. "It's going. The developers have been really happy with our plans and they haven't run into any issues yet. They're planning on everything being complete structure-wise by September."

"Have you decided what you want to do next?"

"Nothing definite. There's another condo project but it's in Raleigh. It seems like a good opportunity but I just don't know. We may also get in on the bid for a hotel a development group wants to put up in Charlotte near the NASCAR Hall of Fame. That's my preference because it's local, but I'm still waiting for something to come along that really knocks me off my feet."

"You never know. Things come along when we least expect them," Pete said.

"I'm keeping my fingers crossed. How's business with you?"

"I can't complain. We're booked out a few months, which is really great. I get to build things and then my wife usually goes in and decorates them. It's a pretty sweet deal." Pete smiled as he took a sip of his beer.

Pete and Laura were certainly a power couple. They had a great business relationship. Laura's interior design business functioned separately from Pete's contracting business but they always ended up offering referrals for each other to their clients. In addition to having that business relationship, they had a really strong relationship from what Danny could see.

"How are things going with Tess?"

He smiled. "We're great. I'm really happy that she decided to give us a chance."

"You had eyes for her for a long time, didn't you?"

Danny laughed a little. "Yeah, I did. I'm just glad that she decided I was worth giving a chance."

He heard the bell chime over the door, and when he looked up, he saw Cooper walking through with another guy. Danny could feel his grip tighten around his beer glass and it took every ounce of control he had to not get out of his seat and put Cooper against the wall.

"Hey, man. Are you okay? You look like you're about to snap," Pete asked, a frown spreading across his face.

"I'm good," Danny replied, gritting his teeth, never taking his eyes off Cooper as he made his way through the bar. He spotted Danny and a creepy grin spread across his face as he walked toward them.

"Boys night out?" Cooper asked as he stopped right beside them.

"You should probably keep on walking," Danny told him.

"Just having a little friendly conversation here."

"I don't think anything you do is friendly," he said through gritted teeth.

"The way I see it, I walked through the bar, spotted a familiar face, and exchanged pleasantries. If anyone isn't being friendly, I'd say it's you."

"This is me being friendly to you, so if I were you, I'd take it and move along."

"You know, men who spend their nights out drinking when they have girlfriends tend to make terrible mistakes. I'd hate to see Tess get hurt because of something you did." Cooper grinned at him manically.

"You're fucking delusional," Danny said in a clipped tone.

"Just making a point. You might want to make sure you don't keep her waiting too long. Too much of that might make her go looking for someone else." Cooper smirked at him.

Danny was about to get out of his chair, but Pete put his arm across his chest to stop him. "I think you should do what he suggested and move along. Enjoy your night."

Cooper glared at him for a minute before he did anything else. "Ya'll have a good one." He smirked at Danny and then walked to the other side of the restaurant with his companion.

"That son of a bitch is asking for it." Danny noticed his hands shaking in front of him.

"What was that all about?"

"Long story."

"I still have a whole beer left. Start talking because it looked like I was going to have to pry you off of that guy as you pounded his face in."

Danny filled Pete in on the situation and when he was finished, Pete looked at him in utter disbelief. "Shit, man. I should've let you beat his ass."

"He honestly believes Tess would be better off with him."

"Don't even think on it. You know that Tess belongs with you, and I'm pretty sure that she knows that too."

Danny drank down the rest of his beer and it eased him knowing what he felt for Tess and what he was pretty sure she felt for him. He glanced over at Cooper on the other side of the restaurant and shook his head. That guy had it coming and Danny was looking forward to watching him get everything he deserved.

Tess had just finished making a batch of raspberry and lemon cream cupcakes for a client when her cell phone vibrated in her apron pocket. She smiled when she saw it was Charlie.

"Hey, girl, what's going on?"

"I just wanted to check in on you. Nick is working late. Teddy is coming over soon with some takeout."

"How's his store doing?"

Teddy had opened a clothing store where he was able to sell his own designs. It was a tiny little place in the Village, but it was his dream.

"It's doing really well. I'm doing a feature in my blog on his spring line next week. He had a small show for New York Fashion week, but still it's great exposure for him."

Tess knew all about how tough it was to get your own business up and running, and Teddy was in an exceptionally competitive field so he relied heavily on exposure and any kind of promotion he could get. "I'm so happy for him."

"So am I. He's been going on about his spring line since November so he's really excited about it. Oh, and Nick and I got the house."

"You did? The one that you fell in love with?"

"That very one. I just got the call a little while ago and we outbid two other couples. Now it feels real that we're coming back home."

"Oh honey, I can't wait to have you back here."

"I'm hoping everything will be finalized within sixty days so I can start getting it ready for us to live in so by the time Nick's fellowship is done it's not a complete mess when we come back here."

"I loved it from the pictures you sent me. I'm sure you've already got ideas for what you want to do to it."

Charlie chuckled. "I do have some plus I've been talking with Laura so I think it's going to be incredible. I'm trying not to get too ahead of myself. Enough about me. How are you doing with all the craziness that's been going on?"

Tess let out a sigh. "I'm okay, but I'd be lying if I said I wasn't waiting for the next bad thing to happen. I'm worried about Danny. I know what he really wants to do is drive over to Cooper's shop and put him through a wall or two, but he's doing what the chief told him and being patient. I know it's eating away at him."

"Is he still having nightmares?"

"Thankfully, no. He hasn't had them since he talked to you about it."

"Well, that's a good thing. I know this has to be so hard on both of you. I wish there was something I could do to help."

Tess felt her shoulders slump as she leaned onto the counter. "I love you for that, but I don't think there's anything any of us can do right now. I just... I can't help but feel somewhat responsible for all of this."

"What? What the hell are you talking about?"

"I misread the signs with Cooper. I thought we were just friends, and all this time that's clearly not what he's had in mind. Now all of these bad things are happening because I didn't see what was right in front of my face."

"Have you lost your mind? Tess Marie Carmichael, you are in no way responsible for that man's craziness. He's an adult; he should be able to understand that no means no. When a woman tells him that she's seeing someone else and she's not interested, that doesn't give him license to start wrecking people's vehicles and such. No, this is absolutely not your fault so don't you even think about it."

Tess smiled into the phone. She loved her best friend's honesty and her ability to see the situation so much clearer than she could. It made her feel so much better just hearing Charlie say that none of what was happening was her fault. "Thank you for saying that."

"That's what I'm here for. Please promise me you'll be careful until this maniac is caught."

"I promise. I miss you."

"Back at you, honey. I'll talk to you soon."

"Bye, Charlie." They hung up and Tess hadn't realized how much she needed to hear from her. She'd been trying to appear like she had everything under control—that was who she was, an in-control person—but what she wanted to do was scream and throw things. She'd finally found some happiness outside of work and now someone was trying to mess with that. After everything she'd been through with Dean and how she was so quick to think she was better off without love, she knew now that she never wanted to be without it again.

She grabbed some of the empty boxes that had piled up in the kitchen and carried them outside to the recycle bin. As she walked out, she started singing "What I Almost Was," one of her favorite Eric Church songs to go along with her good mood.

"Wow, you sound incredible."

Tess jumped at the sound of Cooper's voice behind her.

"Good Lord, you startled me." She clutched her chest.

"Sorry about that," he said, tossing a garbage bag in the dumpster next to the recycle bin.

She eyed him warily and slowly stepped back from the dumpster.

"It's been awhile since we've talked."

"I don't think there's anything for us to talk about."

"We're still work neighbors, aren't we?" he said sweetly.

"Yeah, but that's where it stops."

He shrugged as if he didn't believe her all while keeping the smile on his face.

"You need to understand that nothing is ever going to happen between us beyond having businesses a few doors away from each other."

"Things can change." His tone actually sounded hopeful.

"They won't. I wish you would accept that so you can move on."

He shoved his hands in his pockets and smirked at her. "I'll see you around, Tess."

Cooper walked away, leaving Tess standing there unsure as to what had just happened. That nervous, worried feeling she was just talking to Charlie about was now worse than ever.

Twenty-One

Danny got a call from Jason inviting him to play golf the next day. Jason was getting ready for mini-camp so he wanted to enjoy himself before he got back into the grind. Danny wasn't the type who usually blew off work, but Zack had everything with the condos handled at the moment so he didn't feel too terrible about taking the day off to spend time with his brother.

Danny headed over to Jason's bright and early the next morning and they drove over to a golf course in Charlotte for their eight thirty tee time. Once they were out on the course, Danny felt somewhat relaxed, something he hadn't felt in weeks. He stepped out of the golf cart and grabbed a club from his bag. He wasn't a great golfer by any means, but he could hold his own.

"I'm glad you agreed to play hooky today."

"Well, you sounded so desperate for a golfing partner on the phone, I didn't want to let you down." Danny shrugged.

Jason glared at him and shook his head. "Oh gee, thanks, bro."

Danny laughed as he stepped up to the tee and took his first swing. He hit a pretty decent shot and then stepped back so his brother could put his ball down.

"Honestly, I felt like we needed a day out. I know I haven't had a ton of time to hang out this winter."

"Bro, you just won the Super Bowl, don't even think on it."

Jason shook him off. "I'm just saying that I know I haven't exactly been around and you've had a lot on your plate. You shouldn't have to deal with all of that alone." He took his shot, which looked like it went a little further than Danny's.

"I appreciate that, but I haven't been alone. Tess and I are in this together, and we've had JJ and the chief in on it."

They climbed back in the golf cart and Jason started driving to the next hole. "Not to get all mushy or anything but I am your older brother, and it's my job is to protect you and Charlie. I know you think you're the only one who felt responsible for her getting in that accident, but you weren't. I was sitting at the same table as you and I didn't get up and go after her either. I know your relationship with her is a little different than mine, but I still feel like I'm supposed to watch out for her too. Now you've got some psycho messing with you because he wants to be with your girl. That doesn't exactly sit well with me."

Danny had no idea Jason felt as guilty as he did about Charlie's accident; when it happened, they'd never talked about it. At the time, they were only worried about making sure she was okay, they'd never talked about how they felt. "I wish I could tell you that I feel good about any of this, but I don't. This guy is the worst kind of bastard. To everyone else he looks like a great guy, but he's fucking sneaky and he drops comments to push my buttons. He actually told Tess that she didn't know what she was doing by being with me and that she was making a mistake. He told her that he understands her better than I ever could."

Jason shook his head as he parked the golf cart. "He's lucky he didn't say something like that to me. If anyone said anything like that about Kate, they'd be missing teeth."

"Believe me, I wanted nothing more than to go beat his ass, but the chief insists that I keep my distance and wait until he messes up."

"Dad knows what he's talking about. I know you're at the end of your rope, bro, but being smart about this is the best thing you can do. In the meantime, if you need to blow off some steam, I've got your back. We can play as many rounds of golf or go ax throwing as often as you need."

Danny's shoulders sagged and he reluctantly nodded. "Maybe kicking your ass at golf will make me feel better."

Jason let out a loud laugh. "That's hilarious you think you can beat me."

"It's on, brother."

They both got out of the golf cart and spent the rest of the morning battling it out. Danny was grateful that his brother had offered him a much-needed distraction, but more importantly that he had reminded him that he didn't have to shoulder everything alone.

Tess lay in Danny's bed with her head on his chest and her arm draped over his stomach. He drew lazy circles on her back as he hugged her close to him. After a long day, she was ready to go home and crash, but then Danny texted and asked her to come to his place. When she got there, he had a beautiful dinner waiting: baked halibut, jasmine rice, and roasted vegetables. She thanked him with some stellar shower sex and then they'd collapsed in his bed. Easter was in two weeks and orders had already started rolling in. As always, Tess liked to stay ahead of the rush, which was why she and Penny had worked late, going over some new ideas for specialty items.

"I can hear that beautiful brain of yours thinking."

"Sorry, I was just thinking over some things Penny and I discussed earlier for Easter."

"New items? Do they need to be taste tested?"

Tess laughed and moved a piece of hair off of her face. "Thank you for your generous offer, but I think we're alright."

"I love when you create new things."

"Me too, but I have to say, it's mostly Penny who comes up with these ideas."

"Don't sell yourself short. You execute them, babe, and make those visions come to life."

She turned her head so she could see his face. He was smiling down at her and it made her heart swell. "You are incredible, Danny Moreau. I don't know why you were so patient with me, but I'm really glad you were."

He placed a kiss on her forehead and gave her a squeeze. "I knew you'd come around."

Tess laughed. "Oh really?" She lifted herself up on her hand so she could see him completely.

"Absolutely. You needed to see what you were missing out on." He grinned at her.

"I *was* missing out."

"We both wasted a lot of time, but we're making up for it now."

"Do you feel like waiting to see what happens with Cooper is somehow ruining things?"

Danny's face twisted in confusion and he quickly shook his head. "No, not even a little bit. I hate that he's interfering in our lives, but I don't regret one single second that we've had. Do you?"

"No, I don't."

Danny's body relaxed and Tess settled back into his chest. "I just want to get through the Easter rush and then maybe we can think about taking a vacation."

He rolled her so she was on her back and he was hovering over her. "Really? You want to take a vacation? You realize that means you're going to have to leave the bakery?"

She smiled. "Yeah, I know. I think a few days away would be okay."

"Who are you, and what have you done with Tess Carmichael?"

She giggled and put her hands on his cheeks. "I'm ready to start living. What do you say?"

"I say that I'd go anywhere with you." He lowered his mouth to hers and she wrapped her arms around his neck to bring him closer to her. In that moment, Tess knew she was falling deep and for the first time ever, she wasn't scared.

Tess got out of her Jeep at her parents' house the same time her sister got out of her car. They tried to do family dinner once a week, but sometimes with Amy's work schedule or depending on what Tess had going on at the bakery, they couldn't make it work, but they always made an effort.

"Hey T." Amy smiled, coming up next to her.

Tess pulled her into a hug. "Hi. You look cute."

"Thanks. No work tonight so I get to branch out from scrubs." She wore distressed skinny jeans, a silk white camisole, and a long navy cardigan that hit below her thighs. She paired it with some brown ankle booties and even wore some light makeup.

They entered the house and they were greeted by the smell of their mother's chicken dumplings. "I will never get tired of that smell," Amy said as they walked toward the kitchen.

"Momma, we're here!" Tess called.

"Perfect timing! The dumplings are ready."

When they got into the kitchen, their mother was at the stove, a smile on her face. She wiped her hands on her apron and stepped away from the stove so she could kiss her daughters. Tess and Amy put their purses down and helped their mother put the food on the table.

"That smells so good. Mostly everything I eat comes out of the microwave," Amy said, taking her seat at the table.

"Dumplings are easy. Nothing you couldn't handle yourself."

"It's just so much better when you make them, Momma." Amy grinned.

"Well, if it isn't all my favorite girls?" Keith Carmichael stepped into the kitchen looking freshly showered and happy to have his family all together. He gave both of them a kiss on the top of their heads and then took his seat at the table. "I was hoping you were making dumplings."

"That's because you didn't want another night of eating vegetables."

"Marion, a man can only eat so many vegetables before he loses his mind."

"Then you probably should've thought of that before you ate at that food truck with Wyatt earlier in the week."

He looked at his wife in shock. Tess and Amy exchanged glances and then broke out into laugher. "Wow, Momma's still got it!" Tess said as she took her seat between her parents.

"Yes, still keeping tabs on me."

"Always." She smirked as she started filling plates.

Tess noticed the loving look that passed between her parents. They had never been overly mushy with each other but she always knew how much they loved each other. Mostly it was in small gestures: her father would always make Sunday breakfast and take care of the cleanup so her mother could relax. They would hold hands when they sat on the porch at night listening to records or they would laugh over practically nothing while they got ready in the morning. Even when things weren't easy, Tess always felt that they loved each other, loved her and Amy. It was then that she realized that she wanted that. She wanted those small moments with someone, to truly build a life and she wanted that with Danny. The feeling hit her like a slap in the face, but she wasn't looking to hide from it.

"Tess?"

She looked up and saw that her mother was holding out a plate to her and she shook herself from her thoughts. "Sorry. Thanks, Momma." She took the plate and smiled as she set it down.

"How was everyone's day?" her father asked. Amy started talking about her last shift at the hospital and Tess poured herself a glass of wine. She sat back in her chair and smiled. She wasn't sure how she'd thought she could do without this, but now she knew that she didn't want to.

Tess watched Amy drive away and stood next to her Jeep with her father. He didn't care how old they were, he always walked them out to their cars and waited until he watched them drive away before he went inside.

"Dad, can I ask you a question?"

"Of course."

Tess swiped her ponytail off her shoulder and let out a deep breath. "How did you know Momma was the one?"

He looked at her, eyes wide, clearly surprised by her question. "Well, I knew it from the minute I saw her. She walked into the diner and I was sitting with a few of my buddies and it was like time just stood still. She was with your gram and I remember she ordered a lemonade and a piece of peach cobbler. She was the prettiest girl I'd ever seen, and I couldn't stop watching her smile. She lit up the room and she didn't even know she was doing it. I leaned over to one of my friends and I said, 'I'm gonna marry that girl someday' and the rest is history."

Now it was Tess's turn to look surprised. "You were what, eighteen then? You just knew? Just like that?"

Her father nodded. "I wish I could explain it better, but that's how it happened. I was a bumbling idiot when I introduced myself to her." He laughed. "Thankfully, she didn't really seem to mind. We got to know each other and it only confirmed what I knew all along—that she was it for me. I didn't want to plan a life if she wasn't in it."

Tess dropped her head and shook it. "That's really amazing that you trusted your judgment so easily. I thought I knew what I was doing when I was with Dean and that blew up in my face."

"We all make mistakes, sweetheart. You were following your heart, no crime in that."

"My heart was wrong, and it almost cost me everything." She shuddered at the thought.

He placed his hands on her shoulders and smiled down at her. "You learned from that, and that's all anyone can ask. It also doesn't mean that you're doomed to make the same mistake again. Danny is a good man and I've seen the way he looks at you. That boy has been in love with you for years, and I'm glad you two are finally on the same page."

"I really think I can see a future with him, and normally that would scare the hell out of me, but…"

"You're not scared."

"No, I'm not."

"That's because you know it's right, that he's the one."

Tess looked up at her father and she couldn't help but smile when she saw the look of happiness on his face. He always knew just what to say to her to ease her worry or confirm her feelings. She leaned in and wrapped her arms around him for a hug. "Thank you."

"For what?"

"For listening, just for being you." Tess kissed his cheek before pulling away.

"Anytime. Oh, and Tess, don't wait too long before you tell him how you feel."

"I won't. Night, Daddy."

She got into her Jeep and waved at her father as she backed out of her parents' driveway.

Twenty-Two

Tess walked into the bakery before five. She wanted to get a jump on some of the Easter orders so that she wasn't working too late. That was something she'd never thought about before Danny came along but she liked their time together, and she didn't want to give it up. Betty was waiting for her at the kitchen counter, wearing a concerned look.

"Hi, Betty. Is everything okay?"

She shook her head. "When I came in, I went to turn the ovens on like I normally do, but two of the wall ovens are out. They're not turning on."

Tess's eyes went wide. "Two of the wall ovens?" Each wall oven had three separate ovens which meant that six of them weren't working.

"I'm afraid so. That leaves us with three ovens…"

"Three ovens to do the daily baking plus orders." Tess dropped her face in her hands and sighed. "Okay, we can make this work. Did you call the repair man?"

Betty nodded. "I left Cliff a message, but being that it's not even five, I'm sure the man isn't awake yet."

"Okay, well let's just hope he calls back and can get here soon."

"I'm sorry. This is the last thing I expected to have to tell you first thing in the morning. Everything worked fine yesterday. There wasn't even a hint that something was wrong and this morning it was like they'd been turned off or something." She shrugged, exasperated.

Suddenly, a light went off in Tess's head. "Betty, just get everything else set up for the day. I've gotta make a quick call and then we'll get started on whatever list I know you have." Tess walked into her office and dropped her purse on her desk before digging for her phone. She pulled it out and pressed a number. "Hey, babe. I'm sorry to wake you. I was wondering if you'd help me with something."

———————

An hour later, Danny, Pete, and one of Pete's co-workers showed up at the bakery to examine the ovens. Tess knew that Pete would know someone who would be able to pull the oven out and see what was going on. She could tell by the way Danny was leaning against the wall, pensively watching the other two guys work, that he was thinking the same thing that she was: Cooper had been behind this too.

Tess went to the working oven and pulled a tray of cupcakes out. She shut the door and then paused next to Danny. "Any idea what's wrong yet?"

He shook his head. "Not yet."

"Relax that scowl. We'll figure out what's going on, okay?"

Danny sighed. "You have no idea how badly I want to walk over to his store and throw something through his giant window and watch it shatter."

"Well, I would appreciate if you didn't sink to his level." She gave him a smirk and walked back over to the counter to put the cupcakes down. Tess removed her oven mitts and left the cupcakes to cool while she double-checked her recipe for the icing. Keeping busy had to be better than just standing around watching, at least that's what she told herself.

"Okay, I think we've got it," Pete said, coming out from behind the oven.

Tess and Danny both stepped toward them. "Your gas line was cut off. It looks like it was only to the line for these two units, but it was definitely cut off," Pete informed them.

Tess's mouth dropped open. "The gas line? This has to be a joke."

"I'm afraid not. Fred is the best plumber I know and if he says it's the gas line, it's the gas line."

Fred nodded next to him. "At least it wasn't clogged or anything, you could've had a real problem on your hands then."

Tess turned away and threw her hands up in the air.

"Can you guys get it fixed?"

"Absolutely, I can get right on it," Fred told them.

She turned back around, a relieved look washing over her face.

"Thanks, Fred. I really appreciate it."

"I'm gonna grab my tools out in the truck and I'll be reattaching the gas line from the pipe outside." He headed outside, leaving Pete, Danny, and Tess standing around.

"Does it look like the line was cut or tampered with in any way?" Danny asked, crossing his arms over his chest.

Pete sighed and ran a hand through his hair. "I'm not sure. It didn't look like it was, but it just seems kind of strange that the ovens were working fine when you left and then this morning both units on that wall go out."

"Are there cameras in the parking lot?"

"I don't think so," Tess told Danny.

"There have to be cameras somewhere." Danny reached into his pocket for his phone.

"Even if there are street cameras, it doesn't mean that they would reach the side of the building where the gas pipes are."

"It's still worth a shot. I'll see what JJ can find out," Danny said, going toward Tess's office to make the call.

Pete gave Tess a consoling look. "He worries."

"I know and I want this all to be over just as much as he does." Tess blew out a breath.

"We can't fix everything today, but we can fix your ovens so let us do that and get you back up and running." He smiled as he patted her shoulder and headed outside.

Tess gave him a nod, silently thanking him. She appreciated that Pete was trying to make her feel better by taking care of the problem at hand. Tess looked toward her office and saw Danny getting off the phone. He walked toward her as he tucked his phone back in his pocket.

"JJ will be right over. He's gonna check to see if there's anything around that might lead us to Cooper. I'm gonna tell the guys to hold up on touching anything until JJ gets here."

Tess stepped in front of him and placed her hand on his chest. "Thank you for being here and making sure this all gets taken care of."

He smiled at her. "We're a team, babe. I've got your back." Danny touched his lips to hers and then made his way outside. Tess stood in the middle of her kitchen with one working oven and dozens of orders to get done and somehow she wasn't bothered that much by it. She hated that Cooper was likely the one causing all of this trouble in their lives, but she no longer felt like she had to carry the weight of everything all by herself and that was worth more than all the working ovens in the world.

A few days had passed since the gas line incident at the bakery. Fred and Pete had been able to repair it and get all of Tess's ovens up and running, and JJ had checked the street cameras for any sign of Cooper that night. Unfortunately, the cameras didn't have a clear view of that side of the building, which Danny had no doubt he was well aware of. He kept waiting for Cooper to get sloppy so that they could catch him, but it didn't seem to be happening.

Danny was on his way to meet Pete at the site of his house to walk through some things. They'd broken ground on the land a little over a week ago and now things were really going to start moving along. His phone rang through the speakers of his truck and he smiled when he saw Nick's name on his screen. He pressed accept on the call.

"Hey, Doc."

"What's going on, man?"

"I'm on my way to meet Pete at the site for my house."

"I heard you broke ground and things are moving along. Congrats."

"Thanks. It's literally a giant hole in the ground right now." Danny laughed.

"Gotta start somewhere. Listen, I'm calling because I wanted to see how you were doing with everything that's been happening? I know I've been a little MIA lately. I feel like I've been living in the OR."

"Don't worry about it, I know you're busy. I'm okay. Just pissed that this guy always seems to be one step ahead."

"Man, I don't know how you haven't punched him in the face yet."

Danny scoffed. "Believe me, it's not for a lack of wanting to."

"You're better than me, always have been. This fucker needs to have his ass handed to him."

"That's an understatement." He sighed.

"What? You sound like there's something you aren't saying?"

Danny's grip tightened on the steering wheel and he shook his head. He shouldn't have been surprised that his best friend knew him so well. "I feel like I always know what to do to fix something or I find a way. But I don't feel like I can see a way out of this. I feel like Cooper is going to keep messing with us until he gets what he wants—me out of the picture."

"No, that's not gonna happen."

"How can you be so sure?"

"You have the best people watching your back. Your dad and JJ are all over this, and they aren't going to let anything happen to you or Tess."

He blew out a breath. "That would be a lot more comforting if these things didn't keep on happening. He cut her fucking gas line at the bakery. Why? Was he trying to blow the place up or just inconvenience her? I don't know, but I've had enough."

"I hear you man, and I wish there was something I could do to help."

"I appreciate that, really I do."

"Just keep your eyes open and be careful. I need you at your best if you're gonna be my best man."

Danny blanched for a second, unsure if he'd heard Nick right. "Wait, what?"

Nick chuckled. "Yeah, you heard me right. I would be honored if you'd stand up next to me when I marry your sister. Will is gonna be my other best man, and I've asked Pete to be a groomsman too. This way, I have all my brothers up there with me."

A smile spread across Danny's face. "Wow, I'm honored. Of course I'll be your best man. Well, one of them."

"That's great. I'm glad to hear it."

"Maybe you two could pick a date so this wedding thing could actually get a move on?"

Nick let out a laugh. "Yeah, I know. We're gonna figure that out once we're back in North Carolina, which will be before you know it."

"I can't wait." Danny pulled into the lot where Pete's truck was parked. "I appreciate you calling to check on me."

"You would've done the same if it were me. Don't let that asshole get you down. You'll beat him at his own game."

He turned off his ignition. "I sure as hell hope so. I just got to the lot, so I gotta run, but thanks again for the call and for asking me to stand up for you."

"Anytime. Take it easy."

"You too." Danny disconnected the call and let out a deep breath. He hadn't realized how much he needed that reassurance from his best friend. For most of their friendship, it was usually Danny who had to talk Nick off a ledge or give him the encouragement he needed, but if this whole thing had taught him anything, it was that he couldn't shoulder everything himself and that was okay. He was surrounded by an incredible group of people who he knew had his back. He got out of his truck and closed the door as he waved to Pete. Danny was moving forward with his life regardless of what was or wasn't coming next and this house was the perfect stepping stone to do that.

Twenty-Three

The rest of the week had passed and no other problems had fallen upon them. Danny didn't like that Cooper had such easy access to Tess and her bakery but he tried not to dwell on that. He sat in the conference room with Zack going over some changes to the plans for the last floor of units in the building. They had figured out just about everything they needed to when Danny's phone rang. He removed his phone from his pocket and answered it when he saw that it was JJ.

"Hey man, what's going on?"

"Are you busy, or can you talk?"

Danny got up from his chair and silently motioned to Zack he'd be right back before moving to his office and sitting behind his desk. "I can talk. What's wrong?"

"Nothing is wrong. Well, I wanted you to know that my buddy down in New Orleans, he got back to me with all the information I requested on Cooper."

"Okay, and?"

JJ blew out a breath. "He's not who he says he is."

Danny pinched his eyes shut and clenched his fist. "Just tell me."

"His name isn't Cooper Witter, it's Cooper Richardson. He was never married. Izzy Wheeler wasn't his wife. They did grow up together and from what I understand he was always infatuated with her. He believed that they belonged together, and she always treated him as a friend. Izzy left for college and he stayed local, but when she came back home after she graduated, he decided to put on the full court press."

Danny leaned back in his chair and gripped the arm of his chair. He couldn't believe what he was hearing.

"He started showing up where she was or if she would find herself in a situation where she needed help, he would miraculously be there to save the day. I guess she didn't think anything of it because they were friends, but he kept asking her to go out and she agreed because she thought it was just a friendly thing."

"What did he do?"

"He made his intentions known and I think it freaked her out because she didn't see him like that. She let him down, but he didn't take no for an answer so well. He still kept showing up where she was, but he never did anything other than just sort of creepily be there. A few months later, she started dating someone and that's when things started happening. The guy ended up with flat tires and a bunch of other car problems that would keep him from Izzy. He was definitely trying to break them up."

This all sounded too familiar to Danny and he felt a knot forming in his stomach because he knew there was more to this story.

"Less than a year after Izzy and her boyfriend were dating, they got engaged and I guess that really pushed Cooper over the edge. Apparently, he confronted her one day and told her that she was making a big mistake and no one was more right for her than he was. She must've really gotten freaked out by his behavior because she ended up taking out a restraining order against him. He didn't let that slow him down though. About a month later, Izzy was in a horrible car accident. She'd borrowed her fiancé's car and drove into the metal guardrail on the highway. The brakes weren't working and it had been raining and it was bad."

"Holy shit."

"Yeah, she ended up in a coma and the doctors weren't sure if she was ever going to come out of it. Shortly after it happened, Cooper left Louisiana and never looked back. I guess he just happened upon Belmont and changed his name so no one could ever connect him to what happened there."

"What happened to Izzy?"

"She was in a coma for almost six months. Had to relearn how to walk. From what I hear, she's just starting to get back on her feet. This happened over a year ago."

Danny ran a hand over his face. He didn't know how to process this new information. This guy was a sick bastard and he was going after them. Danny was done playing by the rules.

"Clearly cars are his MO. He's vandalized my truck more than once. He definitely tampered with Tess's Jeep, and then he messed with Natalie's brakes."

There was a pause on JJ's end, and Danny sat up in his chair. "What else?"

"Turns out the car that was registered to Cooper while he lived in Louisiana was a black Bronco."

Danny's grip tightened around his phone. That was the same Bronco that showed up on all the security footage they saw anytime any vandalism was committed. "That's it then. We have to find that Bronco. How fast can you get a warrant?"

"We're working on it."

"How long do you think it's gonna take?"

"I'm not sure. I'm hoping before the end of the day, but it may not be until tomorrow."

"This can't wait until tomorrow! We need to get him today!"

"Danny, you need to calm down. As soon as we have the warrant, we'll go over there and check things out, but until then we're staying put and so are you."

"Don't fucking tell me to calm down. I've been patient for months while he's been planning God knows what. You just told me that he's already put one person in a coma and I'm just supposed to sit on my hands and wait?"

"Yes, that's exactly what you're supposed to do. If we want to put this guy away, then we need to do everything by the book. I will try to get Judge Larkin to move things along but I sure as hell don't want to get on his bad side so I'm not making any promises."

Danny blew out a breath and dropped his head. He knew that JJ was right, but this was their chance to nail Cooper and now they had to wait. It was infuriating.

"Okay, fine. I'll wait to hear from you."

"We're gonna get this son of a bitch, cuz. Don't worry."

"Thanks, JJ. Call me as soon as you hear."

"Will do."

Danny ended the call and stood up from his desk. He paced behind his desk a few times and then his gaze landed on the picture he had on his desk of him and Tess from the Eric Church concert. She was the one, there was no doubt in his mind. Danny had always done the right thing his whole life and now this psycho was threatening to take away the thing he loved the most. He couldn't sit back this time. Danny pushed out of his chair and made his way out of his office. It was time to finish this.

Tess and Penny were finishing up at the bakery when Tess's phone rang. She smiled when she saw Danny's picture appear.

"Hi."

"Hey, baby. Are you done for the night?"

"Just about. Penny and I are just putting away the last of the cookies we just finished. Where are you?"

"I have to make a stop and then I'll be home. Why don't you go back to my place, order some takeout, and I'll be home by the time it gets there."

She frowned. Something sounded off about his voice. "What stop do you have to make?"

"Pete needed me to look at something for the house. It won't take long, but I need to do it before tomorrow."

"Are you okay? You sound, I don't know, not like yourself."

"I'm good, just looking forward to seeing you."

She decided not to push the issue right then. "Okay, I'll see you in a little while."

"Bye." He disconnected the call and Tess clutched her phone in her hands for a minute.

"Tess, is everything okay?"

She snapped back into focus. "Yeah, everything is fine, I think. Danny just sounded a little... off." She shook her head. "I'm sure it's nothing."

"Maybe he just had a busy day?" Penny shrugged as she shelved last tray of cookies.

"It's possible. I'm sure I'll find out once he gets home." Tess removed her apron and hung it back on its hook. "Thanks for staying so we could get those done."

"No problem. I can't wait to decorate them tomorrow. Easter cookies sure are happy-looking cookies."

Tess chuckled. "I can't argue with that." She stepped into her office and grabbed her things. Penny walked out first and then she locked up and headed to Danny's for the night. As she walked to her car, she wanted to believe everything was okay, but the twinge she felt deep in her gut told her that everything was far from okay.

Since Cooper had managed to stay one step ahead of them the entire time, Danny decided not to look for the Bronco at his house. When people wanted to hide things, they often hid them in plain sight. He parked his truck in the back lot near Tess's bakery and walked over toward Cooper's shop. The lot was mostly empty but some people who lived in nearby apartments used the lot if they couldn't find parking. At the very end of the lot, he noticed what looked like a truck covered by a tarp. Danny walked over to it and slowly pulled it back. Sure enough, a black Bronco was underneath it. He felt like a weight had been lifted off his shoulders. He finally had what he needed to get Cooper put away and out of their lives. He pulled his phone out and snapped a few pictures of it, making sure to get a shot of the license plate. Danny sent them to JJ with a text telling him where he'd found the Bronco. As he put his phone back in his pocket and pulled the tarp back down, he couldn't help but grin.

"Got you, you son of a bitch." He couldn't wait to get home and tell Tess that they didn't have to worry anymore, no more looking over their shoulders. Danny felt something smash into the back of his head with such force that he couldn't even speak. His last thought was of Tess and then everything went black.

Tess paced in Danny's kitchen. She kept grabbing her phone to see if she had a missed call or a text from him, but there was nothing. She'd been waiting for almost forty-five minutes. When she felt like she was going to wear a hole in the floor, she grabbed her phone and dialed JJ.

"Hey, Tess. What's going on?"

"JJ, hi. Have you heard from Danny? He called me almost an hour ago and told me to go to his place. He said he had one stop to make and then he'd be here, but he's still not here and I haven't heard from him at all."

"I, uh, spoke to him earlier."

Tess scowled. JJ was hiding something, too. "Nope, that's not gonna cut it. What the hell is going on here, JJ? I have this terrible feeling that something is wrong and if you know something and aren't telling me, so help me, dealing with me won't be pretty."

JJ blew out a breath into the phone. "I found out some information on Cooper and I told Danny we were in the process of getting a warrant."

"A warrant? What kind of information?"

JJ filled her in on everything he'd told Danny. Tess collapsed onto one of the kitchen barstools, unable to hold herself upright any longer. She couldn't believe the things Cooper had done, but at the same time the past few months all made sense now.

"I don't think Danny wanted to wait for a warrant. He wanted to find that Bronco. He texted me about thirty minutes ago. Looks like he found it in the parking lot by Cooper's shop."

Tess's stomach dropped. If he went to Cooper's shop, there was a chance that Cooper had been lingering and caught him snooping. They could've gotten into some kind of altercation. Danny could be in trouble.

"JJ, can you try and ping Danny's cell or something? Try and find out where he is?"

"Why? Where do you think he is?"

"I can't say for sure but if he texted you thirty minutes ago and he still hasn't made it back home, there's a good chance something is wrong."

"Okay, I'll try and get a location on him. Sit tight, I'll get back to you."

"Thanks JJ." Tess got up from the stool and grabbed her purse. She didn't want to go against what JJ had asked her to do, but she wasn't going to sit around and wait. All of this was happening because Cooper wanted to be with her, so maybe if she could talk him down from whatever crazy thing was going through his head, they could all get out of this relatively unharmed. She ran out the door and prayed that she wasn't too late.

Twenty-Four

Danny's eyes fluttered open slowly and he winced as the pain in his head intensified. It smelled like he was surrounded by gasoline. It took him a minute to realize that he was inside Tess's bakery and he was tied to a chair with a liquid trail circled around the floor near his feet. He could feel blood dripping down the side of his face, no doubt from whatever he'd been hit with. Danny tried to move his hands but they were secured by zip ties.

"Well, well, look who's awake?" Cooper came from behind and then stood directly in front of him with a condescending smirk on his face.

"Untie me."

Cooper laughed. "Not a chance. You know, there was a moment there when I thought that you were going to mess up all my plans, but thanks to your need to be the hero, you actually allowed me to put things in motion sooner."

"What are you talking about?"

"Now that you found the Bronco, you know that I've been behind all the things that happened to your car, so I can't very well keep you around."

Danny struggled against the zip ties. He couldn't let Cooper pull off whatever he was planning. He needed to keep him talking long enough to distract him somehow.

"Look, you were just looking out for Tess, right? You didn't want her with just anyone."

"No! I don't want her with anyone other than me! We were made to be together." Cooper started to pace in front of him and Danny tried to think of something else to keep the conversation going.

"I get it. You had a plan and I came along and I ruined it, but if you truly care for Tess, don't you want her to be happy?"

He stopped and crossed his arms over his chest. "Of course I want her to be happy, but you don't know how to make her happy. You don't understand her dedication to her business, I do," he said, jabbing at his chest.

"Maybe I don't understand as well as you do, but I do understand her."

Cooper started laughing again. "You actually think you understand her? You don't understand her at all. Unfortunately, she doesn't have the best judgment when it comes to men, so I have to make the choice for her. Getting you out of the picture will make things easier."

"You do know that Tess likes to make her own decisions, right?"

"Of course I do! I know her! The problem is, she's too nice and she'd never let you go so I'm going to take care of it for her."

"Just like you tried to do for Izzy?"

Cooper's eyes lit up and he looked like he was going to blow steam out of his ears.

"I'm sure you thought that Izzy would've been better off without her fiancé, and that's why you cut the brakes on his car, but you didn't plan on her taking his car, did you?"

"Shut up! Don't you say another word about her!"

"It's true, isn't it? You wanted him gone so you could come in and show her what she was missing, but your plan backfired when she got in that car and ended up in a coma. The woman you claimed to love could've died because you thought you knew what was best."

Cooper stepped forward and let his fist connect with Danny's cheek. His head snapped to the side as he had no other way to brace against the punch. "I told you. Don't talk about Izzy."

Danny spit out the blood that was pooling in his mouth and looked back up at him. "Was that your plan all along when you came to Belmont? Find a woman to replace Izzy? You basically left her for dead anyway so you needed someone else. You saw Tess and you thought she would be the one." That earned him another punch to the face.

"You don't know anything!"

"Oh, I think I do. You're throwing a tantrum because you didn't get your way again. Poor you, the woman you like doesn't like you back."

Cooper reached in his back pocket and pulled out a zippo

lighter. "She can learn to like me. Once you're gone, she's gonna need someone to turn to, someone who understands her and what she needs, and that someone is me. It may take time, but she'll forget about you."

Danny shook his head. "She would never love you, she knows what you are. You're crazy."

Cooper's eyes filled with rage. He flipped the lighter open and closed a few times.

"What are you going to do with that? You're not going to do anything to Tess's bakery. You love her, don't you? Starting a fire in her bakery wouldn't exactly be the way into her heart."

He looked down at the gasoline on the floor and then looked back up at Danny, a smirk on his face. "Don't worry about it. I've got it all planned out. Minimal damage, but enough to get rid of you and maybe even make you look guilty."

"No one would believe that for a second."

"You'd be surprised what people believe," Cooper snarled. He flicked the lighter open again and Danny tried to free his hands, but the zip ties wouldn't budge.

"Cooper, stop!"

Danny looked up and saw Tess walking through the back door. She looked horrified at the sight in front of her but she kept moving forward.

"Tess, what are you doing here? You need to get out," he told her.

"Cooper, what are you doing?" she asked.

"Your boyfriend was snooping where he shouldn't have been. I was just explaining to him why you and I are so much better suited for each other than you two could ever be." He smiled at her like he really believed what he was saying.

"You need to let him go. He's bleeding, and he could be hurt." She took another step toward Danny but he held the lighter closer to where Danny sat, still not lighting it.

"Stay back! He's no longer your concern. He's been coming between us for too long. After tonight you don't have to worry about him anymore, we can finally be together."

"You've done all of these things for the wrong reason. I'm not a prize to be won."

He shook his head. "You made the wrong choice. Can't you see

I'm trying to show you that? Everything I did, I did so that you would know I cared."

"What are all the things you did?"

"Don't pretend like you don't know. I disconnected the battery in your Jeep so you'd need a ride so that we could spend time together. I took most of your supply order from the truck that day so that you would need to come borrow from me. I sent you the pictures of Danny and his assistant so you could really see what kind of person he is and you foolishly went back to him anyway. I hoped the damage to his truck and stealing his blueprints would annoy him but I was really hoping that when I cut the brakes on his assistant's car that he would've walked away from you, knowing I wouldn't stop. You two are both real stubborn you know that?" He looked between them, his jaw hard. "I hoped when I cut the gas line on your ovens that you'd need me again, but instead you turned to him." Cooper back handed Danny hard so that his head slumped forward.

"Stop! Please, don't hurt him."

Cooper snapped his eyes back to her and cocked his head to the side. "What do you mean?"

"I don't want you to hurt him." She looked up at Danny and he could tell she was trying to buy time. He wondered if she'd called JJ and if the police were on their way.

"He's the problem! He needs to go!" he yelled.

She stepped toward Cooper and placed her hand on his forearm. "I know, but I don't want you to get in trouble for any of it so you need to forget about him and then you and I can walk out of here together."

"You want to walk out of here with me?"

Tess nodded. "That's right, but I can't do that if you hurt Danny so you need to put the lighter away."

"You really want to be with me?"

"Of course I do. It's like you said, I just didn't realize it. You don't need to worry about him anymore. Just worry about us."

Cooper turned and looked back and Danny and then back at Tess. A cocky look passed over his face and then he took Tess's face in his hands and lowered his mouth to hers. Danny shook his chair back forth and tried everything to break free, but it was no use.

Tess gently pushed away from Cooper, a small smile on her lips. "Come on, let's get out of here." She tugged on his hand but he didn't move.

Cooper sighed and shook his head. "I'm sorry, Tess, but I can't leave him. He knows too much. You go on outside and wait for me."

Danny watched as Tess's eyes filled with dread. He had to take a chance and make a move, even if it wasn't much of a move.

"No, I don't want to go out there by myself." She tugged on his hand again, turning him toward her. "He's not going to say anything. Danny will be too embarrassed that he lost me to you. Trust me."

Cooper looked like he was deciding what to do so Danny stood up awkwardly, careful to avoid the gasoline on the floor. He had one shot at this. He ran straight for Cooper and rammed him hard into the counter.

"You're dead," Cooper said, straightening up from the counter. He charged at him and knocked Danny over so that the back of the chair was on the ground. Cooper landed a punch across his jaw and Danny's head hit into the floor.

"Stop it! Cooper, stop!"

"You think I'm gonna let you take her from me?" He wrapped his hands around Danny's neck and began squeezing.

Danny could hear Tess yelling for Cooper to stop and at one point she tried to shake him off of Danny, but he just nudged her away. He kept struggling against Cooper but it didn't seem to be doing much good. He could feel the air leaving his lungs. Suddenly, Cooper fell over to the side, unconscious. Danny blinked a few times and when he looked up, he saw Tess standing over them holding her marble rolling pin in her hand.

"Nice move."

She was breathing heavily and not saying anything.

"Tess... Tess."

Her eyes snapped back to his. "I need you to get me out of these zip ties so we can get out of here."

"Do you think he's dead?"

Danny peered over at him. "No, he's still breathing. It's alright. Get me out of this chair, okay?"

She nodded and walked back toward the counter and fumbled for the pair of scissors in the jar in the corner. "I thought he was going to kill you." She bent over and cut the ties from his wrists.

"So did I. Thank you for stepping in like that." Danny got to his feet and shook his head to try and regain his bearings. He pulled Tess to him and laid his lips over hers. When he pulled back, he could see tears shining in her eyes. "Hey, we're okay, thanks to your quick thinking."

She sniffled and wiped at her eyes. "Seeing you tied up like that..."

"It's okay, it's over. Come on, let's go outside and see if JJ is here."

Just as Danny was about to lead Tess outside, he saw Cooper get up and lunge for them. Danny shielded Tess with his body, but Cooper pushed him so that he was up against one of the ovens. He laid his forearm under his chin to hold him in place.

"It's not over. You thought you'd just get away from me." He took the lighter back out and started waving it in front of Danny's face.

"Take it easy," Danny said, straining against Cooper's arm. His heart was pounding in his chest, wanting out of Cooper's grasp.

He slammed him against the oven, making the pounding in his head start all over again.

"I'm gonna enjoy watching you lose."

Danny turned his head to his right to see if Tess was still standing there, but she wasn't. All of a sudden, he saw a metal baking tray in the air. Tess swung it hard at Cooper's head and once again he collapsed to the ground. Danny caught his breath after Cooper's grip had released on him and he stepped toward Tess. "You've got all the moves today."

Tess looked up at him in horror and before Danny could ask her what was wrong, something caught his eye. He turned toward where Cooper lay and that's when he saw it. He'd lit the lighter before he fell and the gasoline fumes had ignited.

Tess had always heard how people became paralyzed in traumatic situations, but she never imagined she'd be one of those people. She watched the fumes ignite and she knew that gasoline didn't burn for very long. But the fire didn't die; instead it grew. The liquid trail stopped in front of the large boxes she'd left out earlier that were filled with supplies like flour, sugar, baking powder, and baking soda. Tess saw the fire catch onto the boxes and the trash that was sticking out of the trash container. She stood unable to move as the fire spread around them. Danny was looking for the fire extinguisher, but he couldn't get to it. The smell of the burning gasoline was strong and the smoke was starting to build. She could feel her eyes and throat starting to burn.

"Tess! Tess! That's not just gasoline on the floor. We have to get out of here! Now!"

She snapped back into focus and looked around. The door leading to front of the bakery was blocked by fire and it was making its way to the back. The smoke was becoming thick, making it difficult to see. She was going to lose everything. "We have to put it out." She started looking around for something, anything to stop the blaze. Her chest felt tight as she watched the fire grow in a space she'd had so many wonderful memories in. This couldn't be happening. Tess could feel her hands starting to shake as she frantically looked for a way to put out the fire.

Danny gripped her shoulders. "Tess, we have to find a way out of here. I promise you it'll be okay, but we have to get out of here first."

She looked around again and saw there was a small opening to the back door. "We can make it out the back. Danny, we can't..." Just as she was about to tell him they couldn't leave Cooper there, she saw him grab Cooper by the arms and start to pull him toward the door.

"Go, I'm right behind you."

"No, I'm not leaving you," she yelled to him.

"Tess, you've gotta get outside and call for help if it isn't already here. I promise, I'm right behind you."

She looked to the door and then back at Danny. She didn't want to walk out that door without him, but she knew he was right and she needed to get help there as soon as possible. He gave her the most reassuring smile he could muster and she let out a deep breath. The fire had caught onto the wall where they had a large corkboard with pictures and notes and it was getting dangerously close to her. Tess made a move for the door and once she got there, she quickly pulled it open. The night air was a welcome smell to her nose. She coughed as she bent over her knees.

"Let me see your hands!"

Tess looked up and saw JJ and three other officers standing behind their squad cars, their weapons drawn and aimed where she stood. She slowly raised her hands. "JJ, it's me. Call the fire department! It's a gasoline fire."

He shouted something into his radio, holstered his weapon and ran over to her. "Shit, Tess, are you okay?"

She coughed again and gave a nod. "Help Danny! He's trying to get Cooper out."

JJ hurried to the door while his fellow officers followed closely behind. With more hands, they would be able to help both of them get out of there more easily. Except they didn't come right out. Tess felt her heart start to pound. They should've been out by now. Danny had only been a few steps behind her.

"Tess!" She turned and saw the chief practically sprinting into the parking lot. He wrapped her in a big hug and then looked her over. "Are you okay? You're not hurt?"

"I'm fine."

"Where's Danny?" he asked, trying to keep his voice calm.

"JJ and some of the others went to help him get Cooper out but they should've been out by now."

The chief grabbed the radio from his pocket. "What's the ETA on the fire department?"

"Thirty seconds out," the dispatcher replied.

"Moreau, what's your status?"

Tess held her breath as she waited for JJ to answer.

"Moreau, do you copy?"

Still nothing. She knew she should've stayed and helped Danny. Now he could be trapped inside the fire with no way out.

"Moreau, you know I don't like to repeat myself. Do you copy?"

Tess felt the tears stinging her eyes. "Come on Danny," she whispered.

As the chief was about to yell into his radio again, JJ emerged from the door with his arm around Danny, supporting him, and the other officers dragging out a still unconscious Cooper.

Tess and the chief ran over to them just as the fire engine pulled in the parking lot.

"Sorry about not answering my radio, but I had my hands full," JJ replied, jutting his chin in Danny's direction.

"We thought we had a clear path out, but then a bunch of cake boxes caught fire. I was lucky these guys came in when they did. Thanks again, man." Danny patted JJ on the shoulder.

"No problem. Let me go see if they need any help in there," he said, gesturing to the bakery.

Tess stepped forward and wrapped her arms around Danny. She didn't want to let him go.

"Are you sure you're okay?"

"Yeah, Dad." He pulled Tess into his side so they were both facing his father.

"What the hell happened?"

"Oh, just your typical Wednesday night. Cooper caught me snooping around for his Bronco and then hit me over the head, tied me to a chair and was going to light the bakery on fire with me in it so he could have Tess all to himself. Then my girl came in and did some fantastic distracting and managed to knock him out."

The chief turned and looked at Tess. "Yeah, but I guess I didn't hit him hard enough because he got up and put Danny in a choke hold up against the wall."

"That's when she hit him with the metal baking tray."

"And that's when the open zippo lighter hit the gasoline and whatever else he threw on the floor."

The chief put a hand on each of their shoulders. "We can go over everything later. Right now, I'm very thankful you're both okay. Go get checked by the EMTs, you may need a visit to the ER."

They didn't dare argue but instead just nodded. Tess watched as Cooper was handcuffed to the stretcher and loaded into the ambulance. Although she didn't imagine it going like this, it looked like he was finally out of their lives. Tess looked up at her bakery and the tears she'd been holding back finally fell from her eyes.

"Hey," Danny said, wrapping her in a big hug. "I'm so sorry this happened, it's all my fault."

She tilted her head to look up at him. "How is it your fault?"

"If I hadn't been so eager to find that Bronco, I never would've come here and he never would've found me and decided to start a fire."

Tess shook her head. "I think we both know if Cooper wanted to inflict some kind of damage onto the bakery, he would've done it. It might not have been tonight with you here, but he would've done it."

"You never said, how did you know I was here?"

She shrugged. "I just had a hunch. He's been so careful this whole time about not leaving any clues behind, so I thought maybe he wasn't hiding things as much as we thought, maybe he kept things in plain sight to throw people off."

"I had the exact same thought." He smirked at her. "Thank you for showing up when you did. You saved me." Danny took her cheek in his palm and she melted into his touch.

"Don't scare me like that again."

"I won't." He held her gaze, assuring her that he meant what he said.

"Promise me no more chasing after crazy stalkers. I think we've had enough of this kind of excitement to last us a lifetime."

"I can agree to that. I know this is a mess," he said gesturing to the bakery. "I don't want you to worry about it, we'll figure it out."

She watched as the firemen walked back outside, the fire looking to be out.

"I'm not worried."

"I wish we'd managed to actually capture Cooper spilling all those confessions before the fire started, there's no guarantee he'll confess once he wakes up."

Tess reached into her pocket and removed her phone. "Well, I guess it's a good thing I pressed record on my phone when I walked in and got the whole thing on tape then."

Danny smiled at her and shook his head. "You really are something. I probably should've told you this a while ago, but I'm crazy in love with you. You're kind, smart, and sexy as hell. You make me laugh and you're incredibly talented. My life is better just by having you in it."

Tess sniffled and smiled at him as she wrapped her hands around his waist. "I'm crazy in love with you too and I have been for such a long time. I'm sorry it took me so long to realize it and to stop being afraid of it. I can't even picture my life anymore without you in it."

"That's good to hear because I don't plan on going anywhere." Danny leaned down and pressed his lips to hers. She rose up on her toes to deepen the kiss. For the first time in she couldn't remember how long, Tess wasn't worried about what was coming next. She no longer felt like she had to handle everything on her own and there was plenty of room in her life for her bakery and Danny.

Twenty-Five

I t had been about a week since the fire, but it felt like it had just happened yesterday. Danny had managed to only get a minor concussion and a few bumps, in addition to a little smoke inhalation. Tess just had some smoke inhalation and the ER doctor was satisfied neither of them were in need of an overnight stay.

Cooper had also escaped with minor injuries: a concussion and a few first-degree burns. He'd been arrested for attempted murder, attempted arson, stalking, and fraud—not to mention the slew of charges he had waiting for him in Louisiana. Thanks to Tess's recording, the police had more than enough evidence to go after Cooper. When the police searched his house, they found his whole setup in the basement where he'd been watching Tess in particular. He had a board filled with pictures and information on Tess and Danny and all the important people in their lives. One thing was for sure, Cooper was going to be locked away for a long time.

Thankfully, the fire had been mostly contained to the bakery kitchen. Since most of it was steel and metal, the majority of the counters and appliances had remained mostly intact, but her office, the supply room, the walls where there had once been wooden boards with lists and pictures, and part of the entrance from the kitchen to the front of the bakery had been destroyed by the fire.

Tess got out of her Jeep and walked into the empty bakery. Instead of it smelling like sugary deliciousness, the smell of smoke still lingered. Today was the first day she felt like she could go in there and accurately determine what the priorities were so they could get back up and running. She carefully walked through the kitchen and shifted what was left of one of the boards that had come off of the wall. Some of the metal on the countertops was melted at the edges, but not completely destroyed. Tess tossed her purse on the counter and took out a notepad and pen. She threw her braid over her shoulder and blew out a sigh. It wasn't easy standing in there, knowing that someone had set out to try and destroy something that she had worked so hard building, but dwelling on that wouldn't change things. Tess needed to focus on what she could do.

Just as she started looking around the room, she heard the back door open. When she leaned back, she saw Danny standing in the doorway.

"Hey, what are you doing here and how did you get in?"

"Leanne let me use her key."

Tess's face twisted in confusion.

"That's because Leanne is here, too," she announced as she moved past Danny.

"Don't forget about me," Penny said, squeezing through the doorway.

"What are ya'll doing here?"

"Well, we knew you were coming to scope out the damage so we wanted to come help," Leanne said.

"That's really nice of you, but I don't know that there's much you can do. I was just making a list of what needs to be done and then was going to prioritize it so we can get back to work."

Penny held up her hand to silence her. "I don't think you understand. When Leanne says 'we,' she doesn't just mean us three."

Tess looked at Danny, confusion all over her face, and then people started stepping through the back door. First was Betty, followed by Tess's parents and Amy, JJ, Alice and the chief, Pete and Laura, Elena, Zack, and Jason and Kate. Tess's eyes went wide.

"Okay, I'm very confused. What's going on?"

"We're here to help. We know how much you suck at asking for help so we figured we'd just offer our services to you," Amy told her.

"We're gonna help you get your kitchen back in order, maybe even give it some improvements to make it run even better," Pete said, stepping forward.

Tess looked to Danny for some kind of explanation, but all he did was smile. "I don't understand. I can figure this out. Ya'll don't need to do anything."

Her father stepped forward. "Honey, this isn't about need. This is about everyone wanting to help you because that's what a community does, they help their own. You'd be the first one in line to help someone if this happened to them, so no one hesitated when you needed help." He smiled brightly at her and Tess felt tears form in her eyes. This was all so overwhelming.

She tried to clear her throat to shake off the emotion. "I don't know what to say."

"You say, 'yes, I'd love to have ya'll help,'" Charlie said, pushing through everyone and stopping right in front of Tess.

She covered her mouth with her hand, trying to contain her surprise. "What are you doing here?"

Charlie wrapped her in a big hug. "It's like your dad said, we're all here to help." She pulled back from her and smiled. "I'm here for as long as you need me."

Tess pulled her in for another hug and the tears that she'd been holding back spilled down her cheeks. Despite everything that had happened, she felt incredibly lucky to have such incredible people in her life who were willing to step in and help her.

She stepped back from Charlie and wiped her eyes. When she looked up, she saw Danny standing next to Nick, the two best friends having their own conversation. Danny's eyes met hers and she knew instantly that he was behind this whole thing.

"Thank ya'll so much for wanting to help. I'm so blown away but also really grateful."

The room filled with applause and then everyone splintered off into their own conversations, making plans about what needed to be done. Tess stepped toward Danny, a smirk on her face.

"What's that smirk for?"

She wrapped her arms around his waist and rested her head against his shoulder. "I know this was all you."

"I don't know what you mean." He squeezed her tighter.

Tess gestured to everyone in the room. "You mobilized everyone. You wanted me to know I didn't have to figure out everything on my own."

Danny shrugged. "I might have suggested that you could use some help."

She let out a laugh. "A few months ago, I probably would've refused help, hellbent on proving I could handle everything myself, but now I see how nice it is to not have to face things alone."

"I told you you didn't have to choose between your bakery and love," Charlie said, leaning over Nick.

"Well, you are the smartest person I know," Tess replied,

reaching her hand across to her best friend. Charlie grasped it and gave it a squeeze, and a knowing look spread across her face. Tess let go and leaned back into Danny's side. He turned so he was facing her, still smirking.

"I'm pretty sure I also told you that we could make this work without your business suffering."

"You might have mentioned it," Tess said, looking away, trying not to smile.

Danny gripped her hips and pulled her to him, making her giggle. "You could just say I was right."

"I could, but I don't want to inflate your ego."

He leaned down and whispered in her ear. "I have ways to make you change your mind."

"I look forward to seeing you try… later, at home." Tess rose up on her toes and planted a kiss on his lips.

"You can count on it," Danny told her as she pulled away from him. "Come on, we've got work to do." He laced his fingers with hers and led her over to Pete, who was already having a conversation with Zack. As Tess listened to their ideas, she squeezed Danny's hand tighter and he winked at her. There was no one else that she'd rather have by her side in any situation than him. He'd shown her that she was capable of so much more than she ever thought possible. More than anything, Danny truly loved who she was, and she knew that he would never try to change her. Tess felt like she was living for the first time, and she didn't want to miss out on a thing.

———

A few days had passed since everyone had gathered at Tess's bakery to figure out what they could do to take care of the damage. In that short time, Pete already had his crew in there working on the plan that Danny had drawn up. Tess was able to work at a limited capacity, but at least she wasn't completely shut down.

Danny sat in his office, looking over the notes he had on both the luxury hotel that was going up near the NASCAR Hall of Fame and the Raleigh project. Deep down, he'd known all along what he wanted to do, it just took a psycho wanting to get him out of the picture to steal his girlfriend for him to finally make a decision.

There was a knock at his door and Zack and Tom stood in the doorway.

"Natalie said you wanted to see us," Zack said.

"Yeah, come on in," Danny told them, waving them inside.

They stepped in and took a seat opposite him. He couldn't help but notice that they both looked nervous.

"Did someone die and ya'll didn't tell me?"

Tom let out a laugh. "No, it just seemed like whatever you wanted to talk to us about was very serious. I guess we were a little worried."

"Yeah, you've definitely had a lot on your plate the last few weeks."

"Thankfully all the crazy is behind us. I'm not quitting my job or anything like that," Danny said, leaning back in his chair.

"It would be totally understandable if you needed some kind of change after, you know, everything," Zack told him sympathetically.

Danny shook his head. "No, but it did help point me in the direction of a decision for what comes next."

They both sat up in their chairs, eager to hear what Danny had to say.

"Tom, I know you brought us the Raleigh project and you're absolutely right, it's a great opportunity in a great area. I think regardless of who gets that project, you should find a way to be the real estate broker because you deserve that. It's just not where I want to be and not the kind of work I want to do right now. I hope you can understand that."

Tom nodded. "Of course, I just know how talented you guys are and thought you would be a good fit."

"I appreciate that, but it's time for a bit of a change." He turned his attention to Zack. "As for that hotel, I think that's something we should focus on. The only reason I think that is because you have designs I know they will love. You should be the lead architect on that project if they decide they want to work with us."

"Me?" Zack asked, pointing to his chest.

"Yeah, you. You're a great architect and I know this is something you can handle. You've more than earned it."

"Wow, I don't know what to say. Thank you, this is really incredible. You really think they'll choose us?"

Danny shrugged. "I think there's a good chance, especially once they see what you can draw up for them."

"Wait, what are you going to do?" Zack asked, leaning forward in his chair.

"If we get the hotel project, I'll definitely help out, but what I really want to do is rebuild houses that have been destroyed by either fire or a hurricane. Some of those people may need a brand new place to live or they may need their current place fixed up so that it's better. There are more areas than you might think not far from here with homes that have been affected by something like that. I've reached out to a few organizations and I'm going to see what I can do to help."

"Wow, that's really amazing," Tom replied, digesting what Danny had just said.

"I want this company to be known for more than designing luxury condos and all the fancy things. It's time to branch out and this is how I want to do it."

Zack and Tom exchanged a nod and then turned back to Danny.

"Not that you need our blessing, man, but we fully support you. You finally look happy talking about work," Zack said.

Danny couldn't help but grin as he leaned onto his forearms on his desk. "Thank you. I am happy, I think this is going to be great. I really appreciate the support."

The men all got to their feet and Danny shook hands with them. He knew this was without a doubt what he wanted to do, at least right now, and he was grateful that he could trust Zack with handling a big project so that he had the freedom to go out and do this kind of work. As they walked out of his office, Zack paused and looked back at Danny.

"Thanks for the opportunity to take on more responsibility, Danny. I really appreciate your confidence in me."

Danny gave him a nod and watched Zack leave his office. Natalie entered and leaned against the door jam. "How did it go?"

"Really great. They're both on board." He leaned against the head of his chair.

"I told you they would be. We're a team, we support each other. You deserve to do work that makes you feel good."

"Thanks, Nat."

She gave him a smile, pushed off from the door jam, and made her way back to her desk. Danny let out a sigh and felt the smile still on his face. A few months ago, this wasn't something he would've ever thought he could do. Danny had worried that if he wasn't taking certain kinds of jobs, he would seem like he couldn't handle it and he never wanted to seem like he couldn't handle something, especially professionally. Now he realized that it had been his own insecurities messing with his mind. It was like Charlie had told him: he held the pencil and was in complete control of his design projects. Danny also thought back to what his father had told him that day in the emergency room—he was a fixer at heart. He was his happiest when he was helping someone out of a situation they couldn't find a way out of. He sat back down at his desk and refocused his attention on everything coming next.

Tess walked into Danny's apartment later that night after work. The smell of barbecue hit her nose before she even made it into the living room. "What smells so good?" She tossed her purse by the couch and removed her coat, placing it on the rack near the door as she made her way toward the kitchen. Danny was standing at the counter drinking a beer with several plates of food laid out in front of him.

"I stopped at the diner and grabbed some ribs, cornbread, coleslaw, and beans for dinner. I hope that's okay?"

"Oh, it's more than okay." Tess walked up to him and tilted her chin up. "It was a very good decision." She pushed up on her toes and placed a kiss on his lips.

Danny chuckled as he went to the refrigerator to grab her a beer. He opened the cap and handed it to her. They tapped bottles and both took a sip.

"How was your day?" he asked, as he put one of the plates in the microwave.

"It was good. Pete's almost finished with the storage room, which will be a huge help. Right now, we've got supplies all over the place. It's making Betty crazy. She runs a tight ship in that kitchen." She giggled.

"I'm sure Betty will be very happy to have a place to store the flour and sugar."

"Don't joke, she knows where everything is. I could ask her in the middle of the day how much flour we have left and she'll give me the exact amount. She's the most organized person I've ever met."

"Oh, I know she is. When I was drawing the plans for the room, she kept reminding me to make sure all the shelves had enough room for certain containers and the bags of flour and sugar." He chuckled.

"I think Pete should have my office finished soon, maybe by next week. It's also starting to smell less like, ya know, someone tried to light it on fire."

Danny took the plate out of the microwave and popped another one in. "Speaking of fires, I told Zack and Tom what my plans are for my next project."

Tess put her beer down on the counter. "How did they feel about that?"

"Good, they were very supportive. Zack was a little surprised that I'd want him to take the role of lead architect if we actually end up getting chosen for the hotel, but he's so talented I know he can handle it."

She stepped up to him and wrapped her arms around his neck. "I know you're going to help a lot of people."

When Danny had told her his plan to help people who had lost their houses or their businesses due to some kind of disaster, she knew he had found what he'd been looking for professionally.

He settled his hands on her hips and grinned. "Thanks, babe. This is gonna be a change, but a good one. I'm sorry it took something like being in the middle of that fire to make me realize what I wanted to do."

"It's often something awful that pushes us where we need to go."

"Not us though... I was pushed to you at Jason and Kate's wedding. It was magnetic, like I couldn't keep my distance from you anymore. That dress you were wearing certainly didn't help matters."

Tess let out a laugh. "That dress pushed you over the edge?" She stared at him, lips pursed.

"Yes and no. You've always pushed me over the edge, but that dress helped things along and everything that followed was pretty great."

"Oh, you mean me showing up to your hotel room and practically jumping you?"

He dropped his head, trying to hide his smile. "Yeah, that was unexpected, but I definitely loved it."

She swatted his arm and he backed her up against the counter. "I will never be sorry that you showed up that night."

His eyes were intense and Tess knew that he meant every word.

"Neither will I."

"I should probably let you know that your T-shirt is currently pushing me over the edge."

Tess looked down at her Southern Sweet Treats T-shirt and laughed. "You're out of your mind."

Danny pushed his hips up against hers and the bulge in his jeans suggested that he was telling the truth. "I can't help what you do to me. You've had a hold on me since you walked on that school bus that first day of kindergarten."

She cupped his cheeks with her hands. "Same for me." Tess pulled his face down to hers and took his mouth in a hard kiss. Danny leaned into her and swept his hands into her hair. The next thing she knew, he'd lifted her onto the counter.

"What about dinner?" she asked against his lips.

"We can reheat it."

She laughed as his mouth traveled down her neck. Tess reached for the button on his jeans just as he reached for the hem of her shirt and yanked it up over her head. As their clothes hit the floor, Tess pulled back so she could look at Danny.

"What's wrong?" he asked, his eyebrows pinching together.

She slid her hands up his chest and smiled. "Everything is exactly the way it's supposed to be."

Danny's lips lifted into a smile just before he lowered his mouth to hers. After the way things began for them just a few months earlier, Tess never would've believed that they would end up where they were. She'd convinced herself that she only had room in her life for one love, her bakery, but the truth was Tess had been scared to open up her heart again.

Taking that gamble had turned out to be one of the best risks she'd ever taken. In opening up her heart, she'd also rediscovered parts of herself that she had kept hidden for too long. Danny had helped her do that because he loved her. Knowing that she had someone who wanted to be there for her while letting her be herself no longer terrified her; it was actually pretty sweet and she planned on enjoying every bit of it.

Epilogue

Two Months Later

Tess stepped out onto the bakery floor with a tray of chocolate and salted caramel cupcakes. She slid them into the case and took a look around. It was close to five o'clock and there were clusters of people buying their sweet treats for the night. All of the repairs and renovations to the bakery had been completed a couple of weeks earlier, and Tess couldn't have been happier with the way things turned out. Danny's design had two doors on opposite ends coming from the kitchen out to the bakery so there was more than one way in or out. He'd also done a redesign on her office that opened up the space more and somehow made it feel brighter. The storage room even felt bigger and the new shelving units they had in there had Betty happier than a clam. Pete and his crew had done a great job executing the plans that Danny had drawn up and she'd never had to close down the bakery. Danny knew how important that was to her and like most things that were important to her, he found a way to help make it happen.

"Are those the new chocolate and salted caramel cupcakes?" Penny asked, walking behind her to ring up a sale.

"Yes. You did a beautiful job piping that icing onto the cupcakes, they look like a picture."

Penny shrugged. "That's no big deal. You made the icing and that is unreal."

"That icing is really good." Tess chuckled. "Still, making the desserts look so beautiful is no small thing. You've got the creative hand."

Seeing the smile on Penny's face made Tess feel good. She truly valued her and she always wanted her to know that.

Leanne popped out of the kitchen door and leaned against the wall. "We just got an order for two dozen macaroons. Customer wants them in an hour. Do we have enough in the case?"

"Let me check." Penny walked down to the other end of the counter to check on the cookies.

Just then, the chimes above the door sounded and Mrs. Perry came sauntering in. "Christ Almighty," Leanne said. "I already have one bossy person on the phone, now we need one in here?"

Tess stifled her laugh. "Good evening, Mrs. Perry. How are you doing?"

"I'm doing just fine, dear. I was on my way home from my knitting group and I wanted to pick up a few things." She adjusted her purse that was hanging off her forearm and started looking in the case.

"Sure, what can I get for you?"

"Lee, we've got enough cookies," Penny called over to her.

Leanne gave her a thumbs up and disappeared back into the kitchen, grinning like a cat at getting to avoid Mrs. Perry.

Tess focused her attention back on Mrs. Perry.

"I'll take a half a pound of the oatmeal raisin cookies and a half a pound of those almond cookies."

Tess grabbed two boxes and started putting the cookies in.

"So, did I hear right? You're changing your business hours starting next week?"

She nodded as she tied each box with string. "That's right. We'll be open Monday through Friday from 6 a.m. until 6 p.m., Saturday from 6 a.m. to 3 p.m. and Sunday from 7 a.m. until 1 p.m."

"Well, I'm sure lots of folks aren't going to like that."

Tess rested her forearms on the counter and plastered a smile on her face. "Well, I guess they're just going to have to get over it then." It wasn't a big change. The bakery was currently open Monday through Friday from 6 a.m. to 7 p.m. and Saturday and Sunday 6 a.m. to 4 p.m.

One of the things Tess had promised herself after her and Danny survived the ordeal with Cooper was that she was going to reevaluate her life, mainly her work-life balance. She wanted to start enjoying her life and their lives together and that meant fewer hours at the bakery. It wasn't as if Tess was quitting work altogether, but she didn't want to always be walking in the door late and exhausted only to have to wake up and do it all over again the next day with no real break on the weekends. She was even planning on taking Sundays off just so that she and Danny could have an entire day to themselves.

Mrs. Perry had a shocked look on her face, but Tess just kept on smiling. She was completely happy with her decision. "Is there anything else I can get you?"

"You know, I think I'll take one of your key lime pies. The ladies at Rotary Club will love that."

Tess nodded and reached into the case for the pie.

"Did I also hear that you've moved in with Danny Moreau?"

She straightened up quickly, a little taken aback by Mrs. Perry's question. Then again, she knew how quickly word got around in town. "Yes, we just moved in together about a week ago."

"Oh my. Do you think that was the wisest decision? No one wants to buy the cow if you're giving away the milk for free, and you aren't getting any younger." She shook her finger at her to emphasize her point.

Tess bit her lip as she tied up the box. When she looked up at Mrs. Perry, she re-plastered the smile on her face. "Don't worry, Mrs. Perry. Danny pays well for his milk. That'll be twenty-four dollars."

For the first time ever, Anita Perry was speechless. She silently handed over the exact amount to Tess and slowly turned and walked out of the bakery.

"What in the hell did you do to Mrs. Perry?" Leanne asked, coming up next to her. "I just saw the stunned look on her face as I was coming out of the kitchen."

Tess filled her in on what Mrs. Perry said and then told her what left her looking so stunned.

"Yes!" Leanne bumped hips with her. "Oh, I wish I could've heard that! It's about time you said something that forced her to clamp her big mouth shut. Good for you! I'm so proud!"

She shook her head as she rang up the sale and Leanne headed back into the kitchen. It did feel good asserting that she was one hundred percent confident in all of the choices she'd made recently. When Danny asked her to move in, it had taken her by surprise, but then she thought about all the years they'd wasted not being together and Tess decided she was done overthinking things. It was an adjustment learning to live with Danny, but she loved going to sleep with him at night and waking up to him in the morning. Everything felt like it was exactly the way it was supposed to be.

———————

A few days later, Danny told Tess he'd pick her up at the bakery after work. He wanted to show her the progress Pete and his crew had made on the house while it was still light outside. Tess hopped right in his truck when he pulled up and they were on their way.

"How was your day?"

"Ugh." She sighed. "I wanted to spend the day finishing the dessert for Nick and Charlie's engagement party since it's tomorrow, but we had two birthday cakes that we needed to get done this afternoon so they took priority. The cupcakes are done but I still have to finish the cake tomorrow morning and make a batch of lemon cookies. Thank God it doesn't start until four."

"You'll get it done, I have no doubt." He smiled over at her.

"Did they land yet? I haven't had a minute to look at my phone."

"Yeah, Nick and Charlie got in a little while ago. My dad went to pick them up. I had a meeting so I couldn't make it to the airport, but they're back at my parents' house. I told them we'd see them later."

"What meeting did you have? I don't remember you mentioning anything?"

Danny cleared his throat. "It was a video chat meeting. I was talking with Ken over at Houses for Humanity about the projects he's possibly going to use me for."

"That's great. How did that go?"

"It was good. There are several houses that need a new design because they've suffered some kind of damage, so I'm excited to get started."

Danny planned on meeting up with Ken next week to look at some of the properties they were looking to repair or rebuild. Many of them were located an hour or so outside of Belmont. Jason had even talked about helping raise money through his foundation so these families could get the best possible repairs or rebuilds.

He pulled up to the lot and parked as close as he could. Danny shut off his truck and they both got out. Within a few steps, the spot where the house was going up was in view. Most of the framing was done and next week they'd likely start putting up the walls.

"Wow, I can't believe how much they got done! It's really

starting to look like a house!" Tess said, stepping forward and taking it all in.

"Yeah, they're moving along pretty well."

She turned back to face Danny. "How are you feeling about it?"

He let out a sigh and shrugged before shoving his hands in his pockets. "I think it's okay so far."

"Just okay? Is something not the way you designed it?"

"No, they're following the design. It's just I can't help but feel like something is missing."

Tess's eyebrows furrowed in confusion. "What could be missing? You've been over this design so many times. It's perfect."

He stepped closer to her and grabbed her hand. "It's not perfect. Well at least not yet. From the very beginning I knew I wanted this kind of house for us, a place where we had enough room to have both of our families over, a kitchen big enough for you to bake as many things as you want at once, and a place where we could build our lives, raise a family, and grow old. I may have gotten a little ahead of myself but I always believed we'd end up right here, together."

"I'm glad you were so confident because I certainly wasn't." She chuckled.

"I've always known how I felt about you, even if it took over twenty years for everything to fall into place." Danny dropped down to one knee and Tess's eyes practically bulged out of her head.

"Danny Moreau, what are you doing?"

"Tess, there is nothing more that I want than for us to share this house and build our lives together. I want to support you in everything you do and I also want us to be able to lean on each other when we need to. I love you. I always have and I always will." He reached into his back pocket and popped open a black velvet box. "Will you marry me?"

She blinked a few times before looking down at the ring and then back up at Danny. Tears were shining in her eyes, and Danny's heart was pounding in his chest while he waited for her to respond. She nodded and then smiled through her tears. "Yes! Yes, I'll marry you."

He took the ring out of the box and slipped it on her finger. Tess admired the thin white-gold band adorned with small diamonds and the beautiful princess cut diamond at the center. It wasn't a huge stone because that wasn't Tess's style. It was beautiful but simple.

Danny got to his feet and she wrapped her arms around his neck, pulling him in for a kiss. "You couldn't have picked out a more perfect ring. It's absolutely gorgeous."

"When I went to go ask your dad for his permission, your mom may have mentioned that you always had a thing for princess cut diamonds." He grinned.

"You went to ask my dad for his permission? When was this?"

"Not long after the fire. I wanted to ask you sooner but I knew it was important for you to get back to one hundred percent operating capacity at the bakery first."

Tess cupped his cheeks with her hands and smiled. "I will never know what I did to deserve you. Thank you for understanding me and showing me what I was missing in my life. You are the best risk I've ever taken."

Danny placed his hand at the back of her neck and drew her in closer to him. "I'd bet on us every time." He pressed his lips to hers and then pulled away. "Come on, everyone is waiting for us at my parents' house." He grabbed her hand and pulled her back toward the truck.

"You realize this news is going to be all over town by tomorrow morning, right?"

Danny shrugged as he started up the truck. "It could possibly be all over town by tonight."

"That reminds me, if you hear anything about how well you pay for your milk, just ignore it." Tess waved him off as she buckled her seatbelt.

Danny stared at her for a minute, eyebrows furrowed. "I don't want to know, do I?"

"No, you definitely don't."

He reached for her hand and kissed her knuckles, loving that his ring was on her finger. Danny had spent most of his life building things or drawing things for other people to build, and now he was going to get to design a life with Tess and there truly was nothing sweeter.

The End

Here's a Sneak Peek at the Next Book
in the Hearts Are Wild Series,
"A Little Bit of Everything"

One

Sutton James made her way through the Charlotte airport, rushing to get to her connecting flight to New York City. Her whole life had felt like a rush the past two weeks; a job opportunity had come up in New York and she had less than a week to quit her job at the hotel she worked at in Kansas City, pack up her life into two large suitcases, and get to New York.

Sutton had been hired by North East Hospitality, a large PR company that operated largely out of New York to join a team that was responsible for setting up events at Tierney's, a five-star beach resort in the Hamptons. She still wasn't sure about this move. Outside of a few family trips to Florida as a kid, she'd never been anywhere other than Kansas City. It didn't bother her that at twenty-seven her world experience was somewhat limited, but her two older sisters didn't share that opinion. Andy and Maggie were both married with great husbands and careers they loved and they wanted Sutton to get out and experience life outside of Kansas City. Her sisters applied for the job at NEH behind her back and when she got the interview, they confessed that they were afraid she'd never leave if they didn't push her to. The truth was, anytime Sutton thought about leaving all she felt was guilt.

She had spent the majority of her teenage years and all of her adult years living with her dad. Her sisters were in and out of the house for college, but Sutton had stayed. She and her dad became like two peas in a pod and she didn't feel right about leaving him. Nathan James was a good man with the patience of a saint, which was saying something considering he had three daughters. He wanted nothing more than for Sutton to get out and experience the world and practically packed her suitcase for her. While she appreciated the support, it felt strange to not be home.

Sutton placed her carry-on on the conveyer belt at the security area. Once she was through the metal detector, she went to grab her bag off the conveyer belt but it wouldn't budge. She looked up into the most beautiful blue eyes she'd ever seen. "That's my carry-on I'm afraid," the blue eyed stranger told her. She didn't answer right away because she was too busy staring. She looked down and realized it wasn't her bag.

"Oh, I'm so sorry. I wasn't paying attention."

"Not a problem."

Sutton grabbed her bag off the conveyer belt and hurried to put her Converse sneakers on. She watched him as he put his own sneakers back on. He towered over her five-foot-five frame. His brown hair looked perfect and she could see the muscles beneath his Fordham T-shirt.

"Thanks for not running off with my bag." He smiled as he straightened up and grabbed his bag by the handles. She felt herself blush and tried to cover it up. She hoisted her bag onto her shoulder, knowing she needed to make her connecting flight.

"Sure thing. If you'll excuse me." She moved past the handsome stranger and hurried to her gate. Sutton had never gotten flustered like that over a man before, but something told her he was used to that reaction. She forced herself to refocus and made her way to the gate.

———

Will Russo was getting sick of airports. This was the third time he'd flown home to North Carolina in the past four months, which was a lot considering he usually only made the trip about four times a year. He'd gone home for his older brother's engagement party and while it had been a relatively small, enjoyable family affair, he was itching to get back to New York and his life.

Some may have thought Will's rush to return to New York was because his brother was marrying Charlie, a girl that he'd dated briefly last year before he'd found out that she'd slept with his brother. They'd both known her since childhood and Will ran into her in New York after not seeing her for almost ten years. When he made it clear that he was pursuing Charlie, Nick made it no secret that he intended to pursue her as well, but Will hadn't planned on losing to his big brother especially since he and Charlie had always been at odds. It had knocked him for a loop but in the end he realized that they truly belonged together and the three of them made their peace.

It was the first time in years that Will remembered having a relaxed and comfortable relationship with his brother, which was a plus since Nick had moved to New York to complete his orthopedic surgery fellowship. Being back in the same city as his brother had allowed the two of them to reconnect and Will was grateful for that, but he was still reminded of what he didn't have and that was someone to share his life with. He had never had any difficulty attracting female company but he was looking for someone with substance and he wasn't sure if he was going to be able to find that again. Romance aside, he was eager to get back to the grind of corporate law which would no doubt distract him from his lacking love life.

As he got onto the plane in the first class section, he checked his ticket and smiled when he saw he was sitting with a very pretty, familiar looking brunette. Will stowed his carry-on bag in the overhead compartment and sat down in the aisle seat. She was flipping through a magazine and didn't even bother to look up when he sat down. Will leaned forward a little bit but she still didn't stop what she was doing which made him chuckle. "Hello again."

Her eyes shot up and met his. At first she looked alarmed but when she recognized him, her body relaxed. "Oh... hi."

"Sorry if I startled you."

"No... I mean I guess I wasn't paying attention."

"Nervous flyer?"

"Not really it's just my first time to New York, so I think that has me freaking out." She tucked her long hair behind her ear and looked down at her hands.

"It just so happens that I've been living in New York for the past twelve years so allow me to ease your worries. I'm Will Russo, by the way." He extended his hand to her and smiled.

"Sutton James." She shook his hand and that was when Will noticed her big, violet eyes. He'd never seen eyes like that and they were stunning, especially contrasted by her dark hair.

"That's a great name."

"Oh, thanks. My dad named me after Roger Sutton, his favorite baseball player growing up. I'm the youngest of three girls and I was his last chance at a boy so I guess I'm just glad he didn't name me

Roger."

Will let out a laugh. "Now that might've been a little more difficult to handle. Where are you from?"

"Kansas City."

That explained the Roger Sutton connection. Roger Sutton started his major league baseball career with Kansas City back in the fifties before being traded to the Yankees in the early sixties. He held the homerun record for a single season from 1961 until 1998. "So is your dad a Kansas City fan or a Yankee fan?"

"We're Royals fans. My dad was just a kid when Sutton got traded to New York, but he always liked him so he followed his career."

"Oh so you're into baseball too?"

"Yes."

"I have two sisters and they don't know the difference between an inside the park home run and walking in a run," Will said with a chuckle.

"My sisters are pretty much the same way. Like I said, I was the last-ditch effort at having a boy, so I think my dad still molded me to like sports so he'd have a buddy."

The flight attendant appeared and took their drink order. Sutton ordered a Jack Daniels on the rocks which made Will smile. He ordered the same and then turned to look at her. "So what brings you to New York?"

"Work. I just got a new job and I'm headed to the Hamptons for the summer."

His eyes went wide. "Really? Who are you working for?"

"Northeast Hospitality… they're a pretty big PR company. I'm working with a small team over the summer to help plan events at a resort and some of their other spots."

"Yeah, I've heard of them," he smirked. They were actually a client of his firm's, his boss's client to be more specific. but Will knew he couldn't disclose that information. "They're a really well-known company."

Sutton shrugged. "I've never done anything like it before so I guess I'll see."

"Why the change?"

"I've been working in hospitality for about six years at a hotel in Kansas City but when this opportunity came along, my dad and my sisters thought I needed to experience someplace new, so they sort of pushed me into it."

Their drinks arrived and Will passed Sutton hers. He held up his glass. "Well, here's to your new job." They clanked glasses and sipped their whiskey.

"Thanks. I'm certainly going to need it. What do you do?"

"I'm a corporate lawyer."

"That sounds scary."

He shook his head. "Nah, most days it's pretty exciting."

"If you've been living in New York what brought you to North Carolina?"

"I grew up here in a small town right outside Charlotte called Belmont. I came home for my older brother's engagement party."

"That's nice. So older brother and two sisters?" She turned toward him, looking like she wanted to know more.

"Yeah, one sister is older and one is younger. Three girls in your family? Your father must be a very patient man," Will said, taking a sip of his drink.

Sutton nodded. "He certainly is."

"I'm sure your mother must have had her hands full keeping everyone in line."

"My mom died when I was thirteen, but up until then she was great at taking care of everyone—just lousy at taking care of herself."

Will's face dropped as he watched Sutton take a long sip of her whiskey. He certainly wasn't expecting that. "Wow, I'm so sorry."

She waved him off. "It's okay. No way you could've known."

"That had to be really hard."

"She had a brain tumor and no one knew. One morning I left for school and when I came home, I found her unconscious on the kitchen floor. I called 911 and waited for the ambulance to show up all while trying to wake her up. Apparently, she'd had a seizure not long before I found her. The tumor was inoperable, she was in a coma, and there was nothing that could be done. My dad knew she wasn't coming back so he pulled the plug and that was it."

Will could see that Sutton tried to speak of her mother's death like it was no big deal but he knew from personal experience that wasn't the case. "So you didn't really get to say goodbye?"

Sutton shook her head. "Not really, no. But I guess that's how she wanted it."

"I understand how awful that can be."

"You don't have to say that."

"I'm not… my dad died a couple years back. He had a massive heart attack and died in the ambulance on his way to the hospital. I was in New York, so I didn't get to say goodbye either and nothing ever really makes up for that does it?"

"No… it doesn't." Sutton finished her whiskey. "I'm sorry about your father."

Will nodded. "Thanks." He emptied his glass and handed it to the waiting flight attended and tried to shake off the unexpected emotion he felt. The captain's voice came overhead to let them know they'd be taking off soon.

"I feel really guilty about leaving my dad. My sisters were in college when my mom died so it was just me, Dad, and Hank."

"Hank?"

Sutton smiled. "Our dog. He's a bullmastiff and a giant mush."

"How did your dad feel about you leaving?"

"He practically pushed me out the door. Well, not exactly, but he wanted me to get out and live my life but I still feel like I'm abandoning him."

"Your sisters are nearby, right?"

Sutton nodded. "Well then I'm sure they've got him covered. I feel bad every time I leave my momma but my sisters are in Belmont and Nick is moving back in July so that'll make it easier."

"Moving back?"

"Yeah, Nick and his fiancé have been in New York while he finishes his orthopedic fellowship. He's got a job waiting at Charlotte General and with the Carolina Panthers as an orthopedic consultant."

"Wow, that's a hell of a job to have waiting."

He leaned back and smirked. "Nick's marrying Jason Moreau's sister so that doesn't hurt."

Sutton' eyes went wide. "As in the All-Pro tight end?"

"That's the one." She certainly kept surprising him. At that moment, the plane took off and Will watched as Sutton sucked in a deep breath. Once they were airborne, he looked over and she had opened her eyes, looking calmer.

"So your brother is a surgeon, you're a lawyer, are your sisters astronauts and firefighters?"

Will chuckled. "Laura, my older sister, is an interior designer.

She owns her own company with her husband who is a contractor, and Elena's a kindergarten teacher."

"Sounds like you all did well for yourselves."

"I'd like to think so. What do your sisters do?"

"Andy, she's the oldest, she owns her own boutique which is really successful. She gets written up in local magazines and on social media all the time. Maggie is a photographer, a wedding photographer specifically. Believe it or not, that's how she met her husband."

"Go on."

"Finn was a groomsman in one of the weddings she was working. He kept busting her chops during pictures and all through the wedding. She gave it right back to him which prompted their whole love connection. Andy met her husband, Eric, when he rescued her on the side of the road after her car broke down in a horrible rain storm. She kept insisting she was fine but he wouldn't hear of it. He helped get her car towed back to his garage and after he fixed her car he asked her on a date and the rest is history."

Will smiled as he listened to her talk. "What about you? Did you leave some poor guy heartbroken back in Kansas City when you decided to leave?"

"No, there's no one—heartbroken or otherwise."

"That's surprising."

She shrugged. "I don't really believe in the whole romance thing."

He looked at her puzzled. "Don't all women believe in love and romance and happy endings?"

"Not this one. I prefer being practical and focusing on things I know I can count on, like work and my family and friends." Sutton didn't meet his eyes.

"Wow… who broke your heart?"

She glared at him. "Broke my heart? No one."

"People always say that when they've had their heart broken."

"Sorry to disappoint you, cowboy, but no one has broken my heart. I just know what I want and what I don't."

The flight attendant appeared to take their food and drink order. They both ordered the grilled chicken wrap and another whiskey. "So when is your brother's wedding?"

"Next June. Charlie, that's Nick's fiancé, she wanted to have the wedding before Jason leaves for training camp and the fall is obviously out since he's in season."

"That makes sense. Well, you've got almost a year before you have to worry about anything. I'm assuming other than a tux fitting all you really need to plan is a bachelor party?"

"That's right."

Sutton rolled her eyes. "Guys have it so easy. I've already been through this with my sisters, and we run around like chickens with our heads cut off while ya'll stand there like it's nothing."

"Hey, the bachelor party is very important. Don't underestimate all that goes into it."

She glared at him. "Yes, booze and strippers. Really detail oriented."

Will couldn't help but laugh; he liked her spunk. "My brother wouldn't go for the whole stripper thing. He loves Charlie way too much for that. I'm going to have to come up with something else."

"That's impressive. I thought the stripper thing was part of all guys' DNA."

"Not Nick. He was never really that guy but now he's really not. If you ever want to see a man that would move mountains for his woman, that's my brother." Will had never said that out loud to anyone before but he knew it was true.

"So what's your story?"

"What do you mean?"

"I know what kind of guy your brother is but what about you? You seem like a heartbreaker to me. I imagine a long line of girls waiting for you to choose them only to find out you have moved on to the next best thing," Sutton smirked as she looked at him and he couldn't help but laugh.

He let out a sigh as he leaned his elbow on the armrest. "As much as I'd love to say you're wrong, that's pretty accurate. I've always been the guy who never wanted to commit to anyone, and I had a reputation for going through women the way most people change clothes, at least until recently."

"What changed?"

"I ran into someone from high school who I'd been horrible to and she completely knocked me over. She wanted nothing to do with me but I was determined to prove I'd changed."

"Had you? Changed, that is?"

"Yeah. I was lucky she agreed to give me a shot."

"Sounds like a pretty amazing woman. Who was she?"

"It was Charlie."

Sutton' mouth dropped in shock. "As in, your brother's fiancé?"

"The very one."

She shook her head and sighed. "Wow... how did that happen?"

Will gave her the abbreviated history of him and Charlie and Nick and after he told her she looked just as stunned as before.

"That's quite a story. You're all okay with each other now?"

"Yeah, we are actually. It took Charlie almost dying for us to pull our heads out of our asses, but once we did that everyone was happier."

The flight attendant showed up with their food trays and drinks and placed them in front of them. "So you still believe in commitment after all that?"

He nodded as he took a sip of his drink. "I'm not saying it isn't complicated ,but I don't think it's awful like I used to."

Sutton took a big bite out of her wrap and Will couldn't hide his chuckle. "Sorry, I haven't eaten in hours."

"No need to apologize." He picked up his wrap and started eating.

"I find it impressive that after everything you just went through that you haven't sworn off women."

"I'm afraid I'm not strong enough for that. Have you sworn off men then?"

"No, not at all but you know it's that old double standard. When a guy says that he doesn't want to get attached and just wants to date around it's completely normal, but when a girl says that she's a tramp, something is clearly wrong with her. My sisters settled down, why can't I? Blah, blah, blah. I'm twenty-seven and I don't exactly feel like that's ancient so if I'm wrong for wanting to live my life without having to deal with the drama of a relationship then I'm okay with being wrong." Sutton took another bite of her wrap and Will sat back in his seat looking her over. She certainly wasn't like anyone he'd ever met before.

He leaned over toward her and grinned. "I commend you for knowing what you want, and I don't think there's anything wrong with worrying about yourself right now."

"Maybe it's a Midwest thing or something with the obsession of settling down."

"No, it's a southern thing." He laughed. "I think you'll find the metropolitan area completely different."

"That sounds refreshing," she said, lifting her drink to her lips.

"What's the plan once you land?"

Sutton leaned back in her seat with her drink resting in her hand. "Renting a car and driving out to the Hamptons. I actually start work tomorrow, so I'm hoping it doesn't take me too long to get out there."

"Talk about not giving you time to settle in."

"I think this week is mostly getting us familiar with what we're going to be doing and then next week we go full speed. Do you ever make it out to the Hamptons?"

"Not really, but I think I may just have a reason to change that," he said with a grin. "The Hamptons are great but you've gotta see Manhattan."

"I don't know if I'll have anything going on in the city."

"Missouri, you can't come to New York and not see Manhattan. It's un-American, or at least it should be."

Sutton let out a laugh. "Missouri, huh? Well I suppose I'll have to find a reason to come into the city then. I'd hate to be called un-American."

They passed the rest of the flight making easy conversation and before they knew it the captain was announcing their descent into La Guardia. Will reached into his pocket for his wallet and pulled out his business card. "Give me a call when you want a tour of the city. My cell number is on the back."

Sutton ripped a page from her magazine and grabbed a pen from her bag. She jotted down a number and handed Will the page. "Call me if you ever make it out to the Hamptons."

Will smiled as he tucked the paper into his pocket. He let Sutton out first and then grabbed his carry-on from the overhead compartment before following her off the plane. He went with her down to baggage claim to wait for her luggage. Once she had her two bags, Will was trying to find a way to delay leaving. "Thanks for waiting with me."

"You're welcome. Are you going to be okay from here?"

"Yeah, I've gotta pick up my car and then I'm off."

"Yeah, but can you find the Hamptons?"

Sutton laughed. "There's this great invention called GPS, so I think I should be okay."

"Just remember people drive differently on these highways than they do in Missouri."

"I'll keep that in mind." She looked down at her feet letting a moment of silence pass between them. "Thanks for making the flight enjoyable."

"Back at you. Good luck with everything. You're going to be just fine."

"Thanks." She smiled as she turned away with her bags, leaving Will alone. He watched her disappear from his sight and he knew that he had to see her again. One thing that hadn't changed was that once he had an idea in his head, there was no stopping him.

Stay tuned for the rest of
A Little Bit of Everything
coming soon!

Acknowledgements

Before I even finished writing *The One That Got Away*, I knew that I wanted the next book to be Danny and Tess's story. I loved Danny's character right away. He's that really good guy who always wants to do the right thing and will go out of his way to help someone, but I felt like there was so much more to him that I wanted to show.

Tess had a great presence in her scenes in *The One That Got Away*, but I wanted to show her as an independent woman who was running her own business successfully and who also had a lot of emotional baggage. It was a lot of fun building the friends-to-lovers relationship between Danny and Tess, and I hope their happily ever after was as satisfying for you as it was for me.

This book was such a struggle for me in so many ways. I kept starting, hating everything, starting over, thinking I finally figured it out, hating everything again, and wanting to cry because I was starting to question if I could really do this whole author thing. And then I finally got myself right. While publishing my first book was scary because I'd never done it before, writing the second book was absolutely terrifying because I was so worried I was not going to be able to live up to all the good feedback I got from the first book. I wanted to give up so many times, but I'm so happy that I didn't.

A giant thank you to my writing family, especially Hazel Kelly, Annalise Delaney, Jacy Mackin, Mal Cooper, and Thayra Rothweiler. Thank you for pushing me, helping me to get on a schedule since I didn't even know what that meant before Inkers Con, and for always believing in me. Thank you for reminding me to "embrace the suck" and keep going. I love you all and don't know what I'd do without you.

Thank you to my amazing beta readers, Colleen Oppenheim, Barb Jack, and Kimberly Harris. I can't tell you enough how much I appreciate your eye for detail and for you always being willing to run through ideas when I got stuck. Thank you for wanting to help make my book the best it could be.

Thank you to my editor, Kelsy Thompson, for helping make my manuscript shine. I feel like we have been talking about this book for such a long time, and I really appreciate your dedication in helping me make it into the best story possible.

Thanks to Erik Gevers, my amazing formatter. You always make my books look so beautiful!

Thanks to my cover designer at eBook Launch, Dane Low. Thank you for your patience and for never getting annoyed when I said, "Just one more change." Thank you for making me such gorgeous covers!

Thanks to my friend, Detective Billy Waldron, for being my official source for any police or fire questions I had.

A big thank you to all my family and friends for all of your support for *The One That Got Away* and the writing of *Make It Sweet*. It means the world to me. A special thank you to my best friend, Michelle, for your constant patience and your encouragement. You had to hear me complain about writing this book more than anyone, and through all my doubts you always believed I would find my way.

To my parents, thank you for your incredible support. Dad, thanks for telling your patients your daughter wrote a book and helping me "market." Mom, thanks for telling practically everyone you see that your daughter wrote a book. It means a lot that I've done something that makes you both so proud.

To all the new writers out there the best piece of advice I can give you is to keep on writing. The more you do it, the better you'll become. Seek out other writers. Having author friends is amazing. You can't even imagine how much you will learn from them and how much you will be embraced by them. We are all here to support each other so please, don't be afraid to reach out.

About the Author

Marisa Scolamiero is a New Jersey girl with a country soul.

Born and raised not far from New York City, she grew up experiencing a lot of what the Big Apple has to offer. She discovered her love of all things southern on a trip to Nashville, Tennessee and now calls Nashville her soul city.

When she isn't rocking out at a country concert with a whiskey in hand, she can be found cheering on her beloved New York Yankees, and if she's really lucky, she's got her toes dug in the Jersey Shore sand.

She's a self proclaimed ice cream aficionado and super hero nerd. She also loves cooking and enjoying a great glass of red wine with her big, loud, Italian family.

Social Media

Come follow me on social media!

Facebook: Marisa Scolamiero

Instagram: marisascolamiero

Visit my website www.marisascolamiero.com for the latest news, blogs and events. I love hearing from readers so never hesitate to reach out to me!

Made in the USA
Middletown, DE
15 January 2020